L.85

C000070323

RUNA FAIRLEIGH, the author of this remarkable novel, and the sole owner of the small island where the manuscript was discovered, remains as shrouded in mystery today as the circumstances (described by L.A. Morse in his introduction) surrounding the publication of the book itself.

L.A. MORSE is the author of two detective novels, *The Old Dick* and *The Big Enchilada*, both of which were widely reviewed and warmly praised. *The Old Dick* won the Edgar Award in 1981 for the best paperback mystery. L.A. Morse lives in Toronto and is a member of the Crime Writers of Canada.

AN OLD-FASHIONED MYSTERY

RUNA FAIRLEIGH

EDITED AND WITH
AN INTRODUCTION BY
L.A. MORSE

 AVON BOOKS OF CANADA
PUBLISHERS OF BARD, CAMELOT, DISCUS AND FLARE BOOKS

AVON BOOKS OF CANADA
A division of
The Hearst Corporation
2061 McCowan Road, Suite 210
Scarborough, Ontario M1S 3Y6

The Lester & Orpen Dennys edition contains the following
Canadian Library Cataloging in Publication Data:

Fairleigh, Runa.
    An old-fashioned mystery

I. Morse, L.A.   II. Title.

PS8561.A47042   C813'.54   C83-094007-3
PR9199.3.F34042

First Avon Printing, October, 1984

AN OLD-FASHIONED MYSTERY

INTRODUCTION:
THE MYSTERY OF RUNA FAIRLEIGH

WHILE *AN OLD-FASHIONED MYSTERY* may well be one of the most extraordinary books of its kind, the mystery surrounding its author is, in its way, equally puzzling and intriguing. Perhaps by accident, but more likely by design, Runa Fairleigh is one of the most enigmatic figures in the world of letters. By comparison, the mysterious, reclusive writer known as B. Traven was chatty, outgoing, and self-promoting.

The few undisputed facts are as follows.

Somewhat over thirty years ago, Runa Fairleigh purchased one of the smaller of the Thousand Islands, a property approximately two acres in size, and located very near the imaginary line that forms the border between the United States and Canada. There was a small but comfortable winterized cottage on the island, which Miss Fairleigh moved into immediately upon completion of the purchase. That was in November 1948, and as far as can be determined, from that time forward she never again had direct contact with or spoke to another human being.

Although Miss Fairleigh's island is not as isolated as "Komondor Island" in her book (one assumes that Komondor is located in the same general area), access to and from it is only by boat. The island has a small dock, but no boathouse, and it seems reasonably certain that Miss Fairleigh did not herself possess a boat. Furthermore—with the one very obvious exception—there is no evidence at all to suggest that Miss Fairleigh ever left the island, even briefly, after taking possession of it.

The island does not have a telephone and, for at least the last ten years of her residency, it appears that Miss Fairleigh wrote no letters. Groceries, what few pieces of mail she received, and any other supplies (most frequently reams of typing paper) were delivered approximately every week by boat from the mainland. Miss Fairleigh never had contact with the person making deliveries, but if she had any special instructions or requirements a typewritten note was left in a box on the dock.*

Bills for her provisions were submitted to a firm of accountants and paid by them. No one currently with the firm had any first-hand knowledge of Runa Fairleigh, and a long succession of junior members merely followed the instructions that had been laid down more than thirty years before. The account out of which the bills were paid was replenished by the receipt, on a regular basis, of a cashier's cheque, the ultimate source of which cannot be traced.

Runa Fairleigh may have seen no one, but she was not herself unobserved. Her neighbours from nearby islands (mostly summer residents) would not infrequently glimpse her while they were out cruising, or travelling to or from their own cottages. Sometimes she would be tending her garden; more often, though, she would be visible through the window, sitting at a table and working at a large, old-fashioned upright typewriter. People passing close to the island when the weather was warm and Miss Fairleigh's windows were open could often hear the sounds of typing. By all accounts, she was a proficient typist.

It is quite common for people who are or act in any way out of the ordinary to become a focus of attention, even when

---

*Although she may have had other contacts with the outside world besides the weekly delivery, investigation has not revealed them. Any information concerning this would be gratefully received.

their peculiarity happens to be a desire for seclusion and privacy. Such was the case with Runa Fairleigh. She had not lived on her island for many years before her extreme reclusiveness was noted and became a subject of gossip and conjecture. Despite their curiosity, most people respected her obvious wish to be left alone. Every so often, however, passersby would see her outside, perhaps working in her garden, and would approach, calling out greetings and introducing themselves. Miss Fairleigh never responded to the shouts. Without fail, though, she would immediately turn and stride briskly into her house, where she would remain until the intruders departed. By all reports, she never appeared in any way panicked by or even hostile to these approaches, but merely totally determined to avoid all contact.

No one seems ever to have got close enough to get a really good look at her, but those who saw her agree that Runa Fairleigh was tall and very thin, with steel-grey hair pulled into a severe bun at the back of her head. Even into what must have been her late sixties, she conveyed an impression of considerable strength—of character as well as physical vitality. It was probably this impression, combined with the fact that she always wore very out-of-date clothes, that made many people say that she reminded them of turn-of-the-century photographs of governesses and elderly maiden aunts.

For a while the Hermit Lady, as she came to be called, was quite famous—so much so that her little island was included in the itinerary of the sightseeing tour boats that cruise the islands during the season. Miss Fairleigh must have quickly learned the schedule of these tours, for after the first boat made its appearance, she was never spotted by an excursionist, not even sitting in the window of her cottage. Whether she was amused, annoyed, distressed, or inconvenienced by this unwanted attention, we have no way of knowing. Eventually her neighbours, deciding either that an inoffensive old lady was being thoughtlessly harassed, or that they themselves were being disturbed, convinced the tour company to remove the island from their route. And so for many years Runa Fairleigh was able to live the life of peaceful solitude—working in her garden or at the typewriter—that she so evidently desired.

Then in the late fall of 1978, almost exactly thirty years after she moved onto the island, Runa Fairleigh ceased being an amusing curiosity and became an utter mystery. It was at this time, in the course of making the weekly delivery of groceries, that the delivery man found the previous week's supplies still on the dock where he had left them.

Naturally he feared that there had been an accident or an illness. For the first time in ten years of making deliveries, he set foot on the island and went up to the cottage. He knocked on the door, but there was no answer. When he tried the handle, he found the door unlocked. Dreading what he was now certain he would find, he bravely went inside. But instead of the body he was anticipating, he found nothing. Not only was there not a dead or dying elderly lady, there was no indication that anyone had ever lived in the cottage. Much relieved but considerably puzzled, the delivery man returned to the mainland and reported the matter to the police.

When the police investigated, they found things exactly as the delivery man had stated. The small house was neat and spotlessly clean. A search revealed that the cupboards, drawers, and closets were empty. As one of the policemen commented, the house had the empty, impersonal feeling of a rental property waiting for the next occupant. The sense of a personality that all residences begin to acquire after being lived in for even a very short period of time—to say nothing of thirty years—was entirely absent.

There were only two things in the house to distinguish it from the countless furnished cottages that are rented out by the week or the season. One was the old typewriter in its customary place on the table by the window, a very brief, bleakly cryptic note still in the roller. The other was on a middle shelf of an otherwise empty bookcase. Neatly stacked inside a box that had originally contained typing paper were the 288 carefully typed manuscript pages of the book you are about to read.

A thorough search of the house and property revealed no clue to what had occurred; nor did an investigation of the surrounding islands, most of which were uninhabited at that time of the year. To this day, there is no evidence as to the nature of Runa Fairleigh's disappearance—whether it was voluntary or coerced, if there was foul play or suicide. The authorities are more or less satisfied that Miss Fairleigh's behaviour over thirty years, coupled with the absence of any indications to the contrary, strongly suggests that she left entirely of her own volition. The supposition is that she completed the work she set out to do—this book—and decided it was time to move on.

The situation was certainly strange, but not suspicious; having no leads to follow and no clear way to develop any, the police put the matter aside pending the emergence of new information. The manuscript was deposited in the station's property room.

There it might still sit had it not been for a series of fortunate events. In May 1982 a crime novel of mine, *The Old Dick*, was given an award by the Mystery Writers of America. This generated some very welcome publicity, and quite a few articles and stories about me suddenly appeared in various newspapers and magazines. This attention, in turn, resulted in my receiving a lot of phone calls and letters from people I didn't know. Most were genuinely friendly, a few were cranks, and all thought they had some information—usually related somehow to mysteries or crime—that would interest me.

While most of this unsolicited assistance was not very interesting, one letter—from the wife of one of the policemen involved in the Runa Fairleigh incident—was a little different. She wrote about the existence of the manuscript and filled in some of the story behind it. Apparently, she was something of a mystery buff, and also, courtesy of her husband, the only person actually to have read the manuscript. She said that she thought it was wonderful, and that she had long felt something should be done with it, but she didn't know how to go about it. Finally, after reading an article about me, she had decided to write and see if I would come and take a look at the book.

I sent a polite, noncommittal reply, but I had no real intention of pursuing the matter. Still, the basic situation was sufficiently intriguing that I didn't forget about it either, and when, six weeks later, it turned out that I'd be in the area, I decided to make some inquiries.

The police thought the request to read the manuscript was somewhat unusual, but agreed to it, provided that the book was not taken out of the station. They put me in an uncomfortably spartan interrogation room, and brought me the box containing the manuscript. I had expected to look at the first chapter or two, then leave. Four and a half hours later, as I turned the last page, I was unaware of the hard wooden chair I was on or the sickly glare of the fluorescent lights overhead. But I was quite conscious of the fact that I'd just had a most extraordinary—and completely unexpected—experience. While the book was hardly a major work of literature, it was none the less clear that the enigmatic Runa Fairleigh had left behind one of the most remarkable mysteries ever written. In what is the highest praise one writer can give the work of another, I can remember sitting, almost stunned, and thinking, "This is a book I wish I'd written."

With the considerable enthusiasm and excitement I felt for the book, it was easy to arouse the interest of this publisher. Over the next ten days, one by one, the entire editorial staff made the 150-mile trip to the police station to read the manuscript.

The decision to publish was unanimous and immediate. Arranging to do so took a bit longer. The legal status of the manuscript and the author was, at best, ambiguous, and for a while it appeared that publication would not be permitted. Eventually, however, the court agreed to allow it. An attorney was appointed to negotiate a contract and to establish a trust fund to be held for Runa Fairleigh (or any heirs she might have in the event her death is confirmed). All this was accomplished without difficulty, and publication was arranged shortly.

It is fervently hoped that the release of this book—which, we must assume, represents Miss Fairleigh's life's work—will cause the author herself to come forward, if not to accept the praise that is due to her, at least to claim the income that has accrued. Failing that, it is hoped that anyone able to offer any information about either Runa Fairleigh's present circumstances or her equally enigmatic past will get in touch with this publisher. Any assistance in this regard will be greatly appreciated, and confidentiality (if desired) will be scrupulously maintained.

That, such as it is, is the story of Runa Fairleigh and how her book came to be published. It only remains to say a few words about the book itself.

Beyond the statement of the basic situation, which appears on the cover of this edition, almost nothing can be said about the story without saying too much. It is hoped that readers and reviewers will recognize this, and avoid spoiling the fun for those who come after them.

The text is exactly as the author left it in the box on the bookshelf in her cottage. There is, of course, no way of knowing how many drafts preceded the version we now have, but it seems likely that there were a great many. Certainly, the present version is quite contemporary in most respects—in the over-all style, the ideas and attitudes of the characters, and the tone of the narrative voice. (This very obvious modernity suggests that Miss Fairleigh had contacts with—or at least sources of information from—the outside world that still remain unknown.) At the same time, however, internal evidence—certain of the characters, some of the stylistic mannerisms, idiosyncrasies of diction, and sentence rhythms—make it clear that there were other, much older versions, and probably more than a few. The combination of the contemporary and the dated results in a curious kind of ambiguity; there is a feeling of timelessness or, more precisely perhaps, a feeling of somehow being "out of time", a quality that, whether intended or not, seems altogether appropriate for this type of story. Thus, no editorial changes other than minor corrections of spelling and punctuation were made.

Runa Fairleigh called her book *An Old-Fashioned Mystery*. However, it might equally well have been titled *The Last Mystery*, since it is most definitely the mystery to end all mysteries. Indeed, it may be the eschatology of the mystery.

> L. A. Morse
> Toronto
> July 1983

AN OLD-FASHIONED MYSTERY

As flies to wanton boys, are we to the gods;
They kill us for their sport.

CHAPTER ONE

"'THIS CHUTNEY TASTES A BIT OFF TO ME,' THE MAJOR *said. These seemingly innocuous words begin one of the most intriguing and challenging mysteries you will ever read.*" Sebastian Cornichon read aloud from the cover of the paperback he held in his hand, then made a rude noise. "No, I won't," he said, and lobbed the book across the large room, where it struck the nose of the moosehead mounted on the wall.

"Really, Sebastian," Violet Cornichon said from her place on a huge, overstuffed, floral-patterned couch.

"'Really', yourself," Sebastian said as he dropped heavily onto a matching couch opposite his sister. "You're starting to develop the precise tone of disapproval that I thought one encountered only in tight-lipped matrons who donate their time to art museums. I'm glad you've finally decided to get some help."

"Help? What do you mean?"

"Binky Edwards told me he saw you coming out of what's-his-name's office—that very *au courant* up-town therapist whose treatments tend to be noisy, painful, and expensive."

Violet sighed, rolling her very large, alarmingly blue eyes. "You're the one who needs treatment if you credit anything Binky Edwards says he saw. That near-sighted butterfly blurs out past the end of his cute little nose. I once saw him having a long conversation with his reflection in a mirror. Probably went away thinking what a nice young man that was—not terribly talkative but a really good listener."

Sebastian laughed. "That's Binky, all right. But if you're not seeing someone, then I think you should. You may not realize it, but you're beginning to act a little peculiar."

"Your concern touches me, Sebastian, but I'm not quite sure how to take being thought peculiar by someone whose every new deviation for the past ten years has been chronicled in the papers."

"That's called trend setting, my dear," Sebastian smiled.

"Only if someone follows you," Violet smiled back.

Sebastian started to say something, stopped, then laughed again. "Score one for the younger of the Cornichon twins, the erstwhile Society-Girl Detective."

They again smiled at each other, similarly ambiguous expressions that were a complex mixture of affection and hostility, maliciousness, understanding, and the kind of respect accorded a long-time adversary who's been found worthy.

An observer would have been struck by the similarity not just of their expressions, but of everything else about them. While, obviously, only fraternal twins, Sebastian and Violet, as occasionally happens, could not have appeared more identical had they in fact been monozygotic. Both were very blond, fair-skinned, and blue-eyed; both had high foreheads, prominent cheekbones, and expressive mouths; both were slender and lithe; and while Sebastian was slightly shorter than average for a man, Violet was a little taller than average for a woman, so they were essentially the same height. Indeed, except for the fact that Violet's hair was a little longer than her brother's, and that Sebastian wore a touch of eye shadow, there was nothing to choose between them. Some felt that perhaps Sebastian was the prettier of the two, while Violet seemed the stronger and tougher, but that was more the result of subjective impressions, not something that could be concretely demonstrated.

Thus, the major difference between them was not physical, but rather that Sebastian was four minutes older than his sister. This slight temporal advantage, combined with several unintended ambiguities in their parents' wills, had made Sebastian, ten years earlier at the age of eighteen, sole heir to the Cornichon fortune. Violet had been left, as Sebastian had put it (merely stating the facts), on her own.

The Cornichons had long been one of the city's leading families. That they could trace their ancestry back to the famous *Ducs de Cornichon* (advisors to the kings of France) only increased the high esteem in which they were held. High esteem, though, did not put bread on the table, and Violet was forced to do something that no Cornichon within memory had done. She went to work.

Violet scraped together some money, mostly borrowed from friends of her parents who felt under some vague obligation to the orphaned girl. Using this small stake, a good deal of energy, intelligence, and imagination, and a little luck, Violet founded a cosmetics company. Contrary to all expectations—except perhaps her own—the company prospered.

There was nothing terribly special about her products, but Violet was an effective and tireless promoter of them. In the early days of the company, when its future was still in doubt, Violet had had the good fortune to be instrumental in helping the police break a difficult case. This generated a fair amount of publicity, but when Violet followed it up by solving a sensational murder on her own, she became a major celebrity, dubbed the "Society-Girl Detective". She was very young, pretty enough not to need the cosmetics she manufactured, from an old, well-known family, intelligent, and a high-powered corporate executive. Thus for a brief period she became the darling of the media.

Violet was smart enough to realize that that kind of attention did not last, and also smart enough to parlay it into making her cosmetics the choice of all the modern young women who identified with her. Inevitably, of course, new darlings of the media came along, and Violet was finding it increasingly difficult to get the attention she needed. If not yet desperate, the situation gave some cause for concern.

Likewise, over the last ten years, Sebastian had worked hard to create a name for himself. It too was Cornichon—but there the similarity ended.

Living as though he would be penalized if there was anything left of the family fortune by the time he reached thirty, Sebastian seemed to want to achieve a reputation for flamboyance and extravagance unrivalled since the days of Caligula. So successful was he in this that an entire brigade of the Socialist Worker's Party devoted itself exclusively to picketing him. Whenever he went out on the street he was greeted by a small group of protesters holding signs and shouting, "Dung-eating parasite! Boot-licking oppressor!" Sebastian would often smile, wave, and say, "Doesn't that sound like fun?" Cynics said that Sebastian had hired them himself by making a large donation to the SWP, but that was probably just cattiness. It was true, however, that one Christmas he gave each of his picketers a small gold pin of a greyhound—in other words, a little yellow running dog.

For a long time, Sebastian, like his sister, was a favourite of the media, and each new adventure was catalogued and analysed at length. Even when he was resting up between excesses, he was sought out whenever a comment or reaction was needed, for he could usually be relied on to provide something quotable, if not absolutely libellous. Early on he was labelled "irrepressible", and that designation stuck to him like a title of rank—as in, "Present were Lord and Lady Hohum and the irrepressible Sebastian Cornichon. . . . "

Perpetually maintaining a position in the forefront of the vanguard was arduous, and Sebastian was finding it harder and harder to avoid being swamped by each succeeding new wave. Violet had even heard rumours—which she'd dismissed as utterly implausible—that her brother was running out of money. It was a fact, though, that one of the leading arbiters of taste—who had previously participated in Sebastian's extravaganzas and called him irrepressible—had written that Sebastian was starting to sound like Joan Crawford doing her Oscar Wilde imitation. Tough times, it seemed, were ahead.

There was no way of knowing if Violet was bitter because her brother had received the entire Cornichon estate, or if Sebastian was envious of the success his sister had achieved on her own. Both had learned early on that there were certain things one kept to oneself. They did tacitly acknowledge that they appreciated each other most in very small doses; active, positive hatred was a real possibility, mainly avoided by their getting together only at infrequent intervals.

"Boring," Sebastian said.

"What?" Violet looked up from the book she had retrieved from the floor below the moosehead.

"Books like that are filled with pages and pages of boring exposition."

"Mostly it's necessary."

"Necessary or not, it's still boring."

Sebastian stood up, walked to the end of the room, and placed himself in front of the roaring fire. Then he moved to examine the rather ratty specimens that filled the wall above and around the immense stone fireplace. The moose was accompanied by parts of several dozen fellow creatures that some lover of nature had once slaughtered.

"Tasteful," Sebastian said.

He turned and walked the twenty or so yards to the opposite end of the lounge. The wall there was covered with a display of the weapons—bows, arrows, spears, clubs, daggers, shotguns, rifles, pistols, machine guns, and mortars—that had caused the destruction he had just considered.

"Charming," he mumbled.

Restlessly, he went over to the French windows that took up most of the room's long outside wall. The bleak November scene spread out before him contained nothing to lift the spirits. The windows opened onto a broad, grey stone terrace that ended in an ornate stone balustrade. Below and beyond the terrace, the land running down to the water's edge was hard and barren, dusted with a barely visible layer of granular snow, the emptiness broken only by the occasional concrete birdbath or toppled piece of statuary. And past the shore, the only things to be seen were the lake and the sky, both the same grim slate-grey colour, so that it was impossible to tell where one started and the other left off. Sebastian thought it was like being inside a giant overturned chamberpot.

This was Komondor Island, site of the Sill family country

house. Located near one of the continent's most famous summer playgrounds (an area which had also bestowed its name on a popular salad dressing), the island was accessible only by a long boat ride, from either the mainland or another island. Urban Sebastian, distrusting any part of nature that could not be put into a food processor, felt slightly uneasy surrounded by so much of it.

The island got its name from a very rough anglicization of a Mohawk phrase, *cho-moun-dhar*, meaning "place of sacrifice". The first Europeans to visit the island found cairns—piles of stones—that apparently had had some ritual function. The precise nature of these rituals was never determined, but Indian legend held that it was extremely bad luck to remain on the island overnight.

Shortly after the American Declaration of Independence, the island served as a temporary refuge for a band of United Empire Loyalists who had stolen a large part of the war chest of the fledgling Continental Congress. Pursued by a revolutionary force led by Aaron Burr, they hoped to escape attention by hiding on Komondor Island. Apparently they were successful. By the time Burr learned their whereabouts and organized an assault, the island was deserted. Whether the Loyalists' stay on the island was lucky or unlucky is not known; where they went, or what happened to them, has never been discovered, and the incident remains an interesting historical footnote.

By the time millionaire magnate Augustus Sill purchased Komondor Island in the early nineteen-twenties, the region had long been a popular summer retreat for the very wealthy. There was something about owning an entire island that appealed to these people whose dominions tended to be more financial than territorial. Not surprisingly, these deep feudal urges resulted in the construction of some of the most fabulous gothic piles ever seen outside a film studio. The prime example of this period—known as Late Robber Baronial—was the mansion out of which Sebastian unhappily gazed. Built according to Augustus Sill's own detailed instructions, his house was a not altogether successful amalgam of a Loire Valley château and Dracula's castle—simple, classic elegance forcibly merged with crenellated battlements, fortified towers, and chortling gargoyles.

Seen from above, Komondor Island is roughly the shape of the stone ceremonial daggers found throughout the Americas, and this is possibly the reason it was known as—used for?— the "place of sacrifice". It is not quite a mile long, and at its widest point—roughly the bottom of the hilt—it is just under half a mile across. The woods at the top half of the island were preserved, and Augustus Sill put his house in the lower part of the "blade". From his observation turret he could survey the water on three sides, and thus would have plenty of advance warning in case any of the less fortunate rabble launched an expeditionary force against him. As near as can be determined from the few existing old maps, the house happened to be built over the site of the ancient ritual cairns.

By all accounts, Augustus was regarded as having quite a sense of humour. He was considered one of the world's great practical jokers, and thought there were few things more amusing than either observing people who didn't know they were being watched, or leaping out at them from a place of concealment when they least expected it. Thanks to the personality of the host, weekend parties on Komondor Island were famous for being hilarious, if slightly tense, affairs. One day, though, Augustus's inveterate kidding caught up with him when he sneaked up on a guest who believed himself to be alone in the room. Unfortunately, the guest had just finished loading a shotgun preparatory to taking a few pops at the local seagulls. The coffin was closed for the ceremony.

Augustus's son, Ripley, did not have much better luck on the island. In the middle fifties, shortly after his young wife died in a freak boating accident, he happened to be unluckily positioned when one of the gargoyles on the observation turret somehow worked its way loose and tumbled down. His two-year-old daughter, Rosa, thus became the last surviving Sill.

For a while the local residents talked about the Curse of Komondor Island. Then Elvis Presley got into the news and they had other things to think about.

Sebastian Cornichon, staring glumly out of the window,

neither knew about any of this interesting history of the place he was visiting, nor much cared to.

"And speaking of boring," he said, going back to the couch, "what could be worse than being in a summer house in the middle of winter? In a grotesque mausoleum apparently decorated by Abercrombie and Fitch, on an island, in the middle of a lake, in the middle of a forest, in the middle of goddamn nowhere. Really! Why did I let you drag me out here?"

Violet looked at Sebastian, nodding her head and smiling. "If you'll recall, when I happened to mention that I was coming up here, you practically begged me to get you an invitation."

Sebastian fluttered his hand, as though to brush away this insignificant detail.

"What's the matter, Sebastian? Can you no longer get invitations from people who know you, only from people who don't?"

"Very funny—especially considering that lately you haven't exactly been *numero uno* in the hearts and minds of the natives. Besides, while I did express some mild interest in this function, I distinctly remember your enthusiastically urging me to join you. It quite surprised me."

"I did not *urge* you."

"You did so." Violet's eyes opened a bit wider as she tilted her head back, and Sebastian quickly held up his hands. "But let's not argue about *this*."

"You mean we'll have better things to argue about?"

Sebastian smiled. "Precisely. And anyway, no matter what, had I known it would take almost ninety minutes in that little boat. . . . And then to end up in a place like this. . . ."

Violet looked at the trophies on the wall and grimaced. "It is a bit remote."

"Listen, New Jersey is remote. This is ridiculous. And why are we here, anyway?"

"I already told you. Weren't you listening?"

"You know I never listen the first time anyone says anything. I only pay attention to things that are important enough to get repeated."

"Yeah," Violet nodded. "It's one of your more endearing qualities. But are you sure it won't be too boring for you to hear it again?"

Sebastian sighed in a long-suffering way. "It probably will be, Violet. But if you do a really good job, it shouldn't be substantially more boring than, say, watching you read, or—" motioning to the wall "—counting the number of creatures who have lost their glass eyes."

"How could I possibly refuse a request like that?"

Sebastian leaned forward, a tremendously intent, serious expression on his face.

"Give it a rest for once, would you," Violet said, and Sebastian shrugged, then sat back. "Okay. Tomorrow is the twenty-fifth birthday of Rosa Sill."

"Many happy returns."

"They will be, all right. Tomorrow is the day that Rosa gets control of the estate that's been held in trust for her since the death of her parents." Sebastian raised his eyebrows. "An estate of which this house and island are only a small part."

"Oh, my. Then this is a celebration?"

"I suppose so. Rosa was very insistent that the people who've been closest to her be present for the occasion."

"But why here?"

Violet shrugged. "It must have something to do with her parents' dying here. She's never been back since that summer. In fact, except for caretakers, I don't think anyone's been here since that time."

Sebastian shuddered. "Yuck. This is certainly not the way I'd celebrate becoming rich."

"I know. Your party lasted eighteen months, and made the evening news three times."

"Don't be like that. You were invited."

"Yes. To look after the refreshments."

"You would've been paid. And it still would have been more amusing than this."

"Well, Mousey obviously doesn't share your appetite for excess and ostentation."

"Mousey?" Sebastian said disbelievingly.

"That's what I called her at boarding school. She was so little and nervous and timid. Just like a little brown mouse."

"Charming," Sebastian said.

"I was a couple of years older than Mousey——"

"Three," Sebastian smiled.

"All right, three years older, and I felt sorry for the poor kid. She was such a plain little thing, and she didn't have any parents, and she always seemed shy and frightened. So I looked after her, helped her along. I was a cross between big sister and best friend—sort of her mentor, you might say."

Sebastian made a face. "Golly, Violet, that's enough to bring on hyperglycemia. Give me a break."

"Well, it's true."

"Oh, I don't doubt it. Nor do I doubt that, out of gratitude, poor little Mousey turned over her allowance to you every month and was your devoted slave."

"Sebastian!"

"Come on, Sis. I was shipped off to a similar institution. I know how these things work."

"Well, it wasn't like that," Violet said, perhaps huffing a little.

Sebastian shrugged. "Okay, it wasn't. But—could it be?— now that poor little Mousey is about to become rich little Mousey you think that maybe she could use another dose of mentoring?"

"Sebastian," Violet smiled, "I know you have difficulty understanding this because you've never had any, but friends help one another, they advise one another, they stand by one another no matter what."

"Even when one friend has the bad luck to become burdened with an immense sum of money?"

"Rosa Sill and I were, are, and will be friends. She's led a sheltered life. There are very few people she can rely on. If, because of my much greater experience in business and society, I'm able to offer her good advice, I'm happy to do so as a friend."

"And perhaps suggest that if she put some of her capital into Cornichon Cosmetics, it not only would be a good investment, but would add another link to the chain of your relationship?"

Violet's ordinarily pale skin flushed momentarily. "She could do worse."

Sebastian, envisaging a helicopter dumping bags of currency above the city, eloquently raised his eyebrows, but decided that any remark he made would result in an escalating round of accusation and denial, counterattack and rebuttal, and he didn't feel up to it just then. So he merely asked who else was going to be there for the festivities.

Violet nodded in acknowledgment of the change of subject, and much of the tension in her attitude relaxed. "As far as I know, her aunt and uncle will be here. They're from her mother's side, and I believe the aunt is Mousey's only living relative. Then I assume her fiancé will be coming. Also the family lawyer who's been her guardian and trustee. And I guess the woman who's been kind of a secretary-companion for Mousey will be here too."

Sebastian shook his head and sighed heavily. "Doesn't exactly sound like Mardi Gras, does it? What about these people? Are they as dull as they sound?"

"I have no idea."

"What do you mean?"

"I mean that I've heard a bit about them, but I've never met any of them."

"Isn't that kind of odd, you being her best friend and all?"

Violet shrugged. "Maybe it's a little strange. But Mousey has always been so shy and unassertive that she likes to keep things small and simple, keep things separate. So I've never met the others."

"Sounds to me as though she wanted to keep all the people who bully her from ganging up."

"Sebastian, you insist upon misunderstanding everything. It's not like that at all."

"Maybe not. But now, suddenly, she's bringing all you people together in one place at the same time. I wonder why? This might turn out to be interesting, after all."

"I doubt it, but I'm sure you'll do your best to make things uncomfortable for everyone."

"Lively, Violet. I make things lively. When are the others due?"

"Any time now, I suppose. Mousey arranged for boats to be at several different places, so the others are probably on their way."

"I hope so. It's about time this show got on the road. Let's see," Sebastian said, counting on his fingers. "There's you, me, aunt and uncle, fiancé, lawyer, secretary. That's seven. Then there's Medusa and the Yellow Peril."

"I assume by that you mean the housekeeper and the cook. And you wonder, Sebastian, why no one invites you anywhere any more."

"And little Mousey herself makes ten," Sebastian concluded, ignoring his sister. "Ten people on an isolated island. Now, why does that seem familiar?"

"Eleven!" a voice shrieked from out of the shadows next to the fireplace.

Startled, Violet and Sebastian jumped, then whirled in the direction of the voice. They saw a tall, gaunt woman in a fusty, robe-like black dress that hung to the floor. Her eyes were dark, darting, burning with an unnervingly intense light. Her hair was grey, wiry, and stood out from her head as though she'd had an electric shock. She reminded Sebastian of Charlton Heston as Moses when he returned from the mountain after talking with God. Either that, or the bride of Frankenstein.

"You forgot me," the voice cackled again. "They always forget me. Eleven! Eleven!" the woman shrieked, and ran from the room.

Violet and Sebastian stared at one another, identical expressions of surprise and confusion on their faces.

Violet was about to speak when the woman reappeared in the doorway. She laughed, an alien, hiccoughing, whining sound.

"Blood runs red!" she cried.

She laughed again, then disappeared.

CHAPTER TWO

"Hmm. Someone's package is not wrapped very tightly," Sebastian said.

"Where the hell did she come from?"

"Apparently she sprang full-blown from the head of the moose."

Violet looked at her brother, then groaned. "Must you?"

Sebastian shrugged helplessly, as though the burdens of a classical education were beyond his control. "More important," he said, "who the hell was that?"

"It could only be Mrs. Argus. Cassandra Argus."

"And who's that when she's not auditioning to be one of the Weird Sisters?"

"From what I've heard, she's always like that. That's Mousey's godmother—her mother's oldest and best friend. Mrs. Argus was with Mousey's mother when she drowned. That must've been pretty distressing. Then Mousey's father—who was also an old friend—was killed shortly after, and that apparently pushed her right over the edge. I had no idea that she was going to be here. What could Mousey be thinking of?"

"Wonderful," Sebastian said, standing up and moving back to the window. "Just what this party needed—a genuine loony."

After a couple of minutes, he announced that two more guests had arrived, and Violet joined him at the window.

Coming up the sloping path from the dock and boathouse, they saw two figures. The man, who walked with a firm stride, rigidly upright, was wrapped in a heavy leather greatcoat and carried a cane. Even at that distance, his stiff military bearing was as evident as his huge, gleaming white moustache. Next to him, much shorter and rounder, wearing a shabby cloth coat and multicoloured knit cap, a woman struggled with two large and obviously heavy suitcases.

"Must be the Dijons," Violet said.

"The aunt and uncle?"

"Yes. Colonel Nigel Dijon and Aunt Beatrice."

"I wonder what his problem is? Bad back? Gimpy leg?"

"Somehow I don't think that's what it is," Violet said coldly, through clenched teeth, as she watched the Colonel pick up the pace and move three steps in front of his labouring wife.

"It looks like a rather good arrangement to me," Sebastian said, and smiled when Violet turned and glared at him. "I know I would have appreciated a little help coming up that hill. Isn't that what equality's all about? After all, Sis, you always bragged about being the stronger one when we were kids." Violet's eyes opened wider, and the blue turned a steely colour. "Besides, you know I've always been kind of fragile."

"Sebastian, the only thing fragile about you is your grasp of reality."

"But still—" Sebastian gingerly rubbed his neck and rotated a shoulder.

"Did you just see that!" Violet said. "She stopped to rest a minute, and that son of a bitch went back and prodded her with his goddamn cane!"

"He was just encouraging her."

Violet made a couple of strangled sounds, then gave up trying to say anything coherent. Being young, attractive, and female, *and* the founder and head of a not insignificant corporation, Violet often felt that most of her time was spent dealing with leering, condescending, patronizing, porcine, chauvinistic fools. Being also intelligent, tough, and shrewd, she was able to take good advantage of the preconceived notions and blind spots of her male adversaries. Usually they never knew what hit them: they walked into a meeting calling her "honey" and thinking of her as "that cute little blonde", and staggered out, glad to be holding even the short end of the stick, and wondering if certain of their organs were still intact. Still, for all the satisfaction Violet got from such victories, some attitudes never failed to send her right up the wall; she had a pretty good idea of what she would have done with that cane if the Colonel had tried to poke *her* with it. But, Violet thought, trying to calm down, she had enough problems of her own without taking on those of someone who probably didn't want her help in the first place.

By this time, the Colonel and his lady had disappeared from view on their way to the front of the house. Violet and Sebastian were just able to hear the sounds of arrival coming from the vestibule, followed a few minutes later by the entrance of Colonel and Mrs. Dijon, now minus their coats, hats, and luggage, into the lounge.

The Colonel took one look at Violet and Sebastian and strode to the other end of the room where he planted himself, cane tucked under one arm like a swagger stick, before the display of weapons. Even in civilian clothes—country squire tweeds—the Colonel's attitude made it seem as though he was in uniform. His stiffly erect posture testified to a lifetime of stern discipline. Or, perhaps, to an exceedingly tight corset desperately restraining the spread of late-middle-aged flesh. The Colonel's features were a little coarse and thick, and there was a definite tendency to jowliness above the tight white collar. His most striking characteristics, though, were his bushy moustache and dense mane of white hair, both seeming that much whiter by contrast with a complexion that was the colour and texture of rare roast beef. Clear across the room, Sebastian thought he could almost hear the bubbling of the Colonel's blood pressure.

Beatrice Dijon observed her husband's display of good

manners with an expression that indicated she was not exactly surprised by his behaviour, then scurried over to Violet and Sebastian.

She was a plump, middle-aged woman, somewhat younger than her husband, wearing a very dated bright yellow dress with green and blue blotches on it. She smiled at Violet and Sebastian, but seemed flustered and out of breath.

"I'm Beatrice Dijon," she said, "but everyone calls me Budgie."

Violet handled the introductions while Sebastian smiled, biting hard on his tongue to keep from laughing. Aunt Beatrice's nickname seemed to him to be all too appropriate. In that dress, with her large, soft bosom and short, plump legs, her small nose and tiny pursed mouth, and with her bustling movements and determinedly cheerful attitude, she reminded Sebastian of the chirpy but dimwitted little bird with which she shared her name.

"Please excuse my idiot brother," Violet said, motioning to a painfully grinning Sebastian. "When you get to know him, you'll find the discourtesy of his silence is preferable to the discourtesy of his conversation."

"I'm sure that's not true." Budgie smiled at Sebastian, a little uncertainly, then turned back to Violet. "*I'm* the one who should apologize, dear. You see, this kind of weather affects the Colonel's wound, and puts him into one of his moods. It's nothing personal."

Budgie sounded a bit tired and annoyed, as though she had made this excuse more than a few times. Her eyes moved in the direction of the Colonel's back, and her plump little hands formed tight fists, nails digging into her palms. Violet and Sebastian both noticed this and raised their eyebrows at each other.

"Is this wound the reason he didn't help with the bags?" Violet said.

"Mm," Budgie said vaguely, still staring at her husband.

"He looks pretty fit to me. Just what kind of wound is it?"

With an effort, Budgie turned back to Violet and whispered, "Actually, dear, it's not—"

She cut herself off as the Colonel cleared his throat, a low, menacing growl.

Budgie shook her head. "You ask him to do something and he can't hear a word you say. But if anyone starts talking about him, all of a sudden he's got hearing like a bat."

Once more the Colonel cleared his throat, even more insistently.

"We'll talk later, dear." Budgie smiled, but Violet noticed that her hands were again tightly balled.

"So you're Rosa's aunt?" Violet said quickly.

"Yes. Viveca—her poor mother—was my youngest sister." Budgie shook her head. "It was terrible. She was so young, so alive, so happy. And then. . . ."

"It was a boating accident, wasn't it?"

"Yes. Terrible. And I could never understand it, because Viveca and her friend, Cassie, were both such good sailors. They'd won lots of prizes for races."

"How did it happen? Rosa never told me."

"We never knew for sure. I think the sail or the mast or whatever it's called swung around and knocked Viveca out of the boat. It must also have knocked her unconscious, because she'd drowned by the time Cassie got to her. What an awful experience! Poor Cassie was never the same. Kept saying she was responsible."

"She's here, you know."

"Who?"

"Mrs. Argus . . . Cassie."

"Here?"

"Yes. She announced her presence to us just before you arrived."

"Oh, no! I don't understand. What could the child be doing?" Budgie raised a hand to her mouth, and her forehead wrinkled, in either puzzlement or concern.

Violet, who could not help feeling some sympathy for

anyone married to the Colonel, looked at Sebastian for assistance in keeping the conversation moving, but he merely smiled back.

"You know I was at school with Mousey—I mean Rosa."

"You called her Mousey?" Aunt Budgie said. "Isn't that funny. I used to call her Squeak, because of her high-pitched little voice."

"Mousey and Squeak!" Sebastian said, making a face. "I think I'm going to be sick. I can hardly wait to see this pathetic little squeaking mouse of a creature."

"Sebastian!" Violet said.

"You mean she's not here yet?" Budgie said, and Violet shook her head. "That's odd. She should have been here. She was so insistent that we all arrive on time. I hope nothing's wrong."

"I'm sure not," Violet said. "She was probably just delayed a little."

"Still, it's strange. She was always such a prompt, reliable little child—terrified of being late or upsetting anyone." Budgie smiled. "Why, I can remember the times when she visited us during the holidays, how she'd come down to the table fifteen minutes early and stand waiting, knife and fork held straight up in her little hands. She was such a cute little Squeak."

Violet quickly glanced at Sebastian, and jumped in before he could comment. "Why didn't Mousey stay with you permanently after her parents died? You're her only relative, aren't you?"

"That's right, dear. And I wish she had. Especially since I never had any children of my own. But. . . ." Budgie moved her head in the direction of the Colonel.

"I see."

"No, no," Budgie said quickly. "It wasn't the Colonel's fault. We both wanted her, but for some reason poor little Squeak would always get upset when the Colonel was around. It was too bad, because actually the Colonel loves children.

Why, I can still see the happy expression he used to get when he bounced little Squeak on his knee, or when she sat on his lap."

Sebastian raised an eyebrow. "I can well imagine," he muttered to himself.

A low rumble came from the Colonel's direction, and Budgie, with a nervous flutter, snapped back to the present.

"What an interesting outfit you have on, dear," she said to Violet.

The garment she referred to was a very large, very loose-fitting jumpsuit made of dark green canvas, with lots of zippers, pockets, and pouches at odd angles or in odd places. It was the kind of unusual, unexpected statement that Violet was known for, and that her brisk, slender good looks were able to pull off.

"Thanks. It's an original."

"I'll say it is!" Sebastian said. "I keep telling Violet she could be doing maintenance on B-52s."

"Now, now. I think it suits her." Violet smiled. Sebastian sighed heavily and gazed up at the ceiling, and Budgie quickly said to him, "I think your clothes are nice, too, dear. Everything is such a pretty colour. What do you call it?"

"Ta." Sebastian held out his arm so the light could play off the sleeve of his silk shirt. "It's called Dusty Rose."

"Pink!" a throaty, phlegmy voice said from behind Sebastian. The Colonel then walked around and joined the small circle. Violet saw Budgie's soft plump figure tense.

Budgie attempted introductions, but the Colonel was having none of it. His slightly bulging eyes, the whites of which were bloodshot and seemed nicotine-stained, studied Sebastian with an expression of mounting disbelief.

"Pink!" he said again to no one in particular. "The man is wearing all pink."

"Now, dear. . . ."

"I've seen some pretty awful things in my time, but I've never seen anything like that!"

The Colonel lowered his brow, squinted, then pushed his

face close to Sebastian's. Sebastian got a whiff of stale cigars, cheap port, and thirty years of whisky. Up close, the Colonel's nose reminded Sebastian of a large red-skinned potato.

"Make-up!" the Colonel said. "He's wearing make-up!"

"Now, dear. . . ."

"Really! It's just a touch of eye shadow. It's one of my sister's products. I believe in loyalty, showing the family flag, stuff like that."

"Only because I give you free samples," Violet said.

"I didn't spend three years on the Death Railway to end up in the same room with a man dressed in pink and wearing make-up!"

"Now, dear. . . ."

"What he needs is a damned good beating. Yessir, a really good thrashing. That's all it would take to straighten him out."

"Oh, yes. Please," Sebastian said politely.

The Colonel's face moved two shades closer to maroon. He brandished his cane, the heavy silver lion's head on the handle seemingly trying to bite Sebastian on the nose.

Budgie sighed, almost trembling in an effort to maintain control. "I knew this would happen. I shouldn't have let him look at the weapons. Any display of armaments always over-excites him." She looked at her watch and sighed again. "And it's still hours yet before his next Thorazine."

"Watch it, old scout," the Colonel growled. "You know what happens to troopers who tell tales about the C.O."

The Colonel was impervious to the look his wife gave him, her hands again in fists, knuckles white. But Violet noticed. And she had the feeling that beneath Budgie's soft, vague, pleasant, auntly exterior, there was a reserve of tightly coiled strength and determination that would surprise a lot of people—and one in particular—if it ever sprang loose.

Budgie glared at the Colonel, and the Colonel glared at Sebastian, and Sebastian smiled pleasantly while he whistled a snatch of Mozart, and Violet thought she had better say something right away or poor little Mousey's party would be ruined before it ever began.

"Sebastian, why don't you go and see if you can get us some tea."

"Why? I don't really—"

"Sebastian!" ·

"All right, Sis. All right." He held up his hands, then started for the door.

"Wait a second, dear. I'll go with you," Budgie said.

The Colonel stood up even straighter, and hmphed a couple of times. "Remember, old scout..." he started, but Budgie and Sebastian were already out of the room.

Violet let out a deep breath and her body sagged a little. The atmosphere in the room relaxed, but she still felt uneasy. Ordinarily, she was the most clear-headed, coolly rational of people, not at all susceptible to superstition or flights of neurotic fancy. But just then she was aware of an undercurrent...of something wrong...of a presence she couldn't quite identify. She had a feeling of....

"Death and destruction!" Mrs. Argus shrieked from in front of the weapons' display, and then ran cackling from the room.

A small scream escaped Violet's lips, then several most unladylike phrases.

"Damned woman," the Colonel said, eyes bulging, cane quivering. "What she needs is a damned good beating."

CHAPTER THREE

OUTSIDE THE LOUNGE, SEBASTIAN LOOKED DOWN THE LONG hallway at the retreating figure of Mrs. Argus, who had sprung up behind them and nearly knocked them over as she rushed past. He shook his head and made unfriendly noises in his throat.

Aunt Budgie clucked her tongue several times. "Now, now, dear. You mustn't let her upset you. She can't help it, you know. Unlike some people," she added, her voice acquiring a hard edge. "He's always doing that. I hope he didn't bother you."

Never bothered by outrage or hostility that he himself had generated, Sebastian airily waved this off.

"You must be wondering why I put up with it," Budgie said.

Actually, Sebastian had been wondering which of the dozen or so doors off the hallway led to the loo, but he smiled politely.

"Believe me, there are times I wish I didn't have to. And if I were younger—say, your age, dear—I probably wouldn't. But what can I do? I have no money of my own. I can't do anything. The only skill I have is keeping the Colonel more or less pacified, and there's not a big demand for that, is there? So I guess that's it." Budgie sighed wistfully and placed her little hands onto her plump bosom. "But I shouldn't be telling you all this, dear. It's no concern of yours."

Sebastian, who generally preferred to hear intimate details in the form of rumour or innuendo, and who didn't understand why a woman he'd known for only five minutes was unburdening her soul to him in the corridor, couldn't help but agree. "Now, where do you suppose the kitchen is?" he said, taking Budgie by the elbow.

The first door they tried led to the cellar. The next two were closets. Behind the fourth door they heard faint rustling sounds. Opening it, Budgie and Sebastian found themselves in an oak-panelled, oriental-carpeted room that must once have served as the study. The sounds were coming from behind a heavy mahogany desk where a man was bent over, rummaging through a lower drawer and muttering to himself.

Sebastian cleared his throat, and the man hastily sat up, slamming the drawer and looking around nervously. He seemed to be in his sixties, a small, wizened individual in a conservative dark suit that hung loosely on his shrunken, dehydrated body. He had a fringe of grey hair around a high, knobby skull, and his face was so creased and puckered that there didn't seem to be any flesh between the skin and bone. Sebastian thought he looked like an albino prune.

The man's dark eyes, though, were hard and bright, and darted between Sebastian and Budgie with a startled expression. While his uneasiness might have been due to a nervous condition or surprise at the unexpected intrusion, the last time Sebastian had seen a similar expression had been at a cocktail party when he'd flipped on the overhead light in the darkened bedroom that was being used as a cloakroom. Poor Freddy hadn't been able to face him since.

"Who are you?" Sebastian said.

"Who are *you*?" the man replied. His voice sounded as dry and puckered as his face, each word separate and distinct, each a crackling of old parchment.

"I'm the uninvited guest, just making myself at home. And this is Aunt Budgie."

The man sniffed a couple of times as though a disagreeable suspicion had been confirmed. "I'm Drupe. Eustace Drupe, of Drupe, Damson and Taupe. I'm Miss Sill's guardian and trustee. I arrived a few moments ago and was looking for Miss Sill."

"In the desk?" Sebastian asked pleasantly. Budgie swallowed a laugh and poked Sebastian in the arm.

Drupe's hard little eyes narrowed, and behind his compressed lips they could see his dentures slide from side to side, independent of his jaws. "Have you seen Miss Sill?"

"She's not here yet," Budgie said.

"She's not?" Drupe's teeth moved up and down, then clicked twice. "She gave me very precise instructions as to how and when to get here, but she herself has not arrived." Two more clicks. "Most inconsiderate. Most annoying." Drupe's eyes then focused at a spot directly through their bodies and two feet behind them, thereby precluding any possibility of further conversation.

Sebastian looked at him for a long minute, then shrugged. "Well, it was certainly a pleasure. There will be tea in the lounge if we can ever find the kitchen."

"Down the hall; turn left," Drupe said, not changing the focus of his eyes.

"Oh? Ta." They started to leave, then Sebastian leaned back in. "You might try that Chinese cabinet over there."

"What for?" Drupe's raspy voice rose alarmingly, and his glance was suddenly sharp and suspicious.

"For Miss Sill, of course. Given the choice, no one would stay in a desk any more." Sebastian grinned and exited.

Back in the corridor Sebastian said, "What a strange person."

Considering the source, some people might have found this assessment a bit strange too, but Aunt Budgie didn't notice. "Why isn't she here yet?" she said. "I hope nothing's happened."

"I wouldn't worry. Having had the Colonel for an uncle, Violet for a friend, and Drupe for a lawyer, I don't know what more could happen to poor little Mousey Squeak." Sebastian put a comforting arm around Budgie's shoulders and smiled. "If she's got any sense at all, she probably decided not to show up."

Budgie pulled away and looked at Sebastian, very alarmed, her pale watery eyes round and her soft cheeks shaking. "You don't really think so, do you?"

"Well, *I've* been known to give my own parties a miss."

"But that would spoil everything," Budgie said. Then she turned and bustled down the hall, clucking worriedly to herself.

Sebastian watched her, eyebrows raised in mild interest. He had the very rare sensation of feeling that he might well be the least unbalanced person present. He shrugged, then took a few quick strides and caught Aunt Budgie at the end of the corridor.

Off to the left where the passage turned, they heard a rhythmic thumping, as though of a machine on an assembly line, and a weird, high-pitched wailing noise, like that of a cat caught in a drill press. Following the sound, they finally found themselves in the kitchen.

It was a huge, old-fashioned room, filled with giant sinks, great black stoves, and a bank of ovens. Hanging from the beams were oversized utensils (whose original functions were obscure, although they did give Sebastian some interesting ideas) and immense cast-iron pots, seemingly large enough to stew up whole villages. Bigger than most restaurant kitchens, it could easily have accommodated a platoon of sauciers and sous-chefs, and been used to prepare formal dinners for 150 people, or more.

At the moment, though, it held just one person. At the far end of the room, next to what was undoubtedly the door to a walk-in freezer, a man was working at the long butcher's bench. Even from behind, it was obvious he was Chinese, with muscular shoulders and short black hair standing out on his head in spiky tufts.

"That's Mr. Ching," Sebastian whispered. "Our cook."

Mr. Ching was chopping away at something with a large cleaver. The amazing speed and accuracy with which he worked was that of a highly skilled artisan, and the regular chk-chk of the cleaver hitting the chopping block could have come from a precision die-cutter.

Sebastian and Budgie could not see what he was chopping, but from the agonized screeches they heard, they were afraid it was some still-living creature. However, when they moved closer they saw it was merely a slab of meat cut from what appeared to be the leg of a very large beast. The wailing sounds came from a small portable phonograph playing a selection from the Peking Opera along with which Mr. Ching was enthusiastically humming.

Budgie and Sebastian moved close to Mr. Ching, but he was too immersed in the music and his work to notice. Sebastian tried to get his attention, but without success. Finally, after practically shouting "Excuse me" for the fourth time, he got through.

Mr. Ching leapt high in the air and whirled around, his mouth ferociously open in a silent scream of surprise and anger. As he hit the ground, the cleaver came down on the thickest part of the leg and effortlessly sliced completely through it, bone and all, with a terse thwack. Mr. Ching pulled the cleaver from the chopping block and faced Budgie and Sebastian, assuming an attack stance—poised, knees bent, on the balls of his feet, with the cleaver held out to the side.

Budgie whimpered and scurried to stand behind Sebastian. Had Sebastian been quicker off the mark, he probably would have taken cover behind her, but as it was, he smiled and placatingly held out his hands.

"Guess the housekeeper's not here, right?"

Mr. Ching spat out a short, harsh statement in Mandarin tones, and took a half shuffle-step towards them.

"You're right," Sebastian said hastily, still smiling. "She's probably upstairs, and that's where we'll look."

Moving backwards as fast as they could, Sebastian and Budgie got themselves out of the kitchen. In the hallway again, they heard what sounded like a brief laugh, followed by the resumption of the rhythmic chopping.

"Oh, my," Budgie said.

"Hmm," Sebastian said. "He acts like someone used his wok for washing out underwear. Charming."

Going up the back stairway to the second floor, Sebastian paused on the landing to look out the window. He saw a small boat approaching the dock, and then, much farther away, another boat moving slowly through the choppy grey water.

"More company," he said to himself. "And none too soon."

At the same moment that Sebastian was trying to make out who was in the nearer boat, its passenger was gazing up at the Sill mansion—which looked, from that perspective, particularly grim and foreboding. The passenger, warmly wrapped in a full-length wolf's-fur coat, was Derrick Costain, well-known man about town and Rosa's fiancé. His glossy black hair was brushed back from his broad forehead, and fell over the top half of his ears in thick, windswept waves. The tilt of his head, the angle of his firm chin, the thrust of his elegant nose, all suggested that he was at the helm of a sleek ocean-going sloop, rather than huddled on the front bench of a ten-foot dinghy. His deep tan, especially at this dreary time of the year, seemed to speak of Caribbean weekends and polo ponies. Or, perhaps, mid-town tanning clinics.

If, while looking at the house, Derrick saw the vague outline of Sebastian's pink-clad form behind the small landing window, it certainly did not register. His ordinarily smooth brow was creased, a sure sign that he was deep in thought.

"What could little Pinky have been thinking about," he wondered. "Coming up here at this time of the year? I told her, if she wants to go away to celebrate, there are lots of places we could go. I mean, it's not like she couldn't afford it. But no, she insisted. Sure been acting strange lately. And when she gave me the instructions to come out here. That look of hers. Kind of distant and secretive. Like she'd made a decision. Christ! Has she heard something? That's all I need. And after all I've put into this. Maybe my last chance. No, don't even think it.

"Damn! Look at that place. What a dump! But it's worth a bundle, that's for sure. Maybe we can sell it or trade it. And I will get a chance to check out that idea of mine. Wouldn't it be something if that came through? If I'm right, it could solve all my problems. And even if not, I just have to hold on a little longer, and then everything's easy.

"I just wish I knew what was in her mind. Damn silly bitch! It was all going so well. If this falls apart, that could be it for this boy. The old finito. No! She couldn't have heard. Could she? Damn, damn, damn. I'll just have to count on the old Costain luck to pull me through. On the other hand, if I'd had some luck along the way, I wouldn't be in this mess. Well, it should all be clear soon, one way or the other. Oughta be a real fun party.

"Another boat. I wonder which one that is, which lucky guest? I say! From this distance, she looks pretty good. Maybe this won't be so bad after all.

"Here's the dock at last, thank God. I thought this boat trip would never end. I wonder how poor little Pinky's going to take it? She gets seasick walking through puddles. Serve her right. Her own damn fault. Dumb idea. But I'll be so kind and considerate . . . take care of my poor little Pinky Sillikins. That's right. Hang in there, Derrick, old boy. With any luck at all, this time next year you'll be some place a whole lot better."

Meanwhile, in the boat still approaching the island, the passenger shivered once and tried to snuggle deeper into her voluminous, heavy wool Navy-surplus pea jacket. On the lapel, the ornate medals from several long-since-defunct principalities softly jangled together.

Once again, Derrick's finely honed instincts, effective even at considerable distances, had proved to be correct. Cerise Redford, the passenger in the boat, was indeed good looking, though some might feel she tried her best to disguise it.

Her hair was a striking shade somewhere between copper and maroon. Hanging in a series of shaggy layers, it was not unlike a deep-pile nylon bathmat—which was precisely the lo-tech look she wanted. Her face was a smooth oval, and even a heavy application of make-up could not totally obscure its pale, perfect, pre-Raphaelite quality. Lots of black stuff around her clear green eyes turned them into something from an Egyptian tomb inscription, but their wit and intelligence still shone through. Thick dark lipstick made her mouth a startling crimson blotch, but did not cover up the fact that it smiled frequently.

For someone as gloriously, as flagrantly, as antagonistically contemporary as twenty-six-year-old Cerise Redford, the position she held—that of secretary/companion to Rosa Sill— was a curiously old-fashioned one. Still, it was precisely the one she wanted. Or, rather, the one she had to have.

Like Derrick moments before, Cerise examined the manor house as she approached the shore. There must have been something in its grotesque features that prompted ambiguous reveries, for she too grew thoughtful.

"So that's where it happened. Considering the Victorian, maybe even eighteenth-century, nature of it all, that gothic folly would certainly have been an appropriate setting. Christ! Poor Becky. It was a big deal then. As was made very clear to me more than once. Stupid, sanctimonious, small-town bitches!

"But I shouldn't complain. I guess it could've been worse. Apparently, it *was* worse, for *her*. Poor little kid. Shipped off and around. At least Becky cared, did her best. But never got over it. She'd die if she knew I was here. Golly, look at that— turrets and everything. It's funny. I really am kind of glad to see this place, at last. But I can't imagine why *she'd* want to come out here.

"Lately, though, I haven't been able to figure her at all. She seems to be changing. Which, all things considered, might not be so bad. But the way she's been looking at me, acting. I get the feeling she knows. Or suspects.

"Will it make any difference if she does? It shouldn't. I'll get what's mine. One way or another.

"If I still want it.

"What do you mean, 'if'? Don't be an idiot. It's what you've planned for years, especially the last two.

"Except before there was jealousy, even hate. Now I'm not so sure any more. . . . Or sometimes I'm not sure.

"Don't be a jerk. Take what's yours, take what you can. That's what you decided. You're becoming a dishrag. You've been around *her* too long.

"My God! Now I'm talking to myself. I must be cracking up. It's finally getting to me. And it used to be so straightforward. Well, I'll try not to worry about it for just a while longer. I have the feeling that everything will become clear very soon. This promises to be quite some get-together.

"Yeah. And so was the Masque of the Red Death.

"Oh, hell. That guy is waiting on the dock for me. What does he think he's doing? It must be Derrick. At least I hope it is. Two people like that would be too much. Jesus.

"Take a deep one, kiddo. Here we go."

The man running the outboard smoothly manoeuvred his boat up to the dock. Derrick leaned forward, smiling, his large, strong teeth very white against his dark tan. He extended his hand to help Cerise from the boat.

Cerise looked at the teeth, then the manicured hand, then nimbly hopped off the boat without assistance. The boatman handed up her green nylon duffle bag.

After they introduced themselves, Derrick, still smiling confidently, made no attempt to hide the fact that his eyes were moving all over her, from her shaggy, metallic hair to her ragged, blue canvas deck shoes, studying her, sizing her up. Cerise looked back steadily, expressionlessly, her only thought that his magnificent fur coat would've looked a helluva lot better if it was still on its original owners.

When he finished his leisurely examination, Derrick smiled at her with even more self-assurance. "Now I know why Pinky never introduced us."

Cerise coolly looked at him. "So do I," she said.

The small boat started to move off, and she went to the end of the dock. "When will you be back to pick us up?" she called.

The boatman looked up at her, but said nothing. Then he swung the boat around and chugged off.

"Mine wouldn't tell me, either," Derrick said. "You know, a few minutes ago, I couldn't imagine anything worse than being stranded in this place. . . . Now, I'm not so sure." He flashed her another dazzling testimony to his dentist's skill.

"We'd better go up to the house," Cerise said coldly.

Scarcely missing a beat, Derrick moved to pick up her duffle bag, but Cerise jerked it out of his grasp. At that instant, Derrick saw an odd expression flash behind her green eyes. At first he thought she was annoyed, then he thought she was scared. But that didn't make any sense, and before he could make up his mind, the strange look was gone.

"I can do it myself," Cerise said, putting the bag's strap over her shoulder.

One of Derrick's eyebrows lifted as he watched her stride determinedly towards the house. "I'll bet you can," he said softly.

He picked up his own elegant designer bags of honey-coloured leather and followed Cerise.

By this time, in their search for the housekeeper, Sebastian and Budgie had covered the second floor, which held far more bedrooms than would be needed by their small party, and were now going down one of the low-ceilinged corridors on the top floor. This had originally held the servants' quarters, as well as numerous storage rooms. If no expense had been spared on the lower floors, corners had not only been cut but entirely eliminated by the time construction had reached this level. Old Augustus, who had started life selling pickled fish from a barrel, had believed that the lower orders had to be kept in their place. And their place was the attic, in spartan little cubicles that managed to be both airless and drafty at the same time.

". . . and her real name is Mrs. Hook—if you can believe it," Sebastian was saying. "But I call her Medusa, because the way she glares at you she might be trying to turn you to stone."

"Now, dear, I'm sure you're exaggerating."

"You haven't met Mrs. Hook yet. She's the kind of person who regards it as a great imposition—even an affront—to be asked to do any of the things she was hired to do. Makes like she's doing you a huge favour if she does her job. Because really, you see, she was hired so that you could make her life easier, rather than the reverse."

"Well, dear, I wouldn't know because the Colonel won't let me have any, but they do say that good help is hard to find."

"And La Hook does nothing to refute that," Sebastian laughed. "After all, we've been looking for nearly twenty minutes. But I think our goal is near."

He pointed to where the dimness of the corridor was broken by a rectangle of pale yellow light coming out of the open door of one of the storage rooms. They heard sounds of rooting and rummaging, and of objects being roughly chucked about, all punctuated by harsh grunts and guttural curses.

"Sounds like the *grande dame* herself," Sebastian said. He held up a warning finger. "Approach with caution. You thought old Ching was alarming, but you ain't seen nothing yet."

"Now, dear . . ." Budgie clucked, and pushed Sebastian's arm in good-natured reproof. Still, she was careful to position herself behind him as they approached the door.

Looking in, they saw the crêpe bottoms of two sensible shoes, above which was a large rectangular expanse of black rayon tautly stretched across two rather square buttocks.

"Hmm. Like being behind the eight cube," Sebastian whispered, and Budgie pushed him again, a little more roughly this time.

The rest of Mrs. Hook was hidden beneath a large pile of the kind of garbage that is always found in attics. Broken bits of once useful objects; perfectly intact specimens of useless ones; half-empty containers of products whose manufacturers had long since ceased to exist; things of sentimental or potentially pragmatic value, like a box labelled "Pieces of string too short to save"; the usual stuff. Into all this Mrs. Hook burrowed furiously, noisily, like a pig after truffles. A snort of triumph, then she slowly backed out of the heap and stood up. When she turned around and saw Budgie and Sebastian, her eyes went round and her lips pulled back on her crooked and discoloured teeth, as though preparatory to snarling. She quickly recovered, though, and her eyes narrowed in a way that gave Budgie a good idea of what Sebastian had meant. For his part, Sebastian couldn't decide if the gimlet stare that pinned him was one of suspicion or—could it be?—guilt.

Seen in her entirety, Mrs. Hook looked like a cubist's rendition of a housekeeper, all black-and-white rectangular blocks and flat surfaces lumpily stuck together. Broad, mannish shoulders, a stern shelf-like bosom, chunky hands with blunt, stubby fingers, large square hips, and sturdy pillar legs. Her face looked almost completely flat beneath the square little maid's cap that tightly covered her short steel-grey hair. Below a wide forehead overhanging small eyes and a compressed upturned nose with flaring nostrils, the permanent frown of her mouth formed vertical crease lines down her face, making her chin look like that of a ventriloquist's dummy. So great was the impression of large, dense immobility that Sebastian felt it would be necessary to call a taxicab in order to go around her.

With difficulty he forced his eyes away from Mrs. Hook's to the box she held in her hand. It was very dusty from years of abandonment, but there was no mistaking the large skull and crossbones on the front, nor the bold yellow letters announcing RAT POISON. Then Sebastian noticed the other boxes neatly stacked near the door. Each was dedicated to the eradication of a different pest, but each displayed the same clear image of Jolly Roger.

"Charming," Sebastian mumbled.

"We got rats," Mrs. Hook announced, much as some restaurants said that they had three stars. "We got mice. We got roaches. I told Missy it'd be no good coming here. That there'd be nothing but work for a body. Told her there'd be vermin running all over the place." She looked hard at Sebastian as she said this, and he involuntarily backed up a step, bumping into Budgie.

"But does little Missy listen?" Mrs. Hook went on, addressing the bare lightbulb overhead. "No, of course not. Does little Missy care how much work she makes for a body? No, of course not. It's 'Please do this, Mrs. Hook. Please do that, Mrs. Hook. Could you do this if you get the chance? Would you do that if it's not too much trouble, Mrs. Hook?' Never gives a body a chance to rest. Some people just never have any consideration. Think the whole world is there for their pleasure. Well, I told little Missy, I told her, enough is enough. A body's got to draw the line. And this body goes no further." Mrs. Hook heavily stamped her square-toed sensible shoe. "And now we got rats." She again squinted at Sebastian. "Well, what do you want?"

Sebastian's mouth moved soundlessly a few times before he managed the one word, "Tea."

"If it's not too much trouble, dear," Budgie quickly added.

"For seven or eight, I think," Sebastian said.

Mrs. Hook's eyes narrowed menacingly.

"And be sure to make some for yourself, too, dear," Budgie offered placatingly.

Mrs. Hook grunted as she turned her back on them and bent to gather up the boxes.

Budgie and Sebastian looked at one another and silently agreed it was time to leave. As they hurried down the corridor, they heard Mrs. Hook vehemently grumbling about how some people had learned that there's some things a body won't do, and how some other people were just going to have to learn it.

"You see what I mean?" Sebastian said when they were at a safe distance.

Budgie clucked a few times. "Oh, my. She certainly is . . . imposing, isn't she?" She shivered. "You know, dear, I got the strangest sensation just then. I can't explain it. It was one of . . . of. . . ."

"Murder and mayhem!" a voice shrieked immediately behind them, as Mrs. Cassandra Argus leapt out from an unused storeroom. Once again, the black-robed figure nearly knocked them over as she careened down the long hall like a human bowling ball.

"That's one old bat I'd like to get out of this belfry," Sebastian muttered as he attempted to fluff up and smooth down a most disarranged Aunt Budgie.

CHAPTER FOUR

WHEN SEBASTIAN AND BUDGIE RETURNED TO THE LOUNGE, they found the Colonel and Violet separated by most of the room, and standing in postures indicative of considerable tension.

"Not again!" Budgie said to herself, quite annoyed, and scurried over to her husband.

Thinking that this looked promising, Sebastian joined Violet. "What's up, Sis?"

Her blue eyes flashed like valuable sapphires. "That son of a bitch tried to open some of my zippers," she hissed, and checked again that everything on her jumpsuit was securely fastened.

"And?"

"I dissuaded him," Violet said, in a way that made Sebastian think that the Colonel was lucky not to have become the latest addition to the mounted trophies he was so intently studying.

A few minutes later Eustace Drupe, carrying a large, old, and very battered leather briefcase, came into the lounge, but his entrance did nothing to dispel the decidedly frigid atmosphere that had settled on the room. Glancing around and deciding there was little reason to choose either group, Drupe went over to Violet and Sebastian, and the latter performed the introductions.

"I know about Mr. Drupe," Violet said. "He was a presidential advisor and party fund raiser."

The lawyer bowed in acknowledgement, bending far enough to provide a glimpse of his lumpy cranium.

"He also had the distinction," Violet went on, "of being the least-well-known unindicted co-conspirator in that sleazy affair not long ago."

Drupe clicked his dentures twice, and his gaze hardened. "And I am not completely unfamiliar with you, Miss Cornichon. Tell me, what was the disposition of that most interesting case of yours?"

"It has not been decided yet."

"What case is that, Violet?"

"Nothing very important."

"No?" Drupe said. "It seems a young woman who used one of Miss Cornichon's products ended up scarred for life."

"Neither causality nor liability has been determined."

"The case—and its settlement—should create precedent." Drupe clicked his teeth and smiled at Violet. Sebastian thought he'd not seen an expression like that since the last time he watched *The Return of the Mummy* on the Late Show. Drupe again bowed slightly, and left to visit Budgie and the Colonel.

"Mousey'd better count the silver before she lets him leave," Violet said through clenched teeth. "Dessicated old goat. That's one *corpus* it'd be a pleasure to *habeas.*"

Before Sebastian could pursue the most interesting issue that the lawyer had raised, Cerise and Derrick appeared in the doorway. She had on a cheerful red and blue plaid flannel shirt tucked into faded army fatigue pants that were, at the same time, amusingly baggy and intriguingly tight. Far tighter, though, was Derrick's fawn-coloured Italian suit and his fine French shirt in palest yellow. The shirt was open to mid-torso to display curls so dark and thick that they nearly covered the heavy gold chain that nestled on his chest.

"My goodness!" Sebastian said.

Barely pausing, Derrick sized up the situation and made a

beeline right to Violet. He positioned himself in such a way that Sebastian was effectively excluded from the conversation, then he took Violet _____ ___ commenced introductions.

When he hear_ ___let's name, his eyes momentarily widened, but he did n__ __render her hand. "As in Cornichon Cosmetics?" he ___ __?

"Yes, Mr _____ ___?

He smiled broadly, brought his other hand up to cover Violet's, and leaned closer. "Call me Derrick," he said in his most oily manner.

"Gimme a break!" Sebastian said under his breath.

Cerise, who was standing next to him, giggled, and they both immediately recognized that they would be friends. They huddled together, laughing and joking for a bit, then eased themselves next to Violet and Derrick, where yet more introductions were made.

"I just love your jumpsuit," Cerise said sincerely.

"Oh? Thanks."

"Tell me, what surplus store did you get it at?"

Sebastian, who recognized all of Violet's danger signals, quickly ushered away a bewildered Cerise.

"Let me introduce you to the Colonel," he said. "He might shake his cane at you, but at least he won't scratch your eyes out. . . ."

And so, eventually, everyone got to meet everyone else, and discussions of varying degrees of animation and interest took place. As often occurs at gatherings of strangers, the party slowly began to collect itself close together in the centre of the room. Perhaps the proximity of others who are in the same boat in some way mitigates the pall of an otherwise boring or awkward conversation.

Violet, at least, looked as though she'd welcome some fresh input as Derrick escorted her to one of the floral-patterned couches. He pushed aside Drupe's briefcase so they could sit down, but because he was not paying much attention to what he was doing, the case accidentally fell to the floor and popped open, spilling its contents.

A panicked gasp, like the scraping of a harsh desert wind, issued from Drupe, and he dove to retrieve his belongings.

As one of Derrick's few guiding principles was to always, *always* do whatever was necessary to ingratiate himself with people of wealth, power, and influence, he too gasped in horror. Then, uttering profuse apologies, he joined Drupe on the floor to help him gather in the scattered papers. This assistance seemed to upset Drupe even more, but Derrick was bigger and stronger, and insisted upon trying to make amends for his terrible gaffe.

The insignia on the outside of a slender paper wallet caught Derrick's attention, and with friendly curiosity he opened it. "Oh, I say! Going to Rio in two days! Lucky you!"

Two red spots appeared on Drupe's sallow, sunken cheeks. "Give me that, young man!" A claw-like hand shot out and tried to grab the ticket.

"Are you going for business or pleasure? But of course, there's always pleasure in Rio."

"Give me that!" This time Drupe managed to snatch the envelope from Derrick, and quickly shoved it into his briefcase.

"Do you know Rio?" Derrick went on, blind to the lawyer's agitation. "I adore it. I remember the Duchess once chartered a yacht, and we all went down for Carnival. Or *Carnaval*, as they call it down there."

"Oh, shut up," Violet said, though perhaps not loud enough to be heard.

Drupe finished picking up his things and made to sit down.

"You missed something," Sebastian said helpfully, retrieving an object from beneath the couch. It was roughly cylindrical, six inches long, and he looked curiously at it. "Yikes!" he said, as he inadvertently touched the hidden button and a razor-sharp blade sprang out with a menacing swoosh.

"Thank you." Drupe took the knife, closed it, put it in his

pocket, and sat down, clutching his briefcase tightly against his scrawny chest.

An uncomfortable silence, during which no one knew where to look and everyone tried unsuccessfully to think of something to say, settled on the room. It was Aunt Budgie who ended it at last.

"Do you know, our boatman tried to tell us that this island was haunted. Or that there was a curse on it. Something like that. He was a bit vague about the details."

"Mine told me the same thing," Cerise said. "There's an Indian legend that disaster comes to anyone who spends the night here."

"Charming," Sebastian said.

"Balderdash!" the Colonel snorted.

"It is no legend," a voice behind them said. Once again, Mrs. Argus had materialized apparently out of nowhere. This time, however, she did not shriek. Her voice was calm, her manner reasonable; only her words were demented. "It is no legend. Death is in this house, and She——"

"She?" Derrick asked, amused.

"Yes, She. Death is a woman."

"At last! Equality!" Cerise said, and Sebastian giggled.

"Laugh if you want," Mrs. Argus said, and Sebastian no longer wanted to. "But Death is here. And She sits on your shoulders, and yours, and yours...." A long bony finger pointed at each in turn, causing them to squirm uneasily and avert their eyes.

"And yours, too?" Violet asked, but by then Mrs. Argus was no longer to be seen. "Damn! I'd like to know where she keeps popping out of and disappearing to."

"I'd like to know," Sebastian said, his voice unusually hard, "why someone doesn't step on that old hag."

"Hear, hear!" the Colonel said, pounding the floor with his cane.

"Now, dear, don't excite yourself," Budgie soothed. Then her brow wrinkled and she looked around at the others, shaking her head apologetically. "I know I'm being silly—it's probably just this lonely place, and the boatman's stories, and everything—but I have the strangest feeling that something awful is going to happen."

"Well, I hope so," Sebastian said. "And the sooner the better. This is getting awfully tedious."

"Sebastian!"

"Well, it is, Violet." He stood up and went over to the fireplace.

"I don't know about anything awful happening," Cerise said, "but ever since I got here, I've had the feeling we're being watched."

"Of course we are." Sebastian pointed to the trophy wall. "There're thirty-six pairs of glass eyes staring down at us."

"Yucko." Cerise made a face, then shook her head. "No, it's something else."

"It's probably just that time of the month, sweetie," Violet purred, smiling.

"Tea!" Mrs. Hook announced, bringing the trolley to a halt with a clatter that expressed perfectly her opinion of this labour-intensive social custom. "You can serve yourselves. A body's got enough work to do without pouring tea, too."

As she whirled to go, a lacy monogrammed hankie that was sticking out of a pocket in her uniform caught on a corner of the tea trolley and fell to the floor.

Another of Derrick's principles was that you always wanted the servants on your side, and so he quickly scooped up the frilly article, and said, "Mrs. Hook". He had to repeat this, in successively louder tones, three times before she stopped her march across the room and turned around.

"You talking to me?"

"Your name's Mrs. Hook, isn't it?"

The housekeeper's eyes narrowed suspiciously, and Derrick felt himself growing a bit rocky around the edges. He held up the hankie. With a sound like a vacuum seal being broken, Mrs. Hook sucked in a breath, then stormed across the room, grabbed the hankie, and headed out.

"Mrs. Hook?" Cerise said tentatively, but this time the

housekeeper stopped right away and turned again. "Did she—Miss Sill—say when she'd be arriving?"

Mrs. Hook looked expressionlessly at Cerise. "Dinner's at eight," she said, and left.

With that, they all seemed to want to drink their tea as fast as possible and retire until dinnertime.

Soon, only Cerise was left in the lounge, pacing around, trying to determine the origin of that feeling she'd had. After the event, intuitions are often found to have had a basis in reality, and so it was to prove with the sensation Cerise had experienced. However, for the moment she was unable to figure out its cause, and soon went up to her room, again thinking that she must be cracking up.

Even if the others had believed her—or had had similar feelings themselves—it is doubtful if it would have made any difference to what was shortly to happen.

CHAPTER FIVE

THE EIGHT WHO GATHERED FOR DINNER THAT EVENING DID not seem to do so with much enthusiasm or appetite. Whatever the other reasons, the dining room itself certainly did not help. It was gloomy, dark-panelled, and high-ceilinged, and the huge dimly lit chandeliers over the long table seemed designed to cast shadows rather than shed light. Sebastian felt as though he'd wandered into an especially murky German expressionist film.

After some initial jockeying for position, the Colonel sat at one end of the table and Aunt Budgie at the other. Mr. Drupe, Sebastian, and Cerise were down one side, and Mrs. Argus, Violet, and Derrick sat opposite them. Not, perhaps, an ideal arrangement, but probably the best that could be managed, all things considered.

Soon after they were settled, Mr. Ching came in bearing a platter with a large but not very tasty-looking roast on it, and set it between the Colonel and Mrs. Drupe. After a few quick swipes on the whetstone brought the large knife to surgical sharpness, Mr. Ching began carving the joint.

The Colonel grunted appreciatively as he watched the dry, grey slices fall off with perfect uniform precision. He glanced up to see who was doing such nice work, and for the first time saw their cook. His eyes bulged and his face turned a dangerously dark shade.

"He's an Oriental!"the Colonel said, pointing an accusatory finger.

"Golly," Sebastian said. "And I thought you weren't supposed to be very perceptive."

"The last time I saw an Oriental holding a knife, he was coming towards me through the jungle, intending to plant it in my gizzard."

Mr. Ching glared at the Colonel, who frantically groped around the legs of his chair for his cane.

"Now, dear," Budgie said. "It's only the cook."

"Cook my eye! I wasn't in military intelligence for nothing. The man's an enemy agent if ever I saw one!"

Mr. Ching's dark eyes flashed. He spat out a terse Mandarin phrase, then raised the carving knife and fork high overhead like a *banderilla* at a bullfight. The Colonel's eyes bulged even further. He gasped and pushed back in his chair as Mr. Ching suddenly lunged forward.

With a rattle of crockery, the cook plunged the knife and fork deep into the table in front of the Colonel, and stalked out of the room.

Startled silence, then much throat clearing and nervous laughter around the table, until finally Sebastian, who'd always had a well-ordered set of priorities, got things back on track.

"Well," he said, "who's going to carve now?"

"How about Cerise?" Derrick said. "She should be able to do a good job. She went to medical school."

"Did you?" Sebastian asked.

"For a while," she reluctantly admitted.

"Then you're elected."

They managed to get the implements out of the table, and passed everything down to Cerise. She began carving, and, in fact, seemed to be nearly as proficient as Mr. Ching.

"Why'd you leave med school, sweetie?" Violet asked as she watched Cerise work.

"I didn't like it."

"Oh? I thought I heard something else. Maybe I'm wrong, but didn't Mousey tell me there was trouble, or a scandal, or—"

"Carve your own damn roast!" Cerise said. She shoved the platter across the table towards Violet, and sat down heavily, folding her arms and staring stonily up at the cobwebs in the corner of the ceiling.

Violet raised her eyebrows, then shrugged, and began to hack away at the meat.

"Oh, dear," Budgie said as she felt the temperature in the room drop still further. She glanced at Cerise, then quickly turned to Derrick on her left. "Have you been to university, too, dear?"

"Why, yes. I studied history. Mostly Revolutionary War stuff, you know."

"Ah," Drupe said from the opposite end of the table. "If memory serves, I recall that there was an incident involving this very island. Was there not?"

Derrick momentarily went pale beneath his dark tan, then flushed. His brow furrowed deeply. "I'm afraid I never heard about that," he said, staring down at his empty plate and fidgeting with his silverware.

Budgie looked at him, then hastily said to Mr. Drupe, "My husband's read all about that. Haven't you, dear?"

The Colonel, who'd been regarding Derrick with a peculiar expression, started. "What? No! Never heard of it! The woman doesn't know what she's talking about."

"But, dear—"

"I said, old scout, that you don't know what you're talking about."

Budgie held her husband's gaze, her little mouth pursed in tense annoyance, her body stiff, trembling slightly. With an effort she turned to Sebastian, trying to smile. "Did you go to university, dear?"

"No, I didn't. But I do study some chemistry. It's kind of a hobby of mine."

"Oh, that's interesting."

Violet looked up from her carving and smiled. "What Sebastian means is that he takes a lot of drugs."

"Oh." Budgie looked between the identical faces of Sebastian and Violet, and could think of nothing else to say.

The roast and the overcooked vegetables were passed around, and for a while the party ate in silence. Then the

Colonel remarked that the meat tasted suspiciously like water buffalo, and that thought started him recounting, loudly and to no one in particular, his adventures in Mandalay.

Budgie leaned over to Cerise and whispered. "You know, dear, don't you, that the closest he ever got to Mandalay was a tube of Burma Shave."

Cerise looked at Budgie, smiled, then giggled.

The Colonel, however, stopped in mid-sentence and glared furiously at his wife. "Watch it, old scout." His voice was a throaty, threatening growl. "I think it's time you went upstairs and got ready."

"But—"

"Old scout, I said it's time."

Budgie looked at her husband, then, averting her eyes from the others, stood up and left the room, her small, soft body shaking.

This was the kind of incident to which observers could only respond with embarrassed silence, and thus the only sound for a while was that of the Colonel chewing energetically and hmphing from time to time.

Finally, it was Derrick who spoke. "Mr. Drupe, you knew little Pinky's father. What was he like?"

"Why do you ask?"

"Just curious. Little Pinky says she thinks I'm a lot like him."

Before the lawyer could make his usual judiciously non-committal reply, the Colonel looked up and snorted.

"Old Ripley!" he said. "You should be so lucky, old son. Now, there was a man for you. Quite a one for the ladies. I'll say! No creature in skirts who was still warm was safe from him."

Derrick chuckled in a confident, man-to-man kind of way that indicated he too was known to indulge occasionally, and he seemed to puff up a little at the thought.

Violet looked between Derrick and the Colonel, an expression of growing distaste on her face.

The Colonel was now also chuckling. "Oh, yes. Quite

something, I tell you, old son. You, of course, know about the Sill birthmark—that little sort of fin-shaped strawberry mark that every member of the Sill family has. Why, there must be all kinds of little bastards around the countryside with that mark on them. Yessir. Old Rip's gone, but he's not forgotten.''

The Colonel and Derrick again began to chuckle. From across the table, Sebastian saw his sister's blue eyes narrow threateningly and her hand involuntarily contort into a claw. He began a mental countdown, but to his surprise, the explosion occurred to his immediate left.

Cerise leapt to her feet, overturning her chair. ''You pigs! You vile, disgusting pigs!'' she screamed, then ran out of the room.

The Colonel looked after her and snorted. ''Damned girl! What she needs is a damned good spanking.''

Sebastian noted with interest the Colonel's expression as he said this. ''Tell me, Colonel,'' he said pleasantly, ''do you beat Budgie? Or do you have her beat you? Do you wear costumes? Is that what you meant by getting ready? Why, I bet that she has to wear a leather hood, while you put on something like—oh, I don't know, maybe a little frilly tutu.''

Sebastian grinned. From the Colonel's look of mounting shock and horror, he knew he had just made one of those insanely wild shots that somehow end by miraculously hitting the mark dead-centre.

The Colonel's eyes seemed about to erupt out of his head, his face took on the appearance of an over-ripe Concord grape, and those around the table were convinced they were about to witness a massive hemorrhage. Instead, the Colonel made incoherent sputtering noises, and quick-marched from the room, the pounding of his cane marking time with every furious step.

''I'm afraid poor Budgie's going to have her little hands full,'' Sebastian said quietly to himself.

Just then Mrs. Hook set down the silver tray holding cream and sugar for after-dinner coffee. She sighed wearily as she cleared the abandoned plates from the now-empty places, and slowly moved her grievously overworked body towards the door.

Sebastian lifted the lid of the sugar bowl and looked inside, appearing dubious about what he saw. "I hope Mrs. Hook didn't make a mistake and put the rat poison in the sugar bowl," he said with a wink and a smile.

Behind him there was a crash. Mrs. Hook stood as though paralysed, broken dishes scattered around her feet. She stared at Sebastian, a frozen grimace of utter terror and hatred distorting her square, flat features. Then she grunted, shook herself, and stomped out, crunching china beneath her sensible shoes.

For the five remaining at table, what little appetite they'd started with was rapidly waning, and they poked listlessly at the food on their plates.

"Well," Derrick said, looking at his watch, "in just a few hours, my little Pinky becomes one of the wealthiest young women in the country." He paused, then, trying to sound casual and unconcerned, asked, "Just how large is my fiancée's estate, Mr. Drupe?"

The lawyer squinted at him, and clicked his teeth. "Young man, that is hardly a proper question." Drupe rose, picking up his briefcase from beside his chair, and left the room with an odd, crablike gait, as though he expected an assault from behind.

Derrick repeated Drupe's reprimand, attempting not altogether successfully to mimic the lawyer's dry, raspy tones in his own mellow, oleaginous voice. Then he made an angry noise. "Hypocritical crock! One of the first things little Pinky'd better do tomorrow is get herself a new attorney."

"Assuming she shows up to do so," Violet said.

"Yeah. Damn Sillikins. What the hell is she doing?" Derrick paused, and his forehead creased as he suddenly recalled something that had puzzled him. "You know, a little while ago, she told me she'd always wanted to have a surprise party, but no one had ever given her one. Then she got a strange look on her face, and said this year'd be different."

"But that doesn't make any sense," Violet said. "You don't throw a surprise party for yourself."

"I know. But that's what she said."

Mrs. Argus, who'd sat quietly throughout the meal, looked up from the bone on which she was gnawing, her eyes shining manically. "Oh, there'll be a surprise, all right!" She laughed in a way that made the listeners' nerve endings tingle and shrink. "You'll all have a big surprise." She stood up and suddenly turned to Derrick, as though seeing him for the first time. A long, bony finger pointed. "You bet on black. But it came up red. It always comes up red. The colour of blood!" She cackled again, and sailed from the room, her black robe billowing behind her.

"The booby's hatched again," Sebastian scowled. "She should've been put down years ago."

Derrick looked a little green beneath his tan, apparently quite shaken by Cassandra Argus's delphic remarks. "What did she mean by that?"

"Must've been about your gambling, don't you think?" Violet said, offhandedly.

"What are you talking about?" Derrick's voice slid perilously up the scale.

"You're a gambler, aren't you? Haven't I heard that—"

"No, you haven't!" Derrick said, jumping to his feet. "I don't know who's saying such things, but it's a lie. It's a damn lie!" He threw his napkin to the table, and almost ran from the room.

Sebastian watched the departure with raised eyebrows, mumbled something about protesting too much, then turned back towards Violet. "My, my. Everyone seems a bit on edge tonight. Well, I guess now it's just the two of us, Sis."

"Sebastian, I have probably asked you a million times not to call me 'Sis'. It sounds like a slow leak."

With that, Violet stood up and walked stiffly from the room, leaving her brother alone at the long table.

"More wine, Sebastian?" he said out loud. "No, thanks. I don't think I will." He tried to sound cheerful, but the large empty room muffled his voice, making it fall flat as soon as it left his mouth.

He looked up at the high ceiling. The thick shadows on the wall seemed to him to be shaping themselves into pointing fingers and grasping claws.

In the distance, there was a long roll of thunder. It seemed to speak of danger and menace.

Sebastian, ordinarily irrepressible, shivered. He'd suddenly had one of those odd feelings of deep uneasiness that some of the others had already experienced.

He got up and left the dining room, shutting the heavy door.

The chandeliers moved slightly in an unseen draft. The shadows danced.

The thunder rolled again.

Nearer this time.

CHAPTER SIX

AN HOUR OR SO LATER, THE PARTY HAD REGROUPED IN THE lounge. The outbursts of the dinner table had passed, but not without leaving a residue of embarrassment, discomfort, and tension. The feeling that something was about to happen was now more widespread, giving the room the atmosphere of a small-town bus station in the middle of the night, with the inter-state local two hours late and no new estimated time of arrival posted.

Whatever conversations took place were quiet, sporadic, and desultory. Aunt Budgie knitted. Others leafed through the twenty-five-year-old magazines that they'd found. The rest just sat—thinking, dozing, or waiting.

The ancient floor-model radio, as large as a liquor cabinet, was playing. The only station they were able to get featured music from the Big Band era. Reception was poor, with much static and many interruptions, as though the transmission had to come over not only many miles but many years as well.

"I think we're caught in a time warp," Sebastian said to Cerise.

The party seemed to emit a silent collective sigh when the approaching storm finally announced its arrival with a spattering of rain against the french windows. This was shortly followed by the full force of a late-fall storm—howling winds, flashing lightning, and thunder claps growing ever louder, as the storm centre moved closer.

Suddenly there was a tremendous crash and an impossibly brilliant, green-white flare illuminated the room, followed almost instantly by a giant crash of thunder. Then the room was plunged into darkness.

Startled cries and gasps, then laughter at the initial reaction.

"Oh, dear!"

"I say!"

"Too damned close!"

"Not close! Here! *It* is beginning!"

"A fuse must have blown."

"That bat's fuse blew a long time ago."

"Whoever you are, if you don't remove your hand immediately, you're going to lose it."

"You can put it here."

"Shut up, Sebastian."

"I guess a body's got to do this, too," Mrs. Hook said from the doorway. Then they heard her move complainingly down the corridor, open the door to the cellar, and clomp down the stairs.

Silence for a long two minutes. Then a scream of total, absolute terror rose out of the basement, nearly shaking the house with its intensity.

Sounds of surprise and confusion swirled around the lounge— "What was that?" "What happened?" "What should we do?"

"Let Sebastian investigate," Violet finally said.

"Why me?"

"Because you're the one who's explored the house."

"But Sis, you're the one who should be able to see in the dark."

"Sebastian!"

"Meow."

"Sebastian!"

"Oh, all right. I'll go."

Another few minutes passed slowly, then the lights came back on, soon followed by Sebastian's return.

He went over to Violet. There was a curious expression on his face, and he seemed even paler than usual. He held his lightly scented handkerchief up to his nose.

"Your friend, Mousey—" he said, "—does she have short, light-brown hair?"

"Yes. Dull brown."

"And that funny birthmark—sort of here?" He pointed to a spot on his shoulder.

"Yes. What is this? Is she here? Have you seen her?"

Sebastian hesitated, taking another deep breath behind his handkerchief. "Well, I've seen parts of her."

CHAPTER SEVEN

"MY GOD!"

"Look at that!"

"How terrible!"

"I'm going to be sick!"

The entire party, including the cook and housekeeper, stood in a semicircle around a heap of coal in the basement, trying to look anywhere but at the horribly mutilated, dismembered body of Rosa Sill.

"Well," Sebastian said, doing a quick estimate, "I guess that's most of the hostess."

Cerise started to giggle, then quickly swallowed it. She averted her eyes and turned a bright red.

"Sebastian!"

"All right, Sis." He held up his hands and moved to the other side of the basement.

"Oh, dear. What do we do now?" Budgie said.

"I think we'd better examine the...uh...." Violet gestured towards the coal pile.

"What for?" Derrick said, a note of hysteria in his voice "Signs of life? My God!"

"I think it would be preferable not to interfere with anything, Miss Cornichon," Drupe said, squinting at Violet.

"In a homicide investigation," Violet said, evenly but with considerable authority, "the period immediately following the discovery of the body can be crucial. If proper steps are not taken on the spot, vital information could be irretrievably lost."

"Or irrevocably destroyed by blundering amateurs."

"I am not exactly without experience, Mr. Drupe."

"Yes, but of what sort? As an officer of the court, I must——"

"You must do everything you can to further an investigation, not hinder it . . . as you have, from time to time, been known to do."

Drupe started to reply, but then clicked his dentures and fell silent.

Violet turned to Cerise. "Sweetie, you've had the formal training. Do you want to do the examination?"

Cerise's eyes went wide with horror, and she began to step backward. "What are you suggesting? God! How sick! No, I don't! No! No!" She was almost screaming as she fled as far from the coal pile as she could.

Violet looked after her, then shrugged. "Well, I've made a fair study of forensic medicine, so——"

"Why, this looks like a job for the Society-Girl Detective!" Sebastian said enthusiastically.

Violet glared at him for a second, then looked around at the others. "So, if there are no objections. . . ."

The lawyer clicked his teeth again, but there were no other objections.

Examining the ground carefully before she took each step, so she would not inadvertently destroy any minute bits of evidence, Violet slowly approached the coal pile. Then, taking a deep breath, she knelt and began her examination, aided by the portable but extremely powerful magnifying glass she always carried in her purse. Except for some muttered remarks from Sebastian about Sherlock Cornichon, the room was silent for the ten minutes she spent at her grisly task.

"Well?" Derrick asked when she at last stood up, wiped off her hands, and brushed her knees.

"Well, it's a bit hard to tell because the coal is so dark and absorbent, but from the...uh...." She paused, trying to find the most delicate way to express herself. "...the...uh... dampness that I felt, I'd say that it—the...uh...butchering—"

"Ohh," Budgie said, weakly.

"—took place right here, on that spot. I can't be sure about the cause of death—whether it was due to one or more of the...uh...obvious wounds, or whether the...uh... dismemberment—"

"Unh," Derrick grunted, looking a bit greener.

The Colonel huskily cleared his throat, a warning sound suggesting some caution was in order.

"Or whether *it* was done after death. But if so, judging from the...uh...amount of exsanguination, *it* would have to have been done almost immediately after." Violet looked around, but no one seemed inclined to dispute her conclusions thus far. "The...uh...body is still quite warm, and there has not yet been coagulation to any significant degree. The wounds themselves are still moist and glistening; some slight...uh... seepage is still occurring."

Mrs. Hook violently snorted, indicating that there were some things that a body just didn't have to listen to.

"Even considering that it's quite warm down here from the furnace," Violet continued, "the murder must have taken place very recently. Certainly not more than two hours ago, probably within the last hour."

"Oh, dear," Budgie said.

"Claptrap!" the Colonel said. "Damned woman's bonkers!"

Drupe sniffed as though to say, "You see what I mean."

Then Mrs. Argus chuckled quietly—in a knowing sort of way—and everyone else fell silent.

"There's something else," Derrick said, noticing the curious expression on Violet's face. "What is it?" Violet shook her head, but Derrick persisted. "What?"

"Yes. Do tell us what further discoveries you've made," Drupe said.

"Well," Violet sighed, "it's the wounds themselves. They

seem rough, brutal, the result of an insane outburst, a savage hacking."

Drupe sniffed. "How perceptive."

"No. I mean, I think they are *supposed* to look that way. But when I examined them closely using the glass, I believe I saw indications of precision and skill there. What I mean is that I have the feeling that the killer knew exactly what he—or she—was doing."

Sounds of surprise, incredulity—mumbling and foot shuffling.

Violet looked over at Cerise, whose lips may have been compressed slightly, but who steadily returned the gaze.

"Hmm," Sebastian said to himself from behind the pile of old cartons around which he was poking. He glanced at Mr. Ching who was standing slightly behind the others, muscular arms folded, dark eyes expressionless, impenetrable. It was impossible to tell if he understood the proceedings, but somehow Sebastian was sure that he did . . . and that he might even have been enjoying himself.

Mr. Drupe cleared his throat several times, a scratchy kind of sound, then pushed his hand deeper into his jacket pocket and stared unblinkingly at his brown wingtip shoes.

Sebastian waited until things had settled down again before announcing, "I found something, too, Violet. In the corner over there, behind that rubbish."

"Oh? What?" she said, not much interested.

Sebastian smiled and held up a finger to indicate that she should wait a second. He went over to Cerise and showed her a white, business-size envelope. "Is this what's-her-name's writing?"

Cerise looked at the envelope, then at Sebastian, an expression of extreme puzzlement on her face. She nodded her head. "It's hers—Rosa's."

"What is it, Sebastian?" Violet said, putting her hands on her hips and sounding impatient.

"It's an envelope, Sis."

"I can see that, you fool!"

"On the front here it says, 'To be opened in the event of my death.'"

"What! Come on, Sebastian!"

"And someone's followed the instructions."

"Well?"

Sebastian shrugged, then smiled. "Well, it's empty."

CHAPTER EIGHT

WHEN THE PARTY ONCE MORE REASSEMBLED IN THE LOUNGE, it was, understandably, even less chipper than before.

Using the pocket camera with which Aunt Budgie had planned to document her niece's birthday celebration, Violet took several photographs of the ghastly scene in the basement, in order to be able to provide the authorities with a precise and accurate record of what it had been like. The awful remains were then taken upstairs and put into the walk-in freezer for preservation.

Back in the lounge, the topic was, of course, what to do next. Naturally, the telephone had long since been disconnected, so that was out. Cerise then asked if anyone had looked in the boathouse. Derrick quickly jumped to his feet and volunteered to go out and see if there wasn't something there that could take at least a couple of them back to the mainland for help.

As they waited for Derrick's return, the tension in the room was palpable. So this is what they mean by being able to cut it with a knife, Sebastian thought, then grimaced; under the circumstances, there were, perhaps, better metaphors.

Derrick came in slightly winded, drops of moisture attractively beading on his tanned face where it had been exposed to the storm. He shook his head.

"Nothing?" Violet asked.

"Worse." He looked grim. "There was a boat there—two, in fact. And they were in pretty good shape, would've gotten us out of here easily. Until someone chopped big holes in them with an axe."

"Hell and damnation!" the Colonel said.

"Was this done recently?" Violet asked.

"Very. You can see the cuts are fresh."

"Damned fellow! Needs to be taught a damned good lesson! Oh, yes!" The Colonel's eyes gleamed at the thought, and he pounded his cane.

"Now, dear, try to calm down," Budgie said. "Can they be fixed, dear?"

"No. They're completely ruined."

"So that's that," Cerise said.

Derrick nodded. "Oh, yeah...there is some diving gear there—fins, a wetsuit—in case anyone feels up to a five- or six-hour swim in near-freezing water."

"Then we have no choice but to wait," Drupe said. "In any event, it should not be long. A boat should come for us tomorrow."

"Not necessarily," Violet corrected. "Poor Mousey made all of the arrangements, you know, and as far as I can tell, none of us has any idea what they were. Maybe a boat'll come tomorrow, maybe it won't."

"But she specifically told me that—" The lawyer abruptly cut himself off, looked nervously at the others, then put his arms even more tightly around his briefcase.

"Do you mean, Violet," Sebastian said, "that we're here in the middle of nowhere, with a deranged killer running around loose? And that there is no way for us to communicate with the outside world, or get help, or get away? And that we don't know how long we're going to have to stay here? Charming!"

"Hee, hee, hee," Mrs. Argus said to herself, very quietly, as she rubbed her large bony hands together.

"My God!" Cerise said. "What should we do?"

"We should each take some bread, and cans, and stuff," Sebastian said, "then go up to our rooms, and lock our doors, and stay there until somebody arrives."

As things turned out, this might well have been pretty good advice; of course, had they followed it, there wouldn't have been much more of a story to tell.

"Nonsense!" Derrick said, striking a dashing pose. "What we've got to do is mount a search and find the maniac. Flush him out!"

"Hear, hear!" Again the Colonel pounded his cane. "Distribute arms! Beat the bushes! Got enough fire power here to blow the bloody bugger clear to Athabasca!"

"Now, dear."

"The Colonel's right," Derrick said. "There are slickers and sou'westers in the closet, and some flashlights that work. Even with just a few of us, we should be able to stick close together and still comb the island from one end to the other."

"Speaking of maniacs..." Sebastian muttered. "He wants to walk out and announce, 'Here I am, Number Two for the Ripper.' And people call *me* crazy."

"What do you think we should do?" Cerise asked Violet, who'd been listening to all this with a thoughtful expression.

"I suppose we should do as Derrick and the Colonel suggest." She sounded quite tentative—either unconvinced about the approach, or amazed to find herself agreeing with anything that those two might propose.

"Violet!" Certainly Sebastian was amazed.

"Do I take that to mean you won't be helping us?"

"Well, Violet, it is pouring outside."

"Fine. Then you can search the house. You've already had lots of practice."

"But—"

"Now, how should we arrange...."

Eventually it was decided that Derrick, the Colonel, Violet, Cerise, and Mr. Ching would search the island. The others, working as a group and sticking close together, would cover the house from top to bottom. Mr. Drupe seemed disinclined to participate, but was persuaded it was in his own best interest to stay with the group.

In less than three-quarters of an hour, the outside party was back inside, its search completed. The island was not really that big, and even in darkness and a driving storm there simply were not that many places an intruder could hide. The younger members returned muddy and tired. The Colonel, though, seemed exhilarated, despite the fact he'd been prevented from popping a few rounds into the darkness—"just to see what jumps out, y'know."

It took Sebastian and the others nearly as long to go through the large house, but that too proved fruitless. They came upon no one, nor did they discover anything to indicate that any intruder had been there.

Thus it was with considerable relief that the two groups met back in the lounge and exchanged negative reports.

"That takes a load off a body," Mrs. Hook said, dropping heavily into a chair and fanning herself with her hankie. It sounded as though she'd been concerned that the presence of a deranged killer would somehow have made more work for her.

"Cowardly bugger's scarpered," the Colonel said.

"Don't sound so disappointed," Cerise said.

"Yes," Derrick agreed. "I don't mind admitting that I for one am pretty happy we didn't find him. He must've cleared out right after."

"Not necessarily," Violet said slowly, as though thinking out loud.

"What do you mean, dear?" Budgie asked, worried.

Mr. Drupe sniffed. "Miss Cornichon is just trying for more theatrics."

Violet stared at the lawyer until he looked away, then turned to the others. "I mean, the killer might be here."

"Nonsense!" Derrick said. "He couldn't be hiding. We've looked everywhere."

"Yes, Violet. We have, you know," Sebastian said.

Violet paused, then shook her head. "No. I mean here." She pointed to the floor. "In this room. The killer may be one of us."

CHAPTER NINE

"WHAT!"

"I say!"

"Hell's bells! Damned woman's gone right 'round the twist!"

"Oh, dear."

"Surprise, surprise," Mrs. Argus giggled.

"Well," Sebastian said, leaning forward, eyes round and gleaming. "This is more like it."

"Perhaps Miss Cornichon would be good enough to explain," Drupe said, his tone suggesting that clearly no explanation was possible.

"It's not that difficult to understand, Mr. Drupe—even for a trained legal mind." Violet smiled coldly at the lawyer, and held up a finger. "One: there's been a murder. Two: all evidence suggests that it took place quite recently. Three: even though we instituted a prompt search, we did not find the supposed intruder. But even more important—Four: we found no traces that anyone other than the people in this room has been on this island."

"We might have missed something," Derrick said.

"A few minutes ago everyone was certain that nothing had been overlooked. You can't have it both ways." Violet turned to the housekeeper. "Mrs. Hook, you and Mr. Ching arrived two days ago to get things ready. Was there any sign that anyone had been on this island recently?"

"Nothing. Dust an inch thick all over. Far too much work for a body to do. I told Missy. I told her she'd be sorry."

"Hee, hee, hee," Mrs. Argus chuckled.

"I meant, it wouldn't be ready on time. I meant—" Mrs. Hook glared around the room, then folded her arms and took refuge in a stony silence.

Violet nodded. "So no one was here before Mrs. Hook arrived, and we have no reason to think that anyone came after—besides us, that is. And finally, we have that envelope that Sebastian found. Several of us here mentioned that poor Mousey had been acting strangely recently—making cryptic remarks, and so forth. And it seems that she considered this gathering to be particularly important. Though precisely why we don't know. Perhaps she had reached an important decision, or was going to make an announcement. Perhaps someone here would not have been happy about what Mousey was going to do. Perhaps that person tried to stop her."

"Pure speculation," Drupe said.

"Perhaps. But the envelope is not speculation, it is fact. And it indicates that Mousey thought something might happen. Why else would a normal, healthy young woman on her way to her birthday celebration prepare something like that? Why indeed?—unless she had a reason to think she might not survive?"

"Ah," Drupe said, as though a magnificent vista had suddenly opened up before him. "The key words in your... uhm... most ingenious analysis are 'normal' and 'healthy'. While it grieves me to speak ill of the dead—"

"Sure it does," Violet muttered. "They don't fight back."

"—I must inform you that, in my opinion, Miss Sill was neither normal nor healthy. You yourself commented on the fact that she'd been acting strangely. I, too, had been aware of that for some time, and had reluctantly reached the conclusion that Miss Sill was suffering from a number of severe mental and emotional disorders that most frequently manifested themselves as schizophrenic fantasy, paranoid delusion, and/or persecution mania. I had urged her for a long time to seek assistance, but she saw my solicitude merely as another aspect of the supposed plot against her. In short, my ward was a grossly disturbed young woman, and thus the envelope—to the existence of which you attach such importance, Miss Cornichon—is only evidence of her illness."

The stunned silence that followed this startling revelation was broken by Sebastian who cleared his throat and smiled pleasantly at Drupe. "Except that the bits and pieces of her are now in the meat locker. I mean, I'm the only one here who didn't know little Pinky Mousey Squeak, or whatever. For all I know, your diagnosis, Doctor, is correct, and she did suffer from all those things. But so what? Don't we all? I know I do. I know Violet does. I'd be surprised if any of you didn't." Sebastian had to pause a minute for the angry denials and outraged protests that greeted what was one of his typical, cavalierly sweeping generalizations. He held out his hands. "What's the big deal? After all, what's raging dementia but another aspect of life's varied tapestry? Anyway, the point is that events proved little Squeaking Pink Mouse correct. Didn't they? Apparently, someone *was* out to get her."

"Yes, you disgusting old coot!" Derrick said to Drupe. "How dare you say such things about my fiancée!"

"Ah, yes," Drupe said drily. "Your fiancée—who recently came to me to see what could be done to ensure that you could not touch any part of her estate in the event that you two married."

"That's a lie!"

"Even in the midst of her delusions, there were apparently lucid moments during which Miss Sill had the presence of mind to want to guard herself against a fortune hunter."

"That silly bitch! No! She didn't say that! I don't believe you, Drupe, any more than the federal prosecutors did."

"Fortune hunter!" The Colonel came out of his half-doze with a start. The phrase in some way seemed to agitate or alarm him severely, and he repeated it. Then he noticed that everyone was looking at him, and he cleared his throat several times.

"Gad, sir! That's disgusting. A thrashing's too damned good for your sort. Nothing lower than a fortune hunter."

"No?" Derrick said. "What about a child molester? Pinky told me about when she visited—"

"That's a damned lie, sir! I always said she was called Squeak because she had a screw loose. And if you believe anything that little gooney-bird said, you're just as bad. Why I could—"

But the Colonel couldn't. His face became so congested with dark blood that he was only able to sizzle like a boiler about to burst.

"Oh, dear." Budgie quickly undid some of the Colonel's buttons.

"Well," Violet said, with perhaps a touch of self-satisfaction, "it seems that Mousey may have had some surprises in store for at least a couple of us."

"Three, *sweetie*," Cerise smiled. "She told me about your attempts to get her to bail out that sinking ship of your cosmetics company. She said it was one turkey that would never even make it to Thanksgiving."

"That ungrateful—" Violet cut herself off and looked sharply at Cerise. "She never did! None of that's true, and you know it. I don't know why, but you're making it up. First, Mousey'd never say that. And second, nothing's wrong with my company. We're just fine. Although I will say, sweetie, judging from the amount of stuff that you load on your little puss, if you'd switch to my brand we could show a record profit."

"Well, Violet," Sebastian hastily put in, before the two women began to hiss and claw at each other. "No matter what, you know it couldn't have been me. After all, I never even met the poor girl."

"Since when have you ever needed a reason to do anything?" Violet snapped angrily, then looked at her brother and shook her head. She shrugged helplessly and smiled an apology at him.

Sebastian smiled back. "It's all right, Sis. We're all on edge."

"Yes, we certainly are," Mr. Drupe said. "And yet Miss Cornichon—for motives I do not even begin to comprehend—seems to be trying her best to make things worse."

"All I've been trying to do is to get us to face the facts, so maybe we can figure out what happened. Meanwhile you, Mr. Drupe—for reasons that I fail to understand—seem to want us to do just the opposite."

"Perhaps," Drupe went on as though Violet hadn't spoken, "Miss Cornichon wants this terrible affair to seem more dramatic and mysterious than it actually is, so her own participation in it will be rendered all the more newsworthy. But possibly I do her an injustice." Drupe smiled in a way that made his mouth resemble that of a snapping turtle. "My own motives are simple. I have tried to employ my many years of training in the law to look at things coolly and objectively, and to provide a calm, rational, and logical perspective on events. Nothing more. And in Miss Cornichon's melodramatic—but wholly unsubstantiated—leap to the conclusion that one of us must be the perpetrator, she has overlooked the simple, undramatic, unspectacular fact that none of us could have done it, because we were all together in the lounge."

"Not quite," Cerise pointed out. "Mrs. Hook and Mr. Ching weren't with us."

Mrs. Hook snorted and glared ferociously at Cerise. Mr. Ching sat with his arms folded, impassive, apparently unhearing, apparently unaware of the look of naked hostility which the Colonel was sending in his direction.

"Oh, I'm sorry. I didn't mean. . . ." Cerise hunched her shoulders and looked embarrassed and apologetic.

"No, you're quite right," Sebastian said. "And Mr. Drupe, I'm afraid it still looks as though Violet is right, too. You see, we were together when the body was found. And before that, we were together at dinner. But between those two times, there was more than an hour when we were not together. That fits with Violet's estimate of the time of death."

Drupe sniffed his opinion of what that was worth.

"I should also mention," Sebastian continued with a

pleasant smile, "that during that hour or so, I believe that each of us was completely alone for at least part of the time."

"I say! You mean—"

"I mean that I doubt very much that we can, any of us, conclusively prove what we were doing for the entire time between leaving the dining room and coming back here. I don't know about motive and method, Mr. Drupe, but it does look as though each of us had ample opportunity."

From the reactions around the room—immediate vehement denials; then a pause; then a reluctant realization; and finally astonished silence—it seemed that Sebastian's analysis was correct.

Violet nodded an acknowledgment to him, and turned to the lawyer. "What do you say now, Mr. Drupe?"

Somewhere in the house, a clock lugubriously—and, it seemed, interminably—sounded twelve.

Mr. Drupe took out his large gold pocket watch and confirmed the time with a terse nod. "I say that nothing more can be accomplished here, with each of you feeding the others' hysteria. I am going to bed. I suggest that you all do likewise. We will all probably need to be as fresh as possible tomorrow."

Even Violet couldn't disagree with that, and there seemed to be some slight reduction of tension as everyone gratefully welcomed a conclusion to the long and terrible evening. However, the rustling preparatory to their departure was brought to an abrupt halt by the eerie, unsettling laughter of Cassandra Argus.

"Oh, yes! To bed! To bed!" She shrieked and giggled. "Remember the curse of the Mohawks. Misfortune to anyone who stays the night on Komondor. Now to bed! To bed!" She ran to the doorway, her scrawny arms flapping the billowy sleeves of her black robe. She stopped and turned back to the room, this time speaking almost inaudibly "*She* waits, you know. *She* waits. Pleasant dreams."

"Charming." Sebastian stared at the now-empty doorway. "I wonder if she sleeps hanging upside down?"

CHAPTER TEN

THE NEXT MORNING, IF NOT SUNNY AND BRIGHT, WAS AT least much less grimly overcast. The fierce storm of the previous evening had eventually moved off, leaving the grey stone house darkly stained and streaked and most of the island a muddy quagmire.

Violet was late coming down to breakfast. After everyone retired, she had lain awake for several hours, going over events, trying to remember everything that had been said and done, seeing what possibilities she could come up with. It was close to dawn when she reached an interesting conclusion and finally fell asleep. By the time she came downstairs, only Sebastian was still in the dining room.

They smiled greetings at one another, and Violet went over to the long, dark oak sideboard upon which were arrayed numerous covered silver salvers containing scrambled eggs, a kedgeree, curries, smoked fish, bacon, sausage, ham, hash, porridge, potatoes, tomatoes, and congealed slices of last night's joint. An impressive display marred only by the fact that everything looked more or less the same and none of it any good.

"Not exactly *la nouvelle cuisine*, is it?" Sebastian said as Violet cautiously raised, and quickly lowered, the cover of the kedgeree.

"I'll say. Looks like these are leftovers from the morning the Light Brigade charged."

"Maybe that's why they charged. Anything was preferable to facing those scrambled eggs. You know, 'Death Before Dysentery!'"

Violet came over and sat opposite Sebastian. She'd taken tea, some cold toast, and something that, by a process of elimination, she decided must be marmalade. "I can't imagine where Mousey found this cook."

"Probably preparing meals for political dissidents in one of Chiang Kai-shek's prison camp, before Amnesty International got him fired."

Violet took a sip of tea, made a face as she swallowed, and pushed the cup away. "You may be right. Ugh. Have you seen any of the others?"

"All of them. Except for that Argus creature. Fortunately. Probably out getting her broomstick serviced. That woman! Drives me right up the wall!"

"What are the rest doing?"

"I think the Colonel went out for a walk."

"A walk? It must be knee deep in mud out there."

"I know. He said something about the days he used to bivouack in rice paddies and went out. Derrick, I think, is in the library."

"What for? He can't read, can he?"

"I gather that old what's-his-name—Augustus—put together quite a collection of documents concerning the early history of this region. I guess that's what he's interested in. Didn't he say he'd been a history student?"

"And here I thought he never read anything longer than a designer label."

"Gee, Sis, I had the idea you were kind of interested in him."

"You're joking! That macho mannequin?"

"Be fair. Beneath that shallow exterior, there's—"

"What?" Violet challenged, eyes flashing.

Sebastian shrugged. "I don't know. As yet unplumbed depths of shallowness?"

Violet smiled and relaxed. "And the others?"

"Budgie said she was going to work on her comforter. And I don't know about the rest."

"What about Drupe?"

"Don't know. He came in and went out, and didn't say a word. He looked kind of grey. Not much appetite. Though, under the circumstances—" Sebastian waved at the sideboard "—that's understandable. But he appeared to have had a bad night."

"Really?" Violet looked up from the toast crumbs she'd been shoving around.

"Yes. But he's about the only one who looked less than chipper. I must say, considering that the girl was a friend or relative or employer of everyone here, the shock of her death has worn off remarkably quickly. I mean, little Mousey-whatever's removal hasn't exactly left an unfillable gap in anyone's life."

"Not exactly, no. I'm afraid most people saw poor Mousey just as someone who could be manoeuvred or used for their own purposes or convenience, and of no interest or importance beyond that."

"Including you?"

Violet looked up from the tablecloth, shrugged, then looked back down. "I may have been guilty of that, from time to time. But—dammit!—the girl seemed to demand it. Everything about her little washed-out presence said, 'Use me; misuse me; abuse me.' It's as if she existed only to be taken advantage of."

"A born victim?"

"If there is such a thing, then that's what Rosa Sill was."

"Well, she certainly realized her ultimate destiny."

"Didn't she, though?" Violet nodded thoughtfully. "And just when it seemed the worm might be turning. Poor little kid. . . . But you said Drupe looked unwell?"

"Yes. Probably just dyspepsia—he seems the type for it. Or maybe he was worried about old Argus's curse."

"Maybe," Violet said, still pushing breadcrumbs with her finger.

Sebastian noticed she was making a bull's-eye design. After watching her for another couple of minutes, he asked what she planned to do.

"I think," Violet said slowly, "that we should act as though we're going to be on this island for a while yet. As indeed we might be."

"What do you mean?"

Violet lifted her head and looked steadily at her brother. "What did you think of my idea last night?"

"That it's one of us? I don't know. It's kind of creepy to sit around, and look at nine people, and think that one of them's a killer. Hard to accept that. On the other hand, an invisible intruder seems even harder to accept. So I don't know. I guess I agree. Sort of. Why?"

"What you said last night—that you're the only one who didn't know Mousey—was right, of course. And, as you pointed out, that means you're in the clear. You're the only one who I *know* didn't do it, and that's important."

"Golly, Sis, are you asking me to help you investigate?" Sebastian started to act very excited. "Me? Assist the Society-Girl Detective?"

"Give it a rest, Sebastian, would you? I'm serious. Are you interested?"

Sebastian looked into a pair of eyes identical to his own and smiled. "That's probably the most amusing proposition I'm likely to receive around here. Sure. Do you have any ideas?"

"One or two that I want to check out before I say anything. Meanwhile, why don't you go around and chat people up. You know, get them to talk about themselves and their relations with Mousey. Get at any gossip they might have heard about the other people here. You're pretty good at digging seamy bits of information out of people."

"I'll take that as a compliment."

"Why? It wasn't meant as one."

"Oh, ta. You know, you're really a pleasure to work with, Violet."

"The hell with that. If we pull it off, it'll be pleasurable enough."

"You think we can?"

"We might. If we have to stay here long enough. And with a little luck. Yes, I think I may be able to deliver the killer to the police."

"*We*, Violet. *We* deliver the killer. Be fair. We're in this together now."

"Fair? Since when is anything in this world fair? Was it fair that you got everything because you're four minutes older? Was it fair that poor Mousey was hacked to pieces before she got anything? What's fair? You know as well as I do that when a chance presents itself, you've got to grab it. I've no doubt that you can look after your own interests without my being 'fair' as you call it. But just remember which of us is the goddamn Society-Girl Detective, brother dear."

Violet stared into space for a few minutes, a slight smile on her lips, perhaps already envisaging a successful conclusion and what it would mean. At least, Sebastian thought that that was where she'd drifted.

"What are you seeing, Sis? Headlines? 'Society-Girl Detective Does it Again'? 'Cosmetics Queen Cracks Caper'? What are you planning—to put out a new perfume? Maybe call it 'Sleuth'?"

Violet abruptly snapped back to the present. "What a great idea, Sebastian! 'Sleuth Perfume...for those secret places...for the detectives of love.' I love it!"

"Come on, Sis, gimme a break."

"Yeah? I know who'll be first in line for a free sample." Violet stared levelly at her brother. "And, if we pull this off, I know which irrepressible one of us is going to dine out on it for an awfully long time."

The serious look that passed between them was not unlike a handshake, but it contained more mutual understanding and concurrence than any physical gesture could ever convey.

"Did you sleep well?" Mrs. Argus asked with a laugh from

next to the sideboard where she was heaping food onto a plate. "Did you hear *Her*? *She* was here. *She* was walking the halls. Waiting. Waiting. Who will be next? Who?"

"Christ!" Sebastian said, standing up and moving quickly to the door. "Speaking of scrambled eggs. . . ."

CHAPTER ELEVEN

THE OPENING PHASES OF THE INVESTIGATION WERE NOT overly productive. Sebastian talked to Mrs. Hook, Derrick, and Aunt Budgie, but learned nothing of any interest. The housekeeper made all her usual complaints, and would probably still be going on if she had not flared up and stormed off after Sebastian made what he though quite an innocuous joke about her name. Derrick put Sebastian almost to sleep as he mellifluously droned on about such fascinating aspects of colonial life as map-making and cryptography. And Budgie, seeming listless and distracted, told Sebastian much more than he ever wanted to know about the Colonel's many ailments—hypertension, arteriosclerosis, his tendency to throw off thromboses the way most people perspired—and the medication she had to administer to treat them. Surely, Sebastian thought, trying to swallow a yawn, a murder investigation should be more interesting than this; Violet must be keeping the good stuff for herself.

She was, but she didn't get to it right away. First, she tried to engage Mrs. Argus in conversation, but the old woman was too involved in working her way through a huge plate of breakfast to say anything, even to make grim predictions of catastrophe. One person, at least, liked Mr. Ching's cooking.

Then Violet went to see Cerise. She thought it would be better if the two of them could make up and start afresh; beyond that, she wanted to find out whatever Cerise could tell her about Mousey's financial affairs, and also just what it was that had caused Cerise to react so strangely and violently at dinner. The first of these objectives was easily, and happily, accomplished; for the second, all Cerise knew was that Rosa had recently been going over records with a new firm of accountants, and had acted very oddly—Cerise couldn't be more specific than that—when she got the report; and as to the third, Cerise nimbly stepped aside from any probes into her background or private life.

Violet then decided to take advantage of the fact that everyone was engaged elsewhere to do a little snooping on the second floor...in one particular bedroom. Even though she doubted that the object she wanted to look through would be there, she felt it was still worth a try. She was right, it was not there, but, at the back of a dresser drawer, she found something better: something that confirmed her hypothesis; something that solved the murder. Damn! she thought, I've done it again!

She hurried downstairs, trying not to grin as if she'd just won a lottery. She located Sebastian and told him to quietly get everyone into the lounge...everyone, that is, but one.

Luckily for Sebastian, the Colonel was just returning to the house. Red-faced, he was walking awkwardly in a pair of hip waders that were thickly covered in mud for their entire length. Sebastian, curious about Violet, didn't want even to speculate about what the Colonel might have been doing. He merely told him about the meeting, and went to summon the others.

Soon Violet had her assembly, but she kept them waiting as she first looked into each of the eight faces around her. Then she announced, "I know who killed Mousey." The exclamations of surprise, curiosity, and scepticism were more or less what she had expected, and she waited until they died down before continuing. "Last night, I had pretty well figured out who it must be, but I couldn't see what this person's motive could be. Then, this morning, I learned the reason. And I found proof. As I said, I know who did it."

"I assume you mean Mr. Drupe," Sebastian said. "After all, he's the only one who isn't here."

More sounds of surprise, during which Violet glared at her brother, while he smiled innocently back.

"Yes, I mean Mr. Eustace Drupe."

"Nonsense!" Derrick said. "That dried up old crock couldn't have——"

Violet held up a silencing hand. "Let me explain. Last night, when I was going over everything in my mind, there were some things I couldn't understand, that didn't make any sense. Most of them had to do with the way Drupe was acting. Even for a lawyer who became wealthy and famous by obstructing the justice that was due his rich and powerful clients, he seemed particularly loath to have any investigation take place. You remember how he tried to keep me from examining the body, which was the best chance to get an accurate fix on the time of death. Then he tried to discredit my findings. You'll also remember that when we conducted our search, he didn't want to go along. Perhaps he wanted the opportunity to create more confusion, to obscure things further. Then when I said the killer might be one of us, you heard how he mocked the idea, finally ending with that oh-so-reluctant revelation of Mousey's mental imbalance. Well, whether or not she was disturbed was beside the point, as Sebastian correctly pointed out. Drupe was trying to deflect our attention, muddy the waters. And finally, there was his absurd argument that it couldn't be any of us because we'd all been together at the time of death. Now, I could understand some of Drupe's early obstructionism—after all, he and I are not fond of each other, to put it mildly—and some of his points may have a certain validity. But it was those last bits about Mousey's paranoia and our all being together that gave me trouble. I don't like Mr. Drupe at all, but I do know he's far too smart to have believed that was relevant. He raised the issues solely to sow confusion.

"Now, I realize that this in itself is not very much," Violet quickly continued, wanting to present her entire argument before answering objections. "But then I remembered something else. Several times in the afternoon, when inquiries were made about the transportation arrangements, Mr. Drupe either said nothing, or claimed ignorance. Last night, trying to urge us to wait, and do nothing, he said that we'd be picked up today. I pointed out that we didn't know that, and he started to say something like, 'But she specifically told me—' and then cut himself off and looked uncomfortable. I think that was a slip. I think that between the afternoon, when Drupe knew nothing about the arrangements, and the evening, when he did, he'd seen Mousey. He'd seen her, and killed her. And then he tried to divert suspicion, not just away from himself, but off the island entirely."

Violet paused, smiled at the rapt attention she'd generated, and went on. "This seemed to account for what I'd noticed, but I still couldn't see why he'd do it. I had one idea, though, and a little while ago, something Cerise told me seemed to confirm it. Apparently, Mousey'd recently had an audit done and, as Cerise said, reacted oddly to the report she received. My bet is that Drupe, as trustee of the estate, had been embezzling funds for over twenty years. Mousey found out and planned to nail him. Even Drupe couldn't slide out of this one, so he killed her."

"My God!" Cerise said. "The plane ticket! He's going to Rio in two days!"

"Precisely," Violet said, smiling.

"And that knife of his!" Sebastian said. "It's sharp enough to cut through anything."

"Oh, dear! We saw him yesterday in the study," Budgie said to Sebastian. "He was looking through the desk, and seemed upset that we'd seen him."

"You didn't tell me that, Sebastian," Violet said.

"It didn't occur to me. Besides, how was I to know you were interested in him? You kept it to yourself...partner."

"I don't like that foul old coot any better than you do," Derrick said, "but you're just guessing. You have no proof."

Violet nodded. "After I talked with Cerise, I went up to Drupe's room. I wanted to see what was in that briefcase he guards so carefully, but not surprisingly, it wasn't there. I thought I'd take a quick look around anyway, and in the back of a drawer I found this." Violet held up a sheet of note paper with handwriting on one side. "It's Mousey's writing. Unless I'm very much mistaken, this is what was inside that envelope Sebastian found."

"What does it say, Sis?"

"It says, 'I have recently discovered that my guardian, Mr. Eustace Drupe, has systematically removed funds from the estate left me by my father, for which he was trustee. As near as the accountants can determine, all the stocks have been sold, all the property is fully mortgaged, and all the cash and other assets are gone. Apparently, much of this went to support questionable political activities, and the rest Drupe removed from the country for his own use. Because of Mr. Drupe's depredations, the estate which I will inherit on my birthday is worthless.' Is this enough proof?" Violet asked. "The letter certainly provides a motive. And the fact that Drupe had it seems to leave no doubt he's the murderer."

"Damned scoundrel! Should be beaten!" The Colonel moved to pound his cane, then looked confused when he realized he didn't have it with him.

"Nothing?" Derrick said to himself.

Mrs. Hook snorted, Cerise laughed softly and shook her head, and Budgie sighed sadly.

"Hee, hee, hee," Mrs. Argus said.

"One thing, Violet," Sebastian said after looking at the letter. "Why would old Drupe keep this around? Awfully incriminating, isn't it?"

Violet shrugged. "It is. Then again, when have you ever known a lawyer to destroy anything, no matter how damaging it might be?"

"That's true. But still. . . . Couldn't the letter have been planted to cast suspicion on Drupe?"

"I suppose that's barely possible."

"So what if it was planted?" Derrick said. "Between

Pinky's accusations and Violet's analysis, Mr. Drupe has quite a few questions to answer."

"Damned right! Full interrogation!" the Colonel trumpeted, rubbing his hands. "Where's the damned fellow, anyway?"

"Yes, where is he?" Violet asked. "Anyone seen him?"

No reply. Then Mrs. Hook snorted. "The little man, dried up like a dead rat? Saw him going into the study this morning. But a body's got enough to do without having to keep track of the lot of you. A body can't be forever——".

"The study!" Violet said. "Where the papers are kept? Again? He's probably making sure that there's nothing there that will point to his embezzling. Quick!"

They all ran to the study, but the heavy door was bolted from the inside. They pounded and called Drupe's name, but there was no answer.

"I'll go check the windows," Cerise said, and ran out before anyone could stop her. After what seemed to be an awfully long time, she returned, slightly out of breath. "The windows are locked. I could see the back of Drupe's head over the top of the chair, but he didn't turn around when I knocked on the window."

"Stand aside," Derrick said. "I'll open the door."

He moved across the hallway, then ran at the door and kicked just beneath the handle, the full weight of his body behind the blow. With a ripping sound, the bolt pulled out of the wood, and the door was open.

They all rushed into the study. In front of them, Drupe was sitting behind the desk. His little eyes were round, and his lower jaw had dropped open. He looked surprised.

But not at their intrusion.

The lawyer's bald lumpy skull was now a red, pulpy mess, split open like an over-ripe plum.

CHAPTER TWELVE

"WELL, IT CERTAINLY LOOKS LIKE OLD EUSTACE HAS drooped," Sebastian said after the initial exclamations of shock and dismay had died down. "It also looks like you were wrong about him, Sis."

"Yes," Derrick said. "He seems to have established his innocence in a rather conclusive fashion."

"Hmm," Violet said, not really listening. If she was disturbed by this new development, she didn't show it. Instead, her eyes were bright and keen as her gaze darted from point to point, examining the scene before her, trying to take in as many details as possible.

It was curious, she thought, but other than the ghastly centrepiece, the setting was lacking the sense of disruption or chaos that usually accompanies violent death. There was no disorder in the room, no sign of haste, or frenzy, or struggle; no drawers were pulled open, no chairs overturned, no papers scattered about. Even the corpse itself seemed composed, the body seated comfortably in the large leather chair, the hands resting on some papers on top of the desk. Nothing suggested panic or fright or that Drupe had tried to defend himself, or even that he had been aware of the approaching attack. All the more curious, Violet thought, since the position of the wound—high up on the forehead, about where the bald lawyer's hairline must have been years before—made it unlikely that the death blow had come from behind. Well, she'd know more about that when she examined the body.

No, besides Drupe's skull, about the only thing not as it should have been was the wall safe. The large painting that usually covered it was swung to the side on its hinges, as was the round door of the safe. Like the lawyer, the safe looked surprised at what had been done to it, the dark circle of the opening seeming to say, "Ooh!"

As she mentally recorded her important first impression of the crime scene, Violet also took careful note of the reactions of her eight companions. Aside from Sebastian, who was trying unsuccessfully to look appropriately serious and grim-faced, most of the others seemed to display the combination of astonishment, fascination, aversion, distress, and uneasiness that was to be expected. Mr. Ching, though, appeared to be merely curious in a detached kind of way. He looked at the body, his hand absent-mindedly running over his short spiky hair, his expression like that of a man doing a complex mathematical calculation.

The Colonel, too, seemed unmoved as he looked at the bludgeoned remains, grunting once, as though in acknowledgement of something. Then he glanced up at the wall to the right of the desk—the wall opposite the one that held the safe—and suddenly his eyes widened and all colour drained from his face. The intricate network of sclerotic blood vessels across his cheeks and nose stood out darkly against the abrupt pallor, and gasping, panting sounds came from deep in the Colonel's barrel chest.

Sebastian looked up, interested, thinking that a beached walrus had somehow blundered into their little get-together.

Budgie bustled over to support her husband, whose legs seemed suddenly shaky. Soon her body was trembling with the effort of holding him up, and Mr. Ching stepped forward to lend a hand. That was all it took for the Colonel to recover from his fainting fit. Colour returned to his face as he backed away from the cook, making warning sounds and shaking his arm, evidently forgetting that he was still not holding his cane.

Violet noted with some interest the sequence of the Colonel's reactions, and she also saw that she had overlooked something in her initial survey of the study. At eye level on the wall to the right of the desk was a rectangular patch much lighter than the surrounding panelling. Until very recently, something had hung there. Something, a quick glance confirmed, that was no longer in the room.

"Hmm," Violet said to herself, nodding. A silent smile formed itself on her lips as she thought how much more interesting these new developments made the case. With a start, she realized that the others were looking at her expectantly and, returning to the present, she briskly took charge of the situation.

She ordered the others to stand back and to touch nothing. As with the first body, Violet's approach was cautious. She worked her way around the desk in ever-diminishing circles, careful to ensure that she destroyed no piece of evidence, overlooked no tiny clue. But, as before, there was nothing to be seen. The safe was empty. The french windows behind the desk were securely locked and bolted. There were no suspicious bits of ash or dirt or lint on the Aubusson carpet— or at least nothing that could not be accounted for by the less than enthusiastic efforts of Mrs. Hook.

Finally, Violet reached the desk. Still without touching anything, she looked over the papers spread out across the top of it. They mostly seemed to be connected with the running of the estate, account sheets, employee lists, and so forth. All looked to be fairly old, though even a cursory inspection made it clear that only one document was of any potential interest. Carefully lifting Drupe's hand—noticing as she did so that the body was still quite warm—Violet pulled out the sheaf of papers on which it was resting. She quickly skimmed through the dense type, shrugged, then looked up and held it out for Sebastian.

At one time, Sebastian, like his sister, had had considerable experience deciphering testamentary intricacies, and the six pages of this document gave him no trouble at all. When he finished, he turned to Budgie, grinning hugely.

"This is Ripley Sill's will," he said, then paused and made a face. "That's a real tongue twister. 'In Ripley Sill's will, will Ripley Sill will, or won't he?'" He smiled again at Budgie. "Oh, he will, all right, and he did. It says that—except for a few minor bequests—the entire estate goes to his daughter, Rosa. But it also says very clearly that if she should die before her twenty-fifth birthday, it all goes to you as her only living relative. Congratulations! It's all yours!" Sebastian, who knew how exciting it was to inherit, was genuinely delighted about Aunt Budgie's good fortune, but his smile faded when he noticed her sad expression. "Or it would have been all yours if there'd been anything left to get." Sebastian shrugged and looked sympathetically at her. "Oh well. Easy come, easy go. Right?"

Budgie tried to smile at Sebastian, but wasn't quite successful.

Meanwhile, Violet had examined the body, but had discovered very little beyond what was immediately evident. The dead lawyer, a fist-sized hole in his forehead, was a textbook example of what happened when the human skull came into contact with the classic blunt instrument. Violet did, however, determine that there had been just one blow, and that—judging from the depth of the indentation—it had been an exceptionally powerful one. Either the killer was very strong, or the weapon was one that could build up considerable momentum before striking. Like a golf club, Violet thought. She couldn't be sure, but judging from the shape and position of the wound, she thought that the blow might have come from the side, rather than the front. If from the front, the attack would have involved reaching across the large desk, which might have been awkward, and which Drupe would certainly have seen coming.

Violet straightened up and, as she did so, saw the wound from a slightly different angle. She froze where she stood, half bent over, staring at it, an expression of near-disbelief on her face. She used her magnifying glass for another close examination of Drupe's skull. Then she got out a clean handkerchief and carefully, very carefully, let it soak up the blood and fluid that had filled the indentation. She again looked closely at the wound and shook her head, as though she still could not believe her eyes. She looked up at the others, then asked Cerise to join her.

Cerise hesitantly went around behind the desk, and Violet asked her to examine the wound. At first she refused, but finally agreed when Violet kept insisting that was essential that she do it.

"Tell me what, if anything, you notice about it," Violet said. "You may have to look at it from different positions."

Reluctantly, Cerise took the magnifying glass and bent to her unpleasant task. After a couple of minutes she started to stand up. "Nothi—wait!" She bent over again, again looked through the glass for a long time, then straightened and went over to Violet. "There's an imprint there," she said quietly. "It's hard to see at first, but once you spot it, it's very clear. Whatever it was that was used to do this, it left a very precise imprint in his skull." She grimaced.

Violet nodded. "What'd it look like to you?"

"Like some kind of animal head, I think. The deepest part looks like it could be the snout."

"Yeah, like a dog."

"Maybe, but not quite. I think it looks more like...I don't know...like a lion's head, or something." Suddenly Cerise stopped and stared at Violet. "My God! Isn't—"

Violet held up a silencing finger. "Shh."

Cerise looked at Violet, then nodded, and went back to where the others were waiting. She stood apart and gazed speculatively at one particular member of the party.

"Well, has the Society-Girl Detective wrapped up another one?" Sebastian asked pleasantly.

Violet's eyes narrowed as she considered her brother. "Idiot," she muttered, then proceeded to relate her findings, such as they were, omitting only the detail of the imprint.

"So you're saying that once again it could be any of us?" Derrick asked when she'd finished.

Violet nodded. "Apparently no one saw Drupe between breakfast and the time we broke in here. Or, I should say—for a rather obvious reason—no one will admit to having seen him. Did any of you see him?" Heads moved from side to side, and Violet nodded again. "One of you is lying, of course, but I'd hardly expect it to be otherwise. And furthermore, I doubt that any one of us can completely and conclusively account for the way we spent those hours."

Several protests started but quickly died, as everyone realized that Violet was correct, that everyone had been alone for significant portions of the period in question.

"Do you think," Derrick asked, "that the same person killed both of them?"

"At this point there's no way to be sure, but it does seem to be a reasonable assumption. Certainly, the alternative—that Drupe killed Mousey, and then was himself killed—is not very reasonable. Circumstances force us to accept the fact that one of us is a killer, but to think that there could be more than one does seem to be pushing things a bit far."

Most of the group nodded in agreement. It was, as Violet said, reasonable; moreover, they had no way of knowing that Violet's assumption was, simultaneously, both correct and incorrect.

"But why kill Drupe?" Derrick persisted. "You made a good case for why Drupe'd want to kill Pinky, but why would anyone want to kill him?"

"That's the question, isn't it? If we knew why, we'd probably know who."

"Maybe whoever it was wanted something from the safe."

Violet shrugged. "It's possible, I suppose, but I kind of doubt it. I don't think there was anything of importance in there, not after all these years. Just the old records—" she waved at the desk "—that Drupe was looking at."

"Besides," Cerise put in, "it's not just who had a reason to kill Mr. Drupe. If Violet's right, it's who had a reason to kill *both* of them. Mr. Drupe may be central to it all, or he may be incidental. Right now we don't know. So, we're right back at the beginning: who had a reason to kill Rosa?"

"Even minus one," Sebastian said, "there should be no shortage of candidates."

"What makes you say that?" Violet said.

"Mousey's accusation against Mr. Drupe."

"What are you talking about?"

"Well, Sis, there was something there that you didn't notice. Or at least didn't mention."

Violet dug the letter out of her shoulder bag and looked at it. "What are you—"

"Top right-hand corner, Sis."

"Damn! You're right, Sebastian."

"What is it?" Derrick asked.

"The number five," Violet said.

"As in page five," Sebastian added. "Meaning that there are at least four preceding pages. Assuming that the rest of the material is similar to what we've already seen, Mousey made accusations against at least four people besides old Drupey. Golly, for all we know, her letter might have gone up to page nine."

"Why not ten?" Violet said.

"How could it? I'm number ten. I never met her, and she didn't know me, therefore she couldn't have a grievance against me."

"One doesn't have to know you, Sebastian, to have a grievance against you, but I suppose you're right in this case."

"So, now we're right back where we began," Derrick said.

"Not quite," Violet said. "There are a few more lines to follow."

"Such as?"

"Such as—whatever it was that hung on the wall over there, but is no longer in this room."

Eight heads turned in the direction Violet was pointing.

She smiled at the sounds of surprise that her dramatic announcement generated, and particularly at the sputtering, choking noises that came from one of their party.

"Oh, dear," Budgie said, pounding her husband on the back.

"Something else is gone, too, Sis."

"Oh?" Violet said coldly, more than a little tired of the way her brother always seemed to manoeuvre himself into *her* spotlight.

"Yes," he said smiling and pointing. "Mr. Drupe's dentures. Upper and lower."

More sounds of surprise as everyone looked and saw that Drupe's mouth did indeed contain nothing but gums. Violet wrinkled her nose; missing pictures were one thing, missing dentures were something else again. Really! How tacky!

"Do you think it's a clue, Sis? Is this what they mean by the teeth of the evidence?"

"Sebastian! This is not funny."

"You're right, it's not. But it certainly is something to chew on, isn't it?"

Cerise started to giggle, and the others joined in, grateful for even a small release from the growing tension and strain. Violet, tapping her foot impatiently, waited for things to quiet down, then asked if anyone knew what had been on the wall.

There was no response, and Violet was wondering where to go from there, when Mrs. Hook said, "Why don't you ask him?" She pointed at the Colonel, who flushed, then paled, but said nothing.

"What do you mean?" Violet asked.

"I mean, I saw him standing right in front of that spot yesterday afternoon, nose right up against whatever was hanging there. I didn't pay attention to what he was looking at. A body's got enough to do without keeping track of stuff like that. And I'd like to know how many there'll be for dinner. There's enough to do without setting places and then having to take them away."

"I imagine we will all be at dinner, Mrs. Hook."

Mrs. Argus laughed in a most amused way. "No, not all," she said, and ran from the room.

"Maybe the old bat's flying off to Transylvania," Sebastian hissed through drawn lips.

"Well, what about it, Colonel?" Violet asked.

"Hell and damnation! The damned woman's mad as a March hare! All wrong. Never been in this room. Never. Don't know what was hanging there. Never saw it." The Colonel harrumphed a couple of times, then stalked out.

Everyone looked after him, expressions of curiosity on their faces. They all knew he was lying.

CHAPTER THIRTEEN

"OH, DEAR," BUDGIE SAID, AND HURRIED FROM THE ROOM.

Violet hardly hesitated before running after her, and caught up with her in the corridor. The Colonel was nowhere to be seen.

"Tell me about it," Violet said gently.

Budgie looked at the younger woman with pale watery eyes, then looked down, sadly shaking her head.

"It's all right. You can talk to me."

Budgie looked up, seemed about to say something, then again shook her head. "No, dear. It's my problem."

Violet resisted the impulse to take Budgie by the shoulders and shake her until she stopped being a long-suffering fool and realized that even though she had the misfortune to be married to the foul son of a bitch, she could still think about herself every once in a while. Instead, Violet said softly, "If there's a problem, it belongs to all of us now."

Budgie sighed and nodded. "I suppose you're right, dear. But it's not easy." She sighed again, and Violet smiled encouragingly. "You know, dear, the Colonel can be a difficult man to live with."

"I did get that impression."

"Yes. Not everyone understands the Colonel."

Violet, who felt she'd understood everything there was to know about the Colonel the moment she laid eyes on him, merely smiled and nodded again.

"Yes, dear. He does tend to antagonize people."

"So I noticed."

"So everyone notices, dear. Believe me, I am constantly—constantly!—having to get him out of trouble. The man never learns."

"I imagine it's quite a strain."

"You have no idea. He's worse than a child. I have to watch him all the time. I'm always apologizing for him, making excuses. If I leave him alone for a minute, I never know what mischief he'll get up to. And it's been like that for almost thirty-five years. Nonstop."

"Why do you put up with it?"

Budgie looked at Violet and smiled, her expression saying that she'd never be able to make the younger woman understand.

"The Colonel seems to have quite a temper," Violet said.

"That's one way of putting it, dear. He has his own ideas about things, and he doesn't like it if he can't get his way."

"He gets upset?"

"He certainly does, dear." Budgie laughed tolerantly, then looked worried and quickly added, "But, dear, you mustn't think he'd ever hurt anyone."

"No, of course not," Violet said, mentally adding, neither would an unexploded bomb.

Budgie seemed reluctant to continue, so Violet asked about the Colonel's habits.

"Habits, dear?"

"Yes, you know. What the Colonel likes to do . . . you know . . . in private."

Budgie blushed. "Oh, I couldn't tell you that."

"It might be important."

"Really, dear? I don't see why."

"Trust me. Please."

"But I've never told anyone this."

"Then maybe it's time you did."

Budgie sighed. "Well, dear, if you really want to know, I suppose. . . ."

Budgie then proceeded to relate—cheerfully and at length—the Colonel's many curious, albeit harmless, quirks and practices. Violet, who had a low tolerance for peculiarities other than her own, punctuated Budgie's recital several times with incredulous shrieks of "He does what?" or "He likes what?"

By the time Budgie finished, Violet wasn't quite sure who was the sophisticated modern young woman and who was the dowdy Victorian doormat. Still reeling from what she'd heard, Violet barely managed to ask, "But what about children?"

"Oh, the Colonel likes children."

"Ah! You mean, he *really* likes children."

"Yes, dear, he really likes—oh, dear! You mean—what that tan young man said last night?"

Violet nodded, holding her breath.

"Oh, no, the Colonel wouldn't. . . . No, I'm sure he couldn't. . . . At least, I don't think. . . . No, of course not. There was only that one—oh, dear!"

"What? What is it?"

"No, I couldn't tell you."

"Please." Violet sensed she was close to a major revelation, and had some difficulty maintaining her composure.

"Well, all right, dear, but you mustn't make more out of it than it really is."

"Don't worry," Violet said, exhaling slowly. "I'd never do that."

Budgie smiled weakly. "There isn't that much to tell. It was when little Squeak was about ten or eleven. You know, she never really liked the Colonel. She said he frightened her. But she was such a high-strung, nervous little thing that she was scared of nearly everything. You know, she saw monsters in every shadow, and she would never get into her bed until someone looked underneath it and told her nothing was hiding there. I guess she never understood that when the Colonel made those faces at her, it was just to make her laugh.

"Anyway, one day she came to me, very upset, and said the Colonel tried to . . . you know . . . do things to her. I confess, dear, that I didn't take her very seriously. After all, I thought I knew the Colonel pretty well. And I also knew—as I said—that little Squeak had a tendency to overreact to things, and even to make things up if it suited her. She had a very active imagination. And I know it's not nice to say this, but she could be a very nasty little child when she wanted to. Well, afterwards, I talked to the Colonel about this, and naturally he said it was all nonsense. He said he caught her looking through his private things—she was always sneaking around, snooping into things, even if she knew she wasn't supposed to—and he got angry. So angry that he spanked her, but as soon as he did it, he felt awful about it."

I bet that's not all he felt, Violet thought, but remained silent.

Budgie sighed sadly. "I guess poor little Squeak made up that story to get even. After that, the Colonel and I decided that maybe it would be better for everyone if Squeak didn't spend very much time with us. The Colonel was very upset about this. As I told you, he really does like children."

Yeah, Violet thought, especially with a cream sauce and miniature onions.

She'd read enough magazine articles to know that this kind of thing was far more common than was generally believed. Furthermore, in the households where it occurred, there was very often a kind of unspoken conspiracy to ignore it, because that way the appalling fact didn't have to be faced. Since Violet wouldn't trust the Colonel to provide the correct time of day, she saw no reason to believe his version of the affair. Whether Aunt Budgie did or not was moot; in any case, she could not be expected to discuss it any more openly than she had already done. Still, Violet had a strong feeling that Budgie meant her to read between the lines. She also had a good idea about what another page of Mousey's letter was concerned with. Now, *that* was a disclosure that one might well do literally anything to suppress.

"But dear," Budgie said, "what does any of this have to do with the treasure?"

"What?" Violet heard her voice rise in an unfortunate squawk.

"The treasure, dear. Isn't that what you wanted to know about?"

"Treasure?"

"Yes, dear, you know—that missing gold from the Revolutionary War."

"Yes, of course," Violet said confidently, nodding her head, feeling as though she'd opened the door of her house only to discover that she was now in the middle of the Gobi Desert.

"Well, dear, the Colonel has been interested in that for a long time. He did a lot of research, and came up with a theory that the gold was still on the island—buried somewhere. As far as I could tell, he had no particular reason to think this, but when the Colonel gets an idea, he tends to hold onto it pretty tightly, reason or no reason. At first I thought it was just kind of a hobby with him—and I was certainly thankful for anything that would keep him occupied for part of the time. But I'm afraid that eventually—as so often seems to happen with him— it turned into a real obsession. He could hardly think of anything else and became determined to find the treasure, no matter what. Of course, he hadn't a clue what he was doing; he's not very good at figuring out complicated problems—or simple ones, either. Sometimes, dear, I swear he doesn't know his right from his left. But I couldn't tell him that. Instead, I reminded him that even if he found it, it wouldn't belong to him. But even that didn't make any difference. He was consumed by the idea of the treasure, and terrified that someone would beat him to it." Budgie sighed wearily. "So, dear, that's why he's behaving as he is. He's so wrapped up in his crazy schemes that he assumes everyone else is as well." Budgie sighed again and shook her head. "I'm sure he was in the study, as Mrs. Hook said. You see, when your brother and I went in there yesterday, I noticed that there was a very old map of the island hanging on the wall. That's what's missing, dear. That's why the Colonel acted the way he did a few minutes ago.

Believe me, it doesn't mean anything, and you shouldn't pay any attention to him. That man! Sometimes I wish I didn't have to—pay attention, that is. But I told you at the beginning, dear—it's my problem."

Budgie looked at Violet, her expression a mixture of hope and anxiety, but the younger woman didn't seem to notice. The Gobi Desert had turned into a lush oasis, thickly verdant with twining vines ripe with intricate possibilities.

Finally Violet looked into Budgie's pale, expectant eyes. "I'm glad we had this talk. You've accounted for some things I'd noticed and wondered about."

"Oh, that's good." Budgie smiled gratefully, her tense little body at last relaxing.

"There's just one more thing. Have you seen the Colonel's cane?"

"His cane, dear? He had it this morning, I know, but I don't know what—oh, dear! Surely you don't think that—not after what I said. But you said—oh, no! You can't—"

Budgie turned and ran down the corridor, her plump body shaking. She stopped once and turned back, a curious expression on her face. Violet could not decide whether she looked despairing or relieved . . . or a combination of both. Then Aunt Budgie turned the corner and disappeared.

Violet gazed down the empty hall, going over in her mind all the interesting things she'd been told. And she had certainly been told several earfuls. For all her hesitancy, once Budgie got started. . . .

Thinking about it, Violet had the feeling that Budgie was not quite as ingenuous as she seemed, and that—despite what she said—she had in fact not been all that reluctant to talk. Then Violet recalled the look of undiluted hatred that she had seen Budgie give her husband the day before. As Budgie had said, it was her problem. Maybe, Violet thought, she had decided upon a way to deal with it.

For quite some time, Violet slowly walked alone through the long corridors of the big house, considering possibilities, trying to see if there was a way she could make all the different threads weave together into a thick, solid rope. As she turned a corner on the second floor, she saw Budgie and Mrs. Hook standing close together at the far end of the hall, apparently deep in a serious conversation. When they turned their heads and saw Violet, they nervously jumped apart, then quickly walked off in opposite directions.

CHAPTER FOURTEEN

BY THE MIDDLE OF THE AFTERNOON, VIOLET HAD PRETTY well worked out her case. There were still some gaps and spaces, but she was at least ninety per cent sure, and was confident that the remaining ten per cent would fall into place before much longer.

All things considered, Violet couldn't have been more pleased with the result. Of course, it might have been more interesting if the solution had been slightly less obvious. After all, if she'd been told at the outset that crimes of violence would be committed, and then asked to guess who the perpetrator would be, this was the member of their party that she probably would have picked. Still, she couldn't complain. Certainly, if there was to be a murderer among them, Violet was not at all sorry that it had turned out to be the Colonel.

She had detested him on sight, recognizing exactly what he was even at a distance of more than a hundred yards. Calling him a pig was both a slander of a perfectly respectable animal, and a too-generous assessment of his character. Closer observation and contact had not only confirmed the original judgement, but had revealed further and more varied forms of loutishness and social maladjustment. Why, as far as Violet was concerned, anyone who tried to pull a stunt like the one the Colonel had tried in the lounge was capable of just about anything. Goddamn! Her zippers still bristled at the recollection.

Still, Violet knew better than to let her personal feelings interfere, and she again went over what she knew and what she was at least reasonably certain about.

One. Even the little that Budgie had willingly related made it clear the man was a pervert and a degenerate. No matter that Budgie seemed untroubled by his so-called "quirks", and said he was essentially harmless; she had been making excuses for him, covering up, for so long, it was automatic with her, and Violet would not have expected anything else. It didn't take much insight to see that the Colonel was a dangerously diseased personality, a menace to those around him, who should have been neutered years ago, if not put down like a rabid stoat.

Two. The depravity that Budgie acknowledged was nothing compared to the vileness she hinted at. Again, her rejection of the awful truth was to be expected, but Violet could read between the lines, and she could also recognize a *cri de coeur* when she heard one. Violet, who could always and easily believe the worst of anyone, had no trouble casting the Colonel in that most terrible of roles—the child molester.

Three. There was the Colonel's considerable temper; his barely controlled tendency to violence; the near-total absence of any check or restraint on his own desires; his inability to recognize those around him as anything other than objects existing solely for the gratification of those desires; his flaring anger in the face of any opposition; his oft-expressed eagerness to inflict pain and to see it inflicted. To some, the Colonel might seem like a minor character from a British bedroom farce, but Violet had taken an extension course in abnormal psychology, and she knew a psychopath when she saw one.

Four. Like most psychopaths, the Colonel was terrified lest any crack appear in the image that he carefully presented to the world. Reality had to be what he said it was and only what he said it was. Any attack upon that reality must be, immediately squelched. Violet recalled the way the Colonel reacted every time Budgie was about to reveal some innocuous little truth about him, something at variance with the way he wanted to be perceived. How he would have responded to the truly major threat that Mousey's revelation would have posed was anyone's guess. Violet guessed it could well have been with an insanely savage violent outburst.

Five. Poor Mousey was killed in what could only be described as an insanely savage violent outburst. Violet remembered saying that she thought the butchering might have been performed in coolness rather than passion, but that did not necessarily contradict her theory here. After all, one of the marks of psychopathic violence is a kind of detached rage, a purposeful, methodical madness.

Six. If the Colonel's fear of being exposed as the disgusting monster that he was was not a sufficient motivation, there was his obsession with the treasure of Komondor Island. Again, it didn't matter whether there really was a treasure, only that the Colonel thought so, and believed, moreover, that he was being thwarted in his attempt to get it. As Budgie had told him, the gold wouldn't belong to him even if he found it. No doubt, though, he was familiar with the terms of the will and knew Budgie would inherit if his niece died. The treasure would then be his, and so, from his point of view, it would make perfect sense to remove the one obstacle standing between him and his desire. Probably neither motive by itself would have been sufficient; but the two together would be irresistible. There, in the person of poor Mousey, was the one thing that jeopardized both his current well-being and his future happiness. Especially if Mousey, with her new-found aggressiveness and desire to avenge wrongs done to her, had taunted the Colonel. Budgie was right that there'd been a streak of nastiness in Mousey; Violet could well imagine that being goaded by the girl in her whining little voice might have been all it took to push the Colonel over the edge.

Seven. The reason for murdering Eustace Drupe was not quite so clear. Possibly, Violet thought, Drupe knew something about Mousey's accusations; he had seemed quite well informed about a lot of things. Or perhaps the reason had something to do with the will or the treasure map. It was not difficult to come up with a number of plausible scenarios, but which was correct was far from certain. What was certain, however, was that the implement that had killed the lawyer was the Colonel's cane—the cane with a large silver lion's head for a handle, the image of which was so clearly visible in Drupe's crushed skull.

Violet had been walking back and forth on the house's long stone terrace—she found that it often helped to walk when she was considering complicated problems—but now she paused and leaned against the railing, gazing out at the island and the grey water and sky. No, she thought, you don't need a map if you can read the road signs; and Violet had always been a pretty good navigator.

There were still a few details that she'd like to have, but those were not much more than the final decorations on the package. There was the question of the time of Mousey's death. The Colonel had left the dining room about ten minutes after he'd driven Budgie away, and Violet wondered how much time was unaccounted for before he joined her in their room.

She doubted, however, that she could get the information from Budgie. The poor woman obviously knew—or at least strongly suspected—the truth, but a lifetime of conditioning had made it impossible for her to take direct, positive action. Instead, she had gone about it in the only way that would permit her to live with herself; she had relied on Violet to penetrate the veils of her necessary deception. That way Budgie could continue to be the shocked, concerned wife, while Violet acted as Nemesis. No, Violet didn't think she could get more out of Budgie than she already had. Maybe Cerise could help, though; her room was next to the Dijons'.

Then there was the question of the weapons. The Colonel was clearly linked to the murder of Drupe. While it would be useful to know what had happened to the cane, the fact that the Colonel no longer had it—after having previously never been without it—was in itself extremely telling. Indeed, Violet decided, maybe even more damning than if he'd still had it with him.

It wasn't absolutely essential, but Violet dearly wanted to know what had been used to kill poor Mousey. If she could find the weapon, and link it to the Colonel, she would have a case with which even her picayune brother could not easily cavil. Failing that, if she could locate the rest of Mousey's letter, or—shudder—Drupe's teeth, it might be almost as effective. Especially if they turned up in the Colonel's luggage.

Violet paused in her deliberations when she noticed someone approaching the house from the upper end of the island. As the figure got closer Violet saw, with some amusement, that it was Derrick. He'd said he was going to make another search of the island in case they had overlooked anything the night before. Violet doubted that they had, but Derrick certainly seemed to have thrown himself into the task. His trim muscular figure and elegant European clothes were almost entirely covered in a thick layer of dark mud.

He climbed up onto the terrace. "I put my foot into a damn gopher hole and went head first into a mud puddle." He shrugged, and gave an embarrassed laugh. No longer the slick man-about-town, Derrick looked as though he'd just come from some Melanesian tribal ritual, and it was all Violet could do to keep from howling.

"Did you find anything?" she asked.

He shook his head disgustedly, causing cracks to appear where he was starting to harden. "I'd better get inside before the old Guccis are ruined for good."

"Dodo," Violet muttered as he disappeared around the corner of the house. Though he does have rather incredible shoulders, she added to herself, then angrily tossed her head to get rid of the thought.

She considered how best to proceed, and decided to start with Cerise . . . if she could find her. Once again, everyone seemed to have wandered off somewhere.

Suddenly, as Violet was about to go inside to look for Cerise, a scream pierced the chilly late November stillness.

A scream. And another scream. And another.

They came from the wooded portion of the island, and

Violet hurried in that direction. Separately, most of the other members of the party also hastened towards the sounds of terror, and soon all but Derrick and Mrs. Argus were gathered around their source.

Violet had located Cerise, but she was no longer interested in talking to her.

It was Cerise who had screamed. She was standing next to a large, deep hole that had recently been dug in the muddy ground. At the bottom of the hole was the Colonel. He was face down. There was a heavy spade sticking out of his back.

Violet looked down into the pit and shook her head. A dead body naturally generates a certain sense of shock, but Violet was honest enough not to pretend to any sorrow or pity. If she'd felt satisfaction at the prospect of exposing the Colonel as the murderer, she was not about to be distressed when he became a victim. No, about all she felt was relief that she'd not gone public with her hypothesis.

"Well," Sebastian said, "it looks like the Colonel's shoveled off to Buffalo. Oops!" He put a hand up to his mouth, looking sheepishly surprised at what had just popped out. "Budgie, I'm sorry. I—"

Aunt Budgie looked at him, her eyes round and crazy, her cheeks and her bosom quivering. Her little bird-like mouth opened, and she cried something like "Yiiii!" as she ran at Sebastian, plump arms straight out in front of her. She hit him in the chest with her little fists and sent him flying backwards into the hole, where he landed next to the Colonel with a gasp and a viscous splash. Budgie did not hesitate, but turned and ran towards the house, all the way emitting her mad, keening "Yiiii!"

The others went over to the edge of the hole and looked down. Sebastian, covered with sticky mud, was just getting to his feet, trying to shake some of the muck off himself.

"I guess I had that coming," he said. Unthinkingly, he picked up a small piece of cloth that was half under the Colonel's outstretched arm and began to wipe himself off with it.

"Sebastian! Stop it!" Violet cried. "What's that?"

Puzzled, Sebastian looked at the cloth in his hand. "It's just a handkerchief, Sis." Then he did a double-take. "Golly! It's monogrammed!"

"What?"

"I said it's monogrammed. It's got the initials HM on it."

The stunned silence lasted until Violet said softly, almost to herself, "But none of us has those initials."

Mrs. Hook shifted from one square-toed shoe to the other, scowling darkly. "A body's still got work to do, I suppose. You'll be six for dinner?"

"Oh, I do hope so," Sebastian said.

"My God!" Cerise shrieked, the terrible reality of their situation striking her almost like a physical blow. "There must be a homicidal maniac on the loose."

She wasn't, as it turned out, far wrong.

CHAPTER FIFTEEN

DINNER THAT NIGHT WAS NOT EXACTLY A FESTIVE OCCASION. And the meal itself—in keeping with the standard already established by Mr. Ching—did little to improve matters.

For starters there was a soup that Sebastian identified as "cream of flour", and things went down after that. The main course consisted of what were obviously chops, though from what animal it was impossible to say. For a moment, Sebastian wondered if Mr. Ching had taken the wrong piece of meat out of the freezer; atypically, he refrained from voicing this idea.

Still, considering the circumstances and the food, most of the party didn't do too badly. Mrs. Argus was ravenous, as usual, and Derrick positively wolfed down his dinner, having somehow acquired an extremely powerful appetite. Budgie, though, barely pecked at her food, and Violet, looking slightly dazed, listlessly pushed bits of grey meat around her plate.

Sebastian glanced at Budgie. Her eyes were round and glassy, and she seemed oblivious of everything around her. Then he turned to Violet, speaking softly. "Before . . . uh . . . this afternoon, Sis, you were starting to think it was the Colonel, weren't you?"

"What makes you say that?" Violet said, staring down at her plate.

"I saw the expression when you looked in the hole. Like you couldn't believe it."

Violet said nothing, merely prodded a glaucous, resistant substance that might have been mashed potatoes.

"Oh, it couldn't have been the Colonel," Cerise said.

Violet looked up for the first time. "Why not?"

"Well, last night—God! Is that all it was? Last night, after I left here, I went up to my room. I wasn't there very long before I heard Budgie come into her room. I heard her talking to herself. I couldn't tell what she was saying, but she sounded very upset or annoyed or angry. Then not long after—probably not more than ten minutes—I heard the Colonel come in. I don't know when he left the dining room. . . ."

Violet nodded. "About ten minutes after Budgie."

"So there's no way that there would've been time for him to . . . for him to do what was done."

Violet looked at Aunt Budgie, but the poor woman just sat there stunned, giving no indication that she'd heard anything. Violet sighed, slowly shook her head, and again looked down at her plate.

"Ah, the plot thickens," Sebastian said. "Actually, considering the amount of gore around, I suppose one could say that the clot thickens."

Cerise started to giggle, then abruptly stopped. "My God! What's the matter with me? That's not funny."

Budgie, showing her first signs of animation, apparently agreed. She stood up, a wild, crazed look in her eyes, her lips pulled back in a silent snarl. She reached down, grabbed a chop from her plate, hurled it at Sebastian with a wicked side-arm delivery, then ran from the room, again making that strange sound of "Yiiii!"

Sebastian, eyebrows raised in surprise, gingerly touched his temple, then looked at his fingertips. It was just gravy, thank goodness. Fortunately, the chop had only grazed him, or it might have done serious damage.

He shook his head, bewildered. "I probably shouldn't have said that, and I realize that this is all very shocking and upsetting, but still. . . . Considering that yesterday she told me she wished she could leave the Colonel, Budgie does seem to be acting strangely—overly distraught."

"I don't think it's so strange," Derrick said. "Look what's

happened in the last twenty-four hours. Wouldn't you be distraught if your only niece was gruesomely murdered? If, as the only relative, you inherit, but then you find that there's nothing left in the estate? If another person is killed, and everything points to your husband? And then your husband is killed? And if, on top of it all, some silly ass keeps making flippant comments? How would you react after all that? I'd say she's behaving very reasonably."

Sebastian shrugged, looking unconvinced. "Well, given the choice, it's probably less dangerous to be hit with the dinner than to eat it."

Just then Mrs. Hook strode in. She looked at Budgie's empty place, inhaled sharply, and scowled. She turned to go, viciously kicking the fallen chop across the oak floor. She paused in the doorway. "There's brown stuff for dessert if anyone wants it," she informed them, and went out.

No one seemed to feel much like dessert, and they all decided to make an early night of it. Before they separated, Mrs. Argus pleasantly reminded them that *She* was still with them, watching and waiting.

"Oh, good," Sebastian said. "That means we still have enough for a baseball team. . . . Especially since we already have an old bat."

In the middle of the night, Violet awoke from a shallow, restless sleep. It is not unusual, when one is troubled with a difficult problem, for the consideration of it to continue subconsciously, and it is on that level that a solution, or the way to a solution, will sometimes be perceived. Thus it was with Violet, who suddenly sat upright in bed, fully alert, her eyes open wide in that instantaneous flash of recognition.

The discovery of the Colonel that afternoon had so taken her by surprise, so shaken her, that she had been in a kind of stunned fog for the remainder of the day. Still, while she had hardly focused on what was going on around her, conversations and reactions had none the less registered. It was these that her sleeping mind had manipulated like pieces of a jigsaw puzzle until, with an abrupt click, they had fallen into place. Now, sitting up in bed, she realized that she had the key—unknowingly given to her by Derrick, of all people.

As with so many things, she thought, it was all in the way you looked at it. If you had the right angle, the right perspective, the right frame of reference, things that otherwise seemed isolated and incomprehensible were suddenly seen to fit together and make perfect sense. Obviously, the things that were happening on Komondor Island—however demented and inexplicable they might seem—could not be random occurrences, discrete events only coincidentally linked together. No, if three unexpected things happened, one after the other, there had to be a connection; if not, this was not a world of logic and probability, but one buffeted to and fro according to the whims of laughing, indifferent deities. And that, Violet thought with a shake of her head, has not been an acceptable explanation of events for quite a few years.

No, the three murders were not random. There was a connection between them. There was even—dammit!—a chain of cause and effect. And once you saw that, once you looked at it in the right way, it was clear that there was an explanation—an explanation that was not just possible, but plausible, that accounted for everything. Or at least everything of consequence.

There was one very big problem with this explanation, Violet realized. A problem of timing. At this point, it looked like an insurmountable obstacle, but Violet was sure she was on the right trail and therefore convinced there was a way around it. Which, when found, would lead not just to a triple murderer but also, she suspected, to a blackmailer into the bargain.

Oh, yes, Violet thought with a smile as she lay back down and closed her eyes; she'd better have a little chat with Mrs. Hook in the morning.

But Mrs. Hook was nowhere to be found.

It seemed that she had put out the breakfast things and then gone off somewhere. In itself this was no cause for concern, since both the house and the island were large enough to enable one to disappear for long periods of time; indeed, most members of the party had already done just that, and more than once.

Violet was concerned at this development, however, because she was beginning to feel the press of time. Boats could be coming to pick them up at virtually any moment. If the others were eagerly anticipating rescue, Violet was in no particular hurry. Although she was sure that she had enough evidence to allow the police to wrap up the case—and that it would also resound greatly to her credit—she would much prefer to be able to present them with an absolutely air-tight explanation. How much easier and more straightforward it would be for the media if they could say, "Society-Girl Detective does it again", instead of reporting that she'd merely helped the police, or provided them with valuable information. And how much more often her name would appear, each time coupled with the information that she was the founder and head of Cornichon Cosmetics. You couldn't buy that kind of publicity, not for any amount of money, and if that wasn't enough to push her to the forefront once more. . . .

But she was getting ahead of herself. There were still a few matters to be taken care of. The first of which was finding the housekeeper.

As Violet started up the main staircase to the second floor, wondering how best to proceed, she saw Budgie descending. The poor little woman moved slowly, awkwardly, like a wind-up toy that was running down. Her face was an expressionless mask, her eyes were lowered, and she seemed totally unconscious of her surroundings.

Violet stopped on the landing, directly in Budgie's path. The older woman continued down the stairs until she reached Violet, and then she too stopped, again mechanically, like a toy that continues until it reaches an obstruction and can go no farther.

Violet asked how she was feeling, but Budgie did not reply, merely raised her head so that Violet looked into two dull, unseeing eyes. Budgie's gaze seemed directed far away—or deep inside—to another reality or to a terrible empty unreality. This blank, zombie-like stare caused an uncomfortable sensation to travel up Violet's spine.

Violet asked if Budgie had seen Mrs. Hook, and suddenly the blankness lifted. Budgie's eyes grew round, and a tremor shook her body. To Violet, it seemed a look of absolute fear—or, perhaps, absolute hatred. Then, as suddenly as it appeared, it was gone.

"I think I saw her go out of the house, dear," Budgie said weakly, her voice as flat and lifeless as her eyes. Then, her manner once again vague and vacant, she took a step to the side and continued down the stairs.

Violet shook her head. The expression about someone's mind snapping was clearly not just a figure of speech; there *were* limits beyond which one could not be stretched and still remain whole. She again shook her head as she watched Budgie drift in the direction of the lounge. Too bad. But at least Violet now knew where she would begin.

Violet reached the top of the stairs and was about to continue down the hall when a movement caught her eye. She quickly ducked behind a corner, then cautiously peeked around it. A door was slowly being opened, as though by someone who wanted to make sure the hallway was empty before coming out. Then Mr. Ching appeared and carefully shut the door behind him. He glanced nervously around, started to walk towards the rear of the house, then paused. Apparently something had just occurred to him. He took out a small book from his pocket, and jotted down a brief note. Then he hurried off and turned the corner in the direction of the rear stairs.

Violet, while quite curious about what the cook had been doing in Mr. Drupe's room, had much more urgent concerns. She doubted that she'd get a better opportunity than this, and she intended to take advantage of it. She went down the hall, casually stopped outside a door, checked that no one was watching, then quickly went into Budgie's bedroom.

If asked, Violet would have said that she found it most distasteful to violate other people's privacy, but that circumstances sometimes required it. However, she was honest enough to admit (if only to herself) that there was something awfully exciting about being where she shouldn't be—an unknown intruder learning secret things. It gave her a tremendous feeling of power. Of course, she would have been outraged if someone had tried to do it to her, and she took great care that no one got the chance. She sometimes thought that if things had worked out differently she would have made a good spy . . . or a good thief.

Violet didn't know what she was looking for; she could only hope that she'd recognize it if she saw it. Last night she had realized that it was mainly a question of looking at things the right way. If her conclusions were correct, she knew that she must still be looking at something the wrong way, making some fundamentally incorrect assumption. What she hoped to find was the thing that would give her the right perspective.

She knew she should do her snooping as quickly as possible, but she could not help but linger over the large suitcase that contained what Budgie had called the "equipment". Equipment, indeed! Why, there were things there that would make the Marquis de Sade pause. Again, Violet had the uncomfortable feeling that she was very sheltered and naive, maybe even priggish.

Fascinating though it was, however, there was nothing in the suitcase that brought her any closer to resolving that one large problem she had. No, the answer was not there, although there were things whose function she could not even begin to guess at. She must remember to ask her brother about them; his knowledge of certain arcane matters was, she gathered, truly encyclopedic.

A rapid but thorough search of the rest of the room revealed nothing of any consequence. Violet was disappointed, but she knew she couldn't remain much longer. Just a quick glance into the bathroom, then out.

Again, nothing. Only the large case holding the Colonel's

medication. For the sake of thoroughness, though she expected nothing, Violet looked through it quickly, and then turned to leave.

She was all the way to the bedroom door when she experienced the mental equivalent of feeling the earth shift under her feet. Her mouth dropped open in amazement.

"So that's what it was," she said in a husky whisper.

She went back into the bathroom and took something out of the case.

She had found her mistake. She had discovered the proper angle of view. She didn't have to find a way around the obstacle. When you looked at it the right way, there was no obstacle.

Violet was smiling broadly as she came out of the bedroom. Not only did she know the answer, but it was so deliciously intriguing that it would be talked about for years. Oh yes, she thought; the Society-Girl Detective has done it again.

CHAPTER SIXTEEN

"YOU'VE GOT THAT LOOK, VIOLET," SEBASTIAN SAID.

Violet grinned at the five people gathered around her in the lounge. Poor Budgie had floated off somewhere, and Mrs. Hook had not yet turned up, but Violet figured she had all the audience she needed.

"Well, come on, Sis. Out with it. Who is it?"

Violet waited a long minute before saying, "Beatrice Dijon."

"What? Ridiculous!" Derrick said.

"Oh, Violet! No!" Cerise said.

"Aunt Budgie? Come on, Sis. You've really gone off the deep end this time. What've you been doing—taking diving lessons from Mrs. Argus?"

Violet smiled forbearingly at her brother. "She has been saying that Death is a woman. It looks like she was right."

"Hee, hee, hee."

"I assume," Derrick said, "that you're basing this preposterous idea on something more than that?"

"Oh, yes. . . . Look, I'm not saying it gives me any pleasure to reach this conclusion," Violet said, trying hard not to smile. "I think the woman is to be pitied more than anything else—and I hope that will be taken into consideration—but the facts leave no room for doubt."

"We'll see about that."

"You will," she said, looking at Derrick. "After all, you were the one who pointed me in the right direction."

"Me?"

"Yes. Last night at dinner, right after Budgie ran out. Remember? You listed all the blows the poor woman had suffered. Only you gave them in a particular order—an order that was a little different from the one in which we got the information. I didn't notice the difference at the time, but later I realized that your sequence not only was correct, but also contained an explanation for the things that had happened."

"What are you talking about, Sis?"

"Okay. I'll lay it out for you, step by step. I admit there are a few assumptions, but by the time I'm done, I'm sure you'll all agree that they are not at all unreasonable. To begin with, it's not hard to accept the idea that living with the Colonel for thirty-five years took its toll. If Budgie hadn't actually been driven mad by the man, she had certainly been pushed to the point where she could endure no more. We all saw the looks of anger and frustration and hatred she gave her husband. Sebastian, you said she told you that she wished she could leave him."

"That's right. The first afternoon. Only she said there was no way she could manage to support herself if she did, so she was stuck."

"She said that?" Violet said. "I didn't know. I had assumed something like that, but the fact that she said it just makes my case stronger. It provides a solid motive for the action that initiated a terrible chain of cause and effect."

"What action?" Cerise asked. "What chain?"

"The action was the murder of Mousey, of course. That's the beginning. That's the key to it all. Look: Budgie wants to leave the Colonel, but she can't; however, if she had some money, she could; and there's only one way of getting the money. We only learned about the will yesterday, but Budgie has certainly known its terms for years—that she would inherit everything if Mousey died before her twenty-fifth birthday. Only, time was running out, and Budgie saw her last chance for freedom, for a new life—a life without the Colonel—slipping away. So she seized that chance in the only way left to her. She killed her niece."

"Sweet little Aunt Budgie?" Cerise said. "How could she?"

"I'm not saying it was an easy step for her to take, nor am I in any way suggesting that Budgie is an evil person. No, I suspect that by the time she thought of it, she was quite unbalanced. If the murder was not literally an act of madness, it was born of a desperation so great as to be virtually indistinguishable from madness. Maybe it wasn't even premeditated, but a spur-of-the-moment inspiration."

"But her own niece?" Derrick said.

"Statistically, murder is very much a family affair." Violet flashed her brother an enigmatic smile. "Besides, remarks that Budgie made to me indicated that she didn't really like Mousey all that much. Just because she was her aunt is no reason for Budgie to have liked the poor girl any better than any of us did."

"Okay, Sis. So maybe she didn't like Mousey. So maybe she wanted to get away from the Colonel. So maybe she was desperately disturbed. I still don't—"

"Wait. I said there was a chain involved here, and like any chain, this one gets its shape and strength from the links that comprise it. I realized that we couldn't be dealing with isolated events, that they had to be connected. Derrick showed me the way by listing—unwittingly—the events in their true sequence.

"But let me continue. So Budgie kills her niece, and has enough presence of mind to make it look like the work of a maniac. She will never be suspected. 'Who? Little Aunt Budgie? Don't be absurd!' So, she's home free. Then what happens? She finds Mousey's letter, and learns that there's nothing left. There is no estate. Gone. Stolen. Imagine how she must've felt at that moment. Having already committed a ghastly, hideous act, she discovers it was all pointless, to no purpose. Wouldn't that push anyone to the breaking point—and beyond?"

"My God!" Cerise said. "Poor Budgie! So you're saying that—"

"Precisely. To commit murder for money was one thing.

But with the money gone, there was no possible justification. She was guilty of the worst possible crime. Only she was and she wasn't. In her unbalanced state, it would not have been difficult for her to transfer the guilt to the person who was responsible for making her crime meaningless."

"I say! You mean——"

"Yes. Mr. Eustace Drupe, the embezzler. Maybe she decided he was ultimately the guilty party, or maybe she decided that if she couldn't have the money, neither would he. Either way, she decided to get even. As you may know, with multiple murderers the first killing is usually the hard one; after that, it gets progressively easier. I suspect that, by this time, she really was mad. If you'll remember, she seemed strangely subdued yesterday morning. In any event, even if she was mad, she was not crazy. She never lost sight of the reason she had begun this terrible course of action in the first place— to escape the Colonel."

"You mean, she saw a way to kill two birds with one stone," Sebastian said.

Violet looked disgustedly at him. "That's one way of putting it, I suppose. Since she'd determined she was going to kill Drupe anyway, why not make it look like her husband was responsible? That way she could get rid of both the person who had ruined her life and the person who had taken away her future. We know the Colonel's cane was used to kill Drupe. Since subsequent events have shown that the Colonel almost certainly wasn't the one who wielded it, who was the person who would've had easiest access to it?"

Violet paused. Mr. Ching muttered something to himself in his own language, took out his pocket notebook, and scribbled something in it. Violet looked at him, then shrugged.

"You were right, Sebastian," she continued. "Yesterday I did think it was the Colonel . . . in large part because Budgie gave me the information that led me to that conclusion—in fact, compelled me to that conclusion. At the time, I thought that she was much less reluctant to talk than she pretended to be. But I assigned the wrong reason to it. Now I understand.

And I also realize that I made another incorrect interpretation yesterday. That fainting fit of the Colonel's in the study had nothing to do with Drupe. It happened when he noticed the map was missing. I was pleased with myself for spotting that reaction, and assumed that the missing map was somehow connected with the murder. However, I now realize that if the Colonel had killed Drupe, either the map would not have been missing or the Colonel would not have been surprised that it was. On the other hand, Budgie certainly knew her husband well enough to know how he would react. What better way to direct suspicion towards him than to force him to act suspiciously? She gave me the bait, and I grabbed it. I never stopped to think that it didn't make any sense."

"But if she went to all that trouble to frame the Colonel," Cerise said, "why did she kill him? I assume that's where you're headed."

"Yes. And I don't know why. Maybe she was afraid it wouldn't work, that the Colonel would get off. However, I expect she just decided that after two murders she didn't especially want to commit, she might as well kill the one person she'd really wanted dead all along. Once she started on the slide, she couldn't stop. Until now. You've seen the way she is. That's a person who's finally hit bottom. And if her own torments are not enough, I think Mrs. Hook is adding to them. Either she's an accomplice, or she somehow figured it all out and is blackmailing Budgie, or both. Certainly, Budgie is scared of her. Mrs. Hook's saying she saw the Colonel in the study was probably another part of the plan to make the Colonel look suspicious."

"But even if Mrs. Hook helped," Derrick said, "I can't believe it'd be possible. I mean, physically possible. Aunt Budgie's just an elderly little lady."

"Who's also remarkably strong. You didn't see her carrying two big heavy suitcases. No, she most definitely has the physical capability. I noticed right from the beginning that there was a lot of tightly coiled strength beneath that soft, plump exterior."

"I saw that, too," Cerise said. "I thought that that was one surprisingly tough little lady. But what I haven't seen—what I still can't see—is any indication of a violent nature. Even if you flip out totally, you don't necessarily become a murderer, not like we've seen here. No, Violet, I'm sorry. Maybe what you say makes sense, but I haven't seen anything in her character to support your theory."

Violet nodded. "You also haven't seen the suitcase full of—uh—implements with which Budgie and the Colonel amused themselves."

"Oh, really?" Sebastian said, wondering how he could get a peek at that.

"And," Violet continued, "you haven't heard Budgie describe the kind of things the Colonel liked her to do. Believe me, that is one woman who's had a lot of experience with punishment and torture . . . and violence."

Violet smiled as she let this last revelation sink in. She saw heads begin to nod in agreement as the force of her argument became clear and the solid strength of the chain was perceived, each link reinforcing the others.

"There's only one problem," Sebastian said at last. "She couldn't have killed Mousey."

Violet raised her eyebrows, trying not to smile in too superior a fashion.

"The time, Sis."

"I was wondering if you'd notice that."

"Of course!" Cerise said. "I heard her in her room after dinner the first night. At the very time Rosa was killed. So she couldn't have done it."

"That's what I thought at first," Violet said. "That was the problem. I knew she had to be the one, but if you were correct, I also knew it was impossible. Then I realized I had made another mistake. Right at the beginning. I was looking at things the wrong way. Mousey wasn't killed after dinner, she was killed before dinner. Budgie would've had lots of time then."

"But Sis, that contradicts what you said."

"I know. I was wrong. I had to be mistaken either about

Budgie's guilt, or about the time of death. Since I knew Budgie did it, the other had to be wrong."

"But you can't just ignore the evidence if it doesn't fit your theory. The body was still warm."

"It was next to the furnace. That would retard cooling. And at most we're only talking about a couple of hours. The furnace could easily account for that difference."

"But coagulation hadn't even started. You said so."

"Quite right." Slowly, smiling, Violet took a small bottle from her pocket, and held it up between her thumb and forefinger. "I found this in the case containing the Colonel's medication. Budgie made no secret of the fact that he was prone to thrombosis." Violet jiggled the nearly empty bottle. "This is heparin, an extremely powerful anticoagulant used to treat that condition. If even a portion of this bottle had been injected into Mousey just prior to death, bleeding would have been profound, and there would have been no coagulation."

"My God!" Cerise said, turning to Sebastian. "Budgie attacked you right after you made that sick joke about the clot thickening."

Violet smiled. "Precisely. Sebastian, you said you thought she was acting strangely, and you were right. It was a lot more than just nerves. I don't know how you do it, but you have the knack of hitting pretty close to the mark without ever trying to do so."

"Casual grace, Sis."

"More likely idiot's luck. But whatever it was, you were right on target. No wonder she got so upset. Coming on top of everything else, it's amazing she didn't entirely unravel on the spot."

Sebastian sighed and shook his head.

"The poor woman!" Cerise said.

"Yes, it's really very sad," Violet said, looking anything but. "The one consolation is that it's unlikely she'll have to stand trial. We can probably arrange for her to be placed in some comfortable institution. And, after thirty-five years with the Colonel, an asylum might seem pleasant by comparison.

The question is, what do we do with her while we're waiting to be picked up from here?"

After some discussion they decided that the thing to do was to offer Budgie lots of comfort and support, but at the same time make sure that she was kept under careful observation and control. While it seemed likely that her murderous spree had run its course, no one could be entirely certain. After all, she had already twice attacked Sebastian, and given her seriously disturbed state, virtually anything could still happen.

One possibility that they were very aware of was suicide. Beyond whatever sympathy and affection they felt for her, they all realized it would be much better for them if Budgie did not kill herself. Violet may have been looking towards headlines; but the others too saw how much simpler it would be to present the authorities with a live deranged murderer, instead of four bodies and a complicated tale of madness, revenge, and remorse.

No, Budgie had to be kept safe and secure. Two people would stay with her as much as possible. If she had to be left alone, it would be in a room that had been cleared of anything potentially dangerous and then locked from the outside.

But first they had to find her. They decided to start by searching the house. Sebastian would take the attic, Cerise the second floor, Violet and Mr. Ching the main floor, and Derrick the cellar. Whoever found her would be very careful not to upset her, and would get help if it seemed at all necessary. If they didn't locate her inside, they would search the island.

They then split up, leaving Mrs. Argus behind. She waited a moment, then went into the hall outside the lounge. She cautiously looked around, then silently moved down the corridor and disappeared into the study, a sly look on her face.

For several minutes, no sound was heard throughout the house.

Suddenly there was a terrified scream, a crash of breaking glass, a sickening thud.

Within seconds, Violet, Cerise, Derrick, and Mr. Ching had converged on the foyer, where they exchanged questions of confusion and concern and regarded each other with expressions of rapidly mounting panic. This continued for quite a long while, no one knowing what to do, each reluctant to take the lead, until finally Sebastian came down the main stairway. Then, without a word but with a nearly overwhelming sense of dread, they ran out the large front door.

From the landing, Mrs. Argus watched their departure. Her eyes shone merrily. Two red spots brightened her sallow, sunken cheeks. Her head nodded, and her thin lips were pulled back in a rictus grin.

Outside, Cerise screamed, "My God!" and brought her hands up to cover her face in a futile attempt to blot out the horror.

Derrick was pale and seemed to have difficulty breathing.

Violet grimly shook her head, expelling a hiss of air between clenched teeth.

The look in Mr. Ching's dark eyes belied his otherwise impassive exterior.

"Well, Sis, it looks as though you were right," Sebastian said quietly, gazing down at the yellow-clad blob spread out on the flagstone terrace. "Aunt Budgie must have been unbalanced. She just fell off her perch."

CHAPTER SEVENTEEN

"GOD! I CAN'T TAKE ANY MORE OF THIS!" CERISE SOBBED.

Sebastian patted her shoulder and tried to comfort her, but even he was starting to feel somewhat more repressible than usual.

"And we were just talking about this. Too late," Derrick sighed heavily, looking away from the thing at their feet. "She must not have been able to stand it any longer. But what a way to do it! Poor woman. . . . You know, Violet, I wasn't entirely convinced before, but now it certainly seems that you were correct." He sighed again. "At least the insanity's finally over."

Violet grunted in acknowledgement. She shielded her eyes with a hand, and looked up at the façade of the building. Silently she pointed to a dormer window on the top floor. All but a ragged fringe of the glass was gone, giving it a blank, gaping look, and clearly marking it as Budgie's point of departure.

"She must have taken a real run at it," Violet said, "to have landed this far out from the house. It must be—what?—almost twenty feet. Remarkable. That was one determined lady. . . . I guess we should check up there. Maybe she left a note. But first I suppose we'd better put her in with the others."

Derrick and Mr. Ching carried poor Budgie into the freezer, and then the whole group went up to the top floor. The atmosphere, though naturally still sombre and subdued, was definitely less oppressive than it had been, even half an hour earlier.

It took them several tries to locate the correct passageway in the labyrinth of the attic, but when they did so, they found Mrs. Argus waiting patiently outside a door.

"*She* was here," the mad woman said pleasantly. "And *She* must have been quite upset," she added in a tone that suggested this was a fascinating piece of gossip. Her eyes and lips formed perfect circles of delight, then she tittered and ran—almost skipped—down the hall, and vanished around a corner.

"Watch it," Sebastian cautioned the others. "You'll have a nasty fall if you step on any of the marbles she left behind."

They looked in the open doorway and saw the broken window that they had observed from below. Then, one by one, their faces took on stunned, puzzled looks as they saw that everything else in the room was broken as well. Plasterboard had been torn from the walls, revealing the studs behind, and strips of flooring had been pulled up from the supporting joists. The electrical outlets were ripped out, and the wiring lay twisted across the floor like slender yellow and black entrails. What had once been a heavy straight-backed chair was in splinters, and a mattress had been reduced to fuzzy clumps of stuffing and tiny blue-and-white striped bits of rag. Even the thick enamel paint had been pulled away from the ceiling and hung down like decorative crêpe-paper streamers. The chaos was total; it was as though the room had been ripped apart by a giant, unseen hand, a wild, invisible, awesomely destructive power.

"Well, Violet, there was only one flaw in your analysis," Sebastian said quietly. "It was wrong."

"Yes," Derrick said. "I don't care how strong Budgie was. Or how disturbed. She didn't do this."

"And look. The window is three feet off the floor. Aunt Budgie didn't get any running start. No, Sis. Her defenestration was not self-generated, so to speak. She was thrown out."

"It's still going on," Cerise said to herself, almost whimpering. "It's still going on." With a nervous backward glance, she left the small room, followed by Derrick and Mr. Ching.

"Sebastian," Violet said, "you were supposed to investigate up here. Do you mean to say you didn't hear anything?"

"Well, actually, Sis, I never got up here. Call of nature, you know." He shrugged, grimaced sheepishly, then quickly followed the others.

Violet lingered for a moment, speculatively staring at the empty doorway. Her ordinarily unflappable brother seemed unusually uncomfortable, ill at ease. Odd. Notwithstanding his ability to spew out an endless stream of outrageous hyperbole, he'd never been able to lie very convincingly. What, she wondered, was he not saying?

When Violet got back to the lounge, she found Derrick, Cerise, Sebastian, and Mrs. Argus already there. Mr. Ching had gone off to work on lunch, a piece of news that did nothing to lighten the mood in the room.

Cerise paced the lounge restlessly, looking up at the high walls, her teeth pressed into her lower lip. "I still say we're being observed. Someone—or something—is watching us. Is it just me? Am I going crazy? Doesn't anyone else have that feeling?"

"I've noticed it," Derrick said, "but I didn't want to say anything."

"Me, too," Sebastian said.

Mrs. Argus grinned broadly.

"I say, Violet," Derrick said. "You may think this is stupid, but do you suppose there might be anything to that curse business, after all?"

Violet looked at him disbelievingly, wanting to shout that he was right, that she did think he was an incredible dolt, but she contented herself with a slight sneer.

"You can all believe in the supernatural if you want—the ghosts of the Mohawks, or whatever, walking the halls—but I think the explanation will be much more mundane." Violet paused, wrinkling her brow in concentration. By this point, there was every reason for her to be a trifle gun-shy, but it seemed she could no more stop analysing and detecting than she could stop breathing. "I think maybe I got it backwards."

"Huh?" Derrick said.

"I can't yet figure how it goes, but I'm pretty sure Mrs. Hook enters into it, and unless I'm really off the mark, she's pretty close to the centre. I said there was something strange going on between her and Budgie, and I thought that maybe Mrs. Hook was doing a bit of blackmail. But perhaps that's what I got backwards. Maybe Mrs. Hook is the doer, and Budgie found out. Certainly, Budgie seemed very scared of Mrs. Hook."

"And with good reason," Sebastian said. "The woman's an absolute terror. If looks could kill, we'd all be in the freezer by now—but I still can't see any reason for her to have done what you're suggesting."

Violet nodded. "Nor can I . . . yet. However, some possibilities do come to mind. Maybe she and Budgie were in league with each other, and planned to share the estate after Budgie inherited. If there were two people working together, it would explain a number of things."

"But, Sis, if that's what it is, why kill the golden goose? Or in this case, the yellow budgie."

"You saw what happened to Budgie. She cracked up. Maybe she couldn't stand it any longer, and threatened to confess everything, not caring about the consequences. Mrs. Hook would then have had to act out of simple self-preservation. Besides, this particular golden goose—as you put it—had no more eggs to lay."

"A conspiracy? Really, Violet!" Derrick said with surprising vehemence.

Violet stared at him, wide-eyed, until he blushed and looked away.

"Okay," she went on. "It doesn't have to be a conspiracy. Maybe Mrs. Hook found out about the will and acted on her own. Then she went to Budgie, told her what she'd done, and demanded her share. Only Budgie, instead of being grateful, fell apart, and Mrs. Hook had to kill her too. Again, to protect herself.''

"Oh, Sis! Come on."

Violet shrugged. "It wouldn't be the first time something like that had happened. Or, if you prefer, how about a servant who gets fed up and does away with his or her employer? Why, whole households have been wiped out in that manner."

"That's right!" Derrick said. "Wasn't there something like that a few years ago? An entire family killed? It was quite a sensation."

"I wouldn't know," Violet said. "I never read the tabloids."

"No," Sebastian mumbled. "Not since they stopped writing about you."

"What?"

"Nothing, Sis." He held up his hands. "Which do you think it is? A mad servant? A conspiracy? Or what?"

"I don't know. I was merely suggesting three possibilities that occurred to me. I'm not saying it's necessarily any one of them. I do know two things, however. First, of all the people here, no one has had better opportunity than Mrs. Hook. She's the only one of us who could go literally anywhere without arousing any suspicion or curiosity. If any of us were seen going into or coming out of someone else's room, for example, it would cause comment. But not Mrs. Hook. She could go anywhere, be seen anywhere, without anyone thinking twice about it or even noticing it. After all, she's the housekeeper, just doing her job. She has access everywhere, virtually complete freedom of movement. Indeed, we so accept the presence of the housekeeper that we fail really to see her, and that gives her a kind of invisibility."

Mrs. Argus chuckled to herself. "Oh, *She's* invisible, all right."

"Speaking of people who should disappear...," Sebastian grumbled.

"You said there were two things you knew?" Derrick said.

"Yes. The second is that there is something very definitely

not right about Mrs. Hook. I don't know what it is, but if we find it, I think we'll have the solution."

"Well, I think we'd better," Sebastian said. "And fast. I mean, really! We're dropping like flies. If things continue at this rate, there will be a very intimate group for dinner tomorrow."

"My God!" Cerise screamed, looking from face to face, her eyes wild and desperate. "How can you just sit here, calmly speculating about it all? Is it So-and-so? Is it this one? That one? Is this the reason? Is that? My God! Don't you see what's happening? Don't you feel it? It's like we're being manipulated in someone's fiendish game!"

"Hee, hee, hee," Mrs. Argus giggled in a knowing kind of way.

Cerise looked at her, then started sobbing. Sebastian gave the old crone a glare of unrestrained hatred, and led Cerise to a couch where he tried to comfort her. Derrick cleared his throat several times, then got up and turned on the old floor-model radio. Static-laden music filled the lounge, as the five remaining party guests sat silently, each along with his or her own thoughts, conjectures, or fears.

Abruptly, the music was cut off, and replaced by a breathy, excited voice.

"We interrupt our program of dance-band music to bring you an important bulletin. It appears that a menace from the past may be among us again. Officials at the Lakeview Institution for the Criminally Insane have just announced that Francis Hacker, the notorious mass murderer who once slaughtered eight innocent people in this area, escaped from the facility approximately thirty-six hours ago. While there is as yet no indication of the fugitive's whereabouts, local authorities fear the killer may be coming in our direction. It will be remembered that Hacker was employed at the Sill family estate on Komondor Island at the time of the murderous rampage. Chief Bently has warned everyone in the vicinity to be on the lookout for this dangerous maniac, and to report immediately any strange or unusual occurrences.

"When questioned as to why they had waited so long to announce the escape, Institution officials said they had hoped to be able to recapture the fugitive without causing any unnecessary panic. Cries of 'cover-up' are already being heard, and a full investigation is being demanded in high government circles. When asked how a dangerous lunatic could escape from a supposedly maximum-security facility, officials speculated that Hacker was assisted by an outside confederate.

"To repeat, local residents are advised to be on the alert for Francis Hacker, convicted mass murderer of...."

A harsh crackle cut off the announcer's voice and the radio went dead. Derrick's efforts to restore reception met with no success. All eyes in the room were fastened upon the old instrument, but its muteness only served to intensify the stunned silence in the lounge.

Gradually, however, the shock of this latest thunderbolt began to diminish. Held breaths were exhaled, rigid bodies relaxed somewhat, goggling eyes blinked and refocused. In a curious kind of way, there was a sense of relief. The menace had in no way abated, but at last it had been identified; it had a name, it could be understood, the terrible lurking shadow now had substance. And even more, a thought began to dawn on them, which Derrick was the first to speak aloud.

"I say, Violet! This means you were wrong all along. It's not one of us."

"Yes, Sis. I suppose what's been happening here just might be classified as the strange or unusual occurrences they want reported. It looks as though there's an intruder after all."

"Thank God!" Cerise said. "I don't know why that should make me feel so much better, but it does. I guess it's because I can now look at the rest of you and not have to wonder."

Violet looked from Derrick to Sebastian to Cerise, slowly nodding her head. "Are you sure about that?"

"Of course, Sis. You just heard that announcement."

"Yes, I heard the announcement, but I didn't hear anything about an intruder."

"What are you talking about?" Derrick said. "There's this escaped madman, Hacker."

Violet looked at him for a long time before saying very softly, "Who—as far as I can see—could still be one of us."

"I say! Ridiculous! *You* must be mad."

"Yes, Sis, come on. Give it a rest."

"Look," Violet said, "how many times have we been all over this goddamn island and through this goddamn house? And have we seen even one sign of this intruder? No, we haven't. So where the hell is this wraith hiding?"

"Okay, Sis, but that still doesn't mean. . . . I mean, it couldn't be. . . ."

"Why not?" Violet challenged. "Before coming here, we were almost all strangers to each other. Not a single one of us can be vouched for by more than one other person—if that. And even that doesn't mean anything since you all heard that they suspect Hacker had an accomplice."

"So you're suggesting that Hacker is one of us?" Cerise said.

"That's right."

"Well, Violet," Sebastian said, "I trust you know it couldn't be me."

"I don't care what she says," Derrick said. "*I* don't know that it couldn't be you."

"Well, I certainly don't know that it couldn't be you, either," Sebastian snapped back.

"And I don't know for sure that it couldn't be either of you," Cerise said.

"You see what I mean?" Violet said.

They saw, all right, as they stopped talking and considered the implications of this new possibility, which seemed to make matters even worse than before. Instead of an intruder, there was an impostor; instead of terrible but motivated crimes, there was random, unreasoned psychopathy.

Again, it was Derrick who broke the silence. "All right, Violet," he sighed. "I'll admit you have a point, though I'm a long way from agreeing with you. But if you want to go with this theory, you'll have to give up your idea about Mrs. Hook."

"Why?" Cerise asked before Violet could reply. She looked at Derrick with a curious but not very friendly expression in her eyes.

"Why? What do you mean why? They said his name was Francis Hacker."

"Why couldn't it be Frances, with a final 'es', you chauvinist buffoon? What makes you think it has to be a man? Why do you assume that only men are capable of insane homicidal rages? What about Lizzie Borden? Or the girls of the Manson family? Or that mad French countess who killed six hundred young girls? Women are also perfectly capable of violence and murder and mayhem."

Looking at Cerise standing over Derrick, green eyes flashing, fist shaking, voice rising to a shrill pitch, the others were strongly inclined to agree.

"What about—" Cerise suddenly broke off and looked around as though confused or lost. "My God! What am I saying? What's happening to me? I'm sorry. I'm very sorry." Shaking her head and repeating, "What's happening to me?" she went back and sat, slumped, on the couch.

"So it is still any of us, isn't it?" Sebastian said. "We're right back at the beginning again."

"Not quite," Violet said. "For one thing, there're fewer of us. For another, we've just gotten an important piece of information."

"What?" Derrick said. "That one of us is a lunatic murderer? I think we'd already had an inkling of that."

"No. The new bit of information is that one of us is an *escaped* lunatic murderer. Therefore, someone here is not the person that he or she pretends to be. Far from Mrs. Hook being eliminated, she looks more and more likely to me."

"Why, Sis?"

"Haven't you noticed? When you call Mrs. Hook's name, she doesn't always answer right away. Then she acts surprised and flustered. As though she wasn't used to that name. As though it were not her real name, but an assumed one."

"You're right, Sis! She got very upset when I made some harmless little joke about her name. At the time, I just thought she was sensitive about it—and with good reason. I'm sure I'd be sensitive if my name were Hook."

"I said there was something not right about that woman," Violet went on. "I think we may have found what it is. And there's one other significant bit of data."

"What's that?" Derrick asked.

Violet smiled at him, as she would at a particularly dim-witted child. "She's disappeared."

Another tense silence descended upon the room as each of them pondered Mrs. Hook in the role of Frances Hacker, escaped homicidal maniac. She did indeed seem well suited.

Somewhere a clock struck the half hour.

"Will you be wanting your lunch soon?" a voice growled from the doorway.

Cerise shrieked, Sebastian gasped, Derrick turned pale, Violet jumped out of her seat, and Mrs. Argus cackled merrily.

"A simple yes or no would be enough," Mrs. Hook said.

CHAPTER EIGHTEEN

"WHERE THE HELL HAVE YOU BEEN?" VIOLET SAID.

Mrs. Hook glared at her. "What's it to you, little Miss Snoop-into-everybody-else's-business?"

"In case you haven't heard, Mrs. Dijon was killed a little while ago."

"I heard. I guess that means you'll be five for lunch."

"And we also heard," Violet said offhandedly, but keeping a close watch on the housekeeper, "about the escape of Frances Hacker."

Mrs. Hook's face darkened ominously, and she scowled. "So now you're saying there'll be six for lunch? I wish you'd make up your minds. A body's got enough to do without all these changes."

"I'm sure you do," Violet said "But what we'd all like to know is just what your particular body has been doing for, say, the last hour?"

Mrs. Hook directed what Sebastian termed her Medusa stare at Violet, but did not answer.

"Please, Mrs. Hook," Derrick said in his most soothing manner, flashing her an encouraging smile. "It would help if you'd tell us."

The housekeeper looked at him and snorted. "I suppose there'll be no peace until I do. Since it's so important to you, I was out walking in the woods. Looking for mushrooms. A body's got to have some time off, you know. A housekeeper's not the same thing as a slave. Though there's been some that have thought so. But they learned otherwise. Oh, yes, they learned that—" Mrs. Hook cut herself off, frowned, then looked suspiciously from face to face. "Besides, a body doesn't take orders from you. I worked for little Missy, and since she's not here, you can't tell me what to do. I'll do what I was paid to do and nothing more. Understand? So just you tell this Hackman person that if he's going to stay, he can make up his own room. A body's got enough to do with the lot of you, without having to take care of unexpected guests."

"Oh, *She'll* take care of herself," Mrs. Argus cried happily, clapping her bony hands. "And very well, too, thank you."

Violet looked at the others with raised eyebrows, then turned back to Mrs. Hook. "Just how long did you work for Miss Sill?"

"Long enough."

"Long enough for what?"

"Long enough to know—" Mrs. Hook stopped. "Just long enough."

"And where'd you work before?"

Mrs. Hook made a sharp intake of breath, and glared at Violet. Behind the evident hostility, there seemed to be an undercurrent of alarm. "What's it to you?"

Violet shrugged. "Just curious."

"Don't forget what that did to the cat, Miss. . . . And the rat," she added, smiling at the recollection.

Just then Mr. Ching burst into the lounge. He seemed extremely agitated, his eyes round, his face pale, his black hair standing up in tufts that were even spikier than usual. The cook ran up to Violet and handed her a sheet of paper.

Violet looked at the paper, then jerked her head up in surprise. "Where did you find this? In the kitchen?"

Mr. Ching nodded.

"What is it, Sis?"

"It's a note. An old favourite—made from letters cut out of magazines. It says, 'You will cook no more meals.'"

"Oh, good!" Sebastian said. "At last, something positive."

"Sebastian!"

"What does that mean?" Derrick said. "Is that an instruction, or . . . or. . . ."

"Or a sentence?" Violet asked softly. "I don't know."

"It just gets worse and worse!" Cerise cried. "Is there no end? Can't someone do something?"

"Cerise is right," Derrick said. "We've got to do something. We've got to get help."

"And how do you propose we do that?" Violet asked. "Have you changed your mind about swimming for it? The water isn't any warmer, nor the distance any shorter."

"Well, there is some diving gear. . . ." Derrick shook his head. "But no. I wouldn't make it."

Violet nodded. "Neither would I. And Sebastian needs water wings in the bathtub. Cerise? No? Okay, so let's forget about that. Mr. Ching, I won't tell you not to worry, because obviously you should be worried. But at least you've been warned, so if you're careful, you should be able to protect yourself."

Mrs. Argus chuckled quietly, a complacent, indulgent smile on her thin lips.

Mr. Ching looked nervously at each of them, muttered something decisive-sounding to himself in Chinese, and turned to leave.

"Oh, Mr. Ching," Violet called, stopping him. "We were wondering about something just before you came in. Could you tell us how long you and Mrs. Hook worked for Miss Sill?"

Mr. Ching didn't answer but seemed to grow even more nervous. Mrs. Hook snorted viciously and angrily stared at Violet.

"All right, Miss Busybody. I don't suppose there'll be any peace until you find out everything you want to know." Mrs. Hook motioned with her square head towards the cook. "He's only been working for her a few months. I been with Missy two years. Isn't that right?"

She stared hard at Mr. Ching, who stared back, in what might have been either fear or confusion.

"Isn't that right," she repeated. This time it was not a question.

Mr. Ching hastily nodded agreement, then hurried from the room, looking even more desperate and concerned than when he had entered.

"Anything else, Miss?" Mrs. Hook asked Violet, her tone anything but polite, her expression anything but expectant. "If not, maybe a body can go and do her work." Mrs. Hook abruptly turned and left.

After the housekeeper had gone, Violet went to the door to make sure she wasn't still hovering in the corridor outside, then returned to the others.

"Does everyone agree that there's something very strange about that woman? I mean, besides her being extraordinarily unpleasant. Does anyone doubt that she's hiding something? And that exchange with Mr. Ching. She certainly made sure he didn't get a chance to answer freely."

"But that still doesn't mean she's this Frances Hacker," Derrick said.

Violet sighed in acknowledgement, and the group lapsed into yet another uncomfortable silence.

Sebastian rummaged in a pocket and pulled out the mysterious handkerchief he'd found. It was wrinkled and mudstained, but he smoothed it across his knees and studied it.

"'HM'. Her Majesty?" he suggested, then snapped his fingers. "I know! It stands for Homicidal Maniac."

Mrs. Argus laughed happily at this, and Cerise managed only to half-swallow a sob.

"Sebastian," Violet said wearily, "since you clearly have nothing constructive to contribute, do you think you might for once keep quiet."

"What's that?" Derrick pointed to the handkerchief.

"Oh, that's right—you weren't there," Violet said. "Sebastian found that beside the Colonel's body. Just another

145

thing that doesn't seem to make sense, like the missing teeth."

"Let me take a look at that." Derrick crossed the room and took the frilly piece of cloth from Sebastian. "I say! This belongs to Mrs. Hook."

"What! Are you sure?" Violet said.

"Of course I'm sure. That first afternoon she dropped it, and I returned it to her. This is the same one."

"That's right," she nodded. "I remember your doing that. And I also remember that you looked at the thing. Didn't you notice the initials were not correct?"

Derrick shrugged and blushed. "Guess not. I saw an M and an H, and I must have registered it as standing for Mrs. Hook. Silly of me." Embarrassed, he shifted from one leg to the other and looked down at his shiny, expensive shoes.

Violet rolled her eyes and made a face, then followed Derrick's gaze. No wonder he wears loafers, she thought; the dolt probably never learned to tie his shoes. MH stands for Mrs. Hook? Really!

"So," Violet said, looking up. "Mrs. Hook is not who she says she is."

"But, Sis, that still doesn't mean she's the escaped killer. Don't forget—those initials are FH."

"I'd hardly forget that, Sebastian. And I'll admit that I don't understand it. But we've got a lot of things that don't yet seem to fit together. I still believe that they will, though, that there's an explanation that will make sense of them—if only we can find the right perspective from which to look at it all. . . . Unless, of course, that's the point—that there is no point."

"Huh?" Derrick said.

"That all these things that don't make sense are that way intentionally—designed to complicate matters, sow confusion, get us looking in wrong directions and running in circles. In other words, a smokescreen."

Mrs. Argus was again chuckling to herself, but the others nodded in agreement. Violet's analysis undoubtedly seemed reasonable at the time, especially since they could not have known that the alternatives she proposed were in no way mutually exclusive.

Abruptly, Violet stood up and crossed the lounge. In the doorway, she stopped and looked back. "If any of you get the chance, you might try to keep Mrs. Hook occupied for a while."

"Oh, wonderful," Sebastian said. "You want us to engage in idle conversation with a person we believe to be an escaped killer. 'Tell me, Mrs. Hook, what does it feel like when your homicidal urges come on you? Have you always been a deranged lunatic, or is this a recent development?' Thanks a lot, Sis."

But Violet had already gone.

"Where's she off to?" Derrick asked.

"I imagine the Society-Girl Detective is once again going to do some detecting."

"Hmm." Derrick looked around the large room, not really taking in anything, but rather as a kind of transitional activity. He glanced at his watch, cleared his throat, then said with studied casualness that there were a few things he wanted to look into himself, and hastily left without looking back.

Sebastian looked after him with raised eyebrows, then shrugged. "He's probably discovered a new mirror."

Cerise did not reply, nor did she seem to have heard Sebastian's remark or noticed Derrick's departure. She sat with her head down, eyebrows lowered in concentration, lips compressed, hands tightly clasped between her knees, knuckles taut as long maroon nails pressed into the backs of her hands. Finally she sighed, shook her short hair, and turned to Sebastian.

"Do you think the person who's responsible for . . . uh . . . what's been happening knows what he or she is doing?"

"Well, I hope so! I'd hate to think this was all inadvertent."

Cerise shook her head. "No. I meant, do you think this person is aware of these things while he or she is doing them?

Or could this person have no recollection of the murders, perhaps have done them in a sort of fugue state?"

"I guess that's possible. Certainly, that's your basic schizoid defense, isn't it? 'But Your Honour, I have no idea how that smoking gun ended up in my hand. I may have fired it six times, but *I'm* not really responsible.'"

"But do you believe that? I mean, have you ever—you know—found yourself somewhere, and not had any idea how you got there?"

"Constantly!" Sebastian said with a laugh. "I couldn't begin to tell you how many times I've awakened and not had a clue where I was, or how I got there, or who all those people were who were strewn about the place. Believe me, daylight has brought me its share of surprises. Why, I could tell you—no, on the other hand, maybe I'd better not. But that's nothing. A couple of weeks ago I ran into a friend who started talking about the way I had behaved at some recent function, and do you know, I had no idea what he was talking about. Not only could I not remember doing what he said I did, I couldn't recall anything about that function, or that there had even been a function. Total blanko."

Cerise frowned and shook her head. "But doesn't that worry you?"

"Well, the first six or eight times it was a bit disconcerting. . . . Now, I just accept it as another of the miracles of modern chemistry. Frankly, I suspect I'm much better off not knowing what I've done. If I could remember, I'd probably stop doing it. And I wouldn't want that, since by all accounts I usually have a really good time."

"But suppose you—" Cerise cut herself off.

"What?"

"Nothing." She shook her head and looked down. "Nothing." She sat for several minutes, biting her lips and clenching her hands, then looked up at the mounted animal heads and shivered violently. "My God! Make it stop! Please make it stop!" Her face distorted with what seemed to be either pain or fear. She looked wildly about, then ran from the room, a hand clamped over her mouth to hold back the sobs.

Sebastian watched her go, both puzzled and concerned. He turned towards Mrs. Argus, who pulled back her lips in a broad grin, revealing a lot of crooked, discoloured teeth. Sebastian quickly stood up and hurried from the lounge.

Mrs. Argus chuckled to herself a bit, then went over to the French windows. She looked cautiously around, smiled again, opened a door, and went outside.

Meanwhile, Violet had looked through the kitchen, the pantries and the other service rooms on the main floor, but had found nothing of interest.

More to the point, she had seen no one, which was too bad. Since she planned to search Mrs. Hook's room, she would have greatly preferred to know beforehand just where the housekeeper was. Violet didn't fancy being caught in the act, especially by a person who might be a psychopathic killer.

But she had no idea where Mrs. Hook was, so she'd have to chance it. Indeed, the stakes—all of them—were sufficiently high to justify certain risks.

As she went up the back stairs, Violet looked out the landing window and saw Mr. Ching heading in the direction of the boathouse. He was walking very fast, almost running, in fact, and he kept looking back nervously over his shoulder. He seemed extremely agitated. And not without reason, Violet thought. Assuming that the note he found was legitimate, Mr. Ching looked like an excellent candidate for number five. Since at least two of the first four seemed to have been taken unawares, the killer clearly must be feeling pretty confident if he or she was willing to provide a warning and thus give up the edge that surprise provided. On the other hand, Violet knew that the delusion of invincibility and omnipotence was a common characteristic of the personality type with which they were undoubtedly dealing. (What Violet did not yet know was that it was not precisely a delusion.)

She reached the second floor, and proceeded cautiously down the empty hallway, alert for any sound of Mrs. Hook, but she heard nothing. She knocked twice on Mrs. Hook's door, and when there was no reply, quickly entered the room.

Violet noted with a slight frown that Mrs. Hook had installed herself in one of the better bedrooms. It must originally have been intended for one of the family or the guest of honour, as opposed to the rooms to be used by ordinary visitors. Violet, who had a well-developed sense of propriety, was not amused by this, particularly since she herself had been given a rather tatty little room near the rear that even had a shared bath. Still, Mrs. Hook's presumption in her choice of accommodation did not necessarily make her a homicidal maniac.

Nor did Violet's initial glance around the room reveal anything more sinister than the evidence that the housekeeper kept her own room much cleaner and shinier than the rest of the house. Hell, Violet thought, you could probably eat off the floor here, whereas she'd been somewhat reluctant even to eat off the plates that Mrs. Hook had supposedly washed.

Violet looked into the large closet, but it held only three black and white uniforms in some synthetic, quick-drying material, and three pairs of rubber-soled, square-toed white shoes. She went next to the dresser, and found it contained mostly underclothes—of a sort which Violet had not realized were still being manufactured. No wonder they were once known as foundation garments, she thought; they made Mrs. Hook look as though her body was moulded out of concrete. Why, compared to some of these contraptions, Aunt Budgie's paraphernalia seemed positively innocent, almost naive. In the top drawer, Violet did find a neat stack of frilly handkerchiefs, each identical to the one Sebastian had picked up, each with the monogram HM, but there was nothing else of interest in the dresser.

On the nightstand next to the bed, there was a pile of scientific papers, all printed in small dense type, with numerous graphs, charts, and lengthy chemical formulae. On looking through the pile, Violet saw they were all reports giving test results of recently developed poisons—pesticides, herbicides, fungicides, and so on—all identified only by a combination of letters and numbers. The reports, of a highly technical nature, presented information concerning such matters as potency, half life, primary and secondary target populations, optimum dispersal techniques, MLDs (Minimum Lethal Dosages), interaction in the food chain, and much more. To Violet this seemed awfully peculiar bedtime reading, but she knew that there were some people who found mysteries to be boring and stupid, so there was no accounting for tastes. Peculiar, yes, but nothing more; now, if it had been a manual on home butchering. . . .

Violet quickly went through the rest of the room and the attached private bath, but found nothing else out of the ordinary. Which was probably to be expected, Violet thought; even totally wigged-out psychos could be amazingly cunning when it came to self-preservation. Indeed, the utter innocuousness of Mrs. Hook's room struck Violet as being a bit fishy. However, she couldn't make a case out of that. Disappointed that she was no closer to finding out what bothered her about Mrs. Hook, Violet started to leave.

As she waited by the door, listening to make sure no one was coming along the corridor outside, Violet suddenly realized that she had not seen something that should have been there. She returned to the centre of the room, took another quick look around, then went over to the bed, dropped to her knees, and lifted the edge of the bedspread. You're getting slow, Violet, she told herself, as she pulled out a large, battered old suitcase.

Luckily, the clasps were not locked. Taking a deep breath, Violet raised the top. The first thing she saw was a shapeless, short-sleeved, square-necked shift made of dingy grey, much-washed coarse cotton. It might have been the kind of smock that is worn to protect the clothes when doing dirty or messy work like heavy cleaning; but Violet recognized, with a nod and a slight smile, that it was also precisely the kind of gown that was regulation issue for female inmates of prisons and other similar public institutions.

Beneath the gown was the only other item in the suitcase, a fairly new and expensive leatherette scrapbook. Opening the cover and flipping through the pages, Violet saw that it was filled with newspaper clippings about a very sensational murder and trial that had occurred a couple of years earlier. She also noticed, from the smudges and the wear, that the book had been examined a good many times.

Violet had to do no more than read the lead sentence of the first article to see that a great many questions were now answered. Quickly going through the book, she saw that one large question still remained, but she figured that would take care of itself soon enough.

She was about to get to her feet when she stopped. "Damn!" she said out loud as she realized with a combination of disgust and amazement that her brother once again had hit a bull's eye without knowing he was even aiming at a target. When was it, she wondered; oh, yes—dinner the first night. Incredible! And even Derrick, not twenty minutes before, had put his finger right on it—though of course he'd had no idea he'd done so.

If she only had some of that blind luck, Violet thought, there was no telling what she could do. She looked down at the scrapbook and smiled broadly. On the other hand, she wasn't doing all that badly without it.

She pushed the suitcase back under the bed, put the scrapbook under her arm, got to her feet, and left the house-keeper's room after making certain the coast was clear.

It was a good half hour before Derrick, Cerise, and Sebastian separately straggled back to the lounge where Violet was waiting. Derrick seemed slightly flushed and perhaps more excited than usual, while Cerise seemed quieter, vague and distracted, as if in a state of mild shock. Sebastian displayed his customary air of faintly supercilious amusement that Violet usually found so annoying. Under the circumstances, though, she was not really unhappy that he was taking their situation so casually; if anyone had a chance of beating her to the solution, it would be her brother, and this was one race where, if she was not first, she would be literally out of the money.

Violet smiled at the others, took the scrapbook from beside her, and put it on her knees. She opened the cover and began slowly turning the pages, a smug look on her face.

"Oh, come on, Sis."

Violet let her brief flare of anger subside, then coolly looked up at the others as she closed the scrapbook with a nice dramatic thunk.

"I know what the initials HM stand for," she said and waited a beat. "Have any of you heard of Helga Milch?"

Cerise shook her head.

"That sounds familiar," Sebastian said, "but I can't place it."

"I say! That's her! That's who I was telling you about!" Derrick gushed.

"Who? What?" Sebastian said.

"That's the woman who killed the family she worked for."

"That's right," Violet said. "All nine of them."

"Nine! My God!" Cerise said, coming to life for the first time.

"Charming. You know, Sis, I'm not exactly surprised. I've said all along that the only sensible thing about Mrs. Hook was her shoes. . . . But if this is true, what's this Milch woman doing loose? Did she escape too?"

Violet shook her head and opened the scrapbook to the back. "No. It seems the jury believed her story that it was all a terrible accident, that the rat poison somehow got into the sugar bowl by mistake. She was acquitted."

All the colour drained from Sebastian's face. "Rat poison? Sugar bowl? But I——! Didn't I——? Isn't that what I——?" He put a hand up to his throat.

"Yes, you did," Violet said. "The first night at dinner. You made a little joke about that very thing when Mrs. Hook brought in the coffee service. If you remember, her reaction was to drop the dishes she was carrying."

Sebastian moved his mouth, but nothing came out. Violet smiled at him.

"But Violet," Derrick said, "are you sure that Mrs. Hook is really Helga Milch?"

Violet hesitated before replying. "Well, there are more of those hankies with HM on them in her room. There's a stack of reports about the latest poisons next to her bed. And there's this scrapbook filled with newspaper stories about the arrest and trial of Helga Milch."

"I say!"

Sebastian raised his eyebrows and nodded as the colour returned to his face. "So that means that Mrs. Hook is Helga Milch, and not this escaped killer, Frances Hacker."

"Not necessarily."

"Huh?" Derrick said.

"That's why I didn't answer you right away," Violet said. "I'm sure that Mrs. Hook *was* Helga Milch. I'm not positive that she still is."

"Huh?"

"Look, it's not that complicated. Suppose after Frances Hacker escaped, she somehow came into contact with Mrs. Hook, and found out what she was doing and where she was going. It would have been almost impossible to resist. Remember, the news report said that Hacker worked here at the time of the murders."

"So, Sis, you're saying that this Hacker killed Mrs. Hook and took over her identity. But all the time Mrs. Hook was not Mrs. Hook, but was really Helga Milch. And thus it turned out that Hacker, who is a convicted murderer, is posing as a woman who was herself playing a part to hide the fact that she's an acquitted murderer. What a delicious irony!"

Violet nodded. "I'm not certain that's the case, but it is a real possibility."

"It is real confusing, is what it is," Cerise said.

"I'll say it is!" Derrick agreed. "I assume there are no pictures of this Milch woman in those newspaper clippings."

"Unfortunately not. That would resolve the matter one way or another."

"So is there in fact any reason to think that Mrs. Hook is really Hacker?"

"There are a few things. First, there's this business of Mrs. Hook not always answering to her name. If she'd been playing the role for a couple of years, you'd think she'd be more comfortable in it. Then, there was the smock-like thing I found in her room, just the kind of dress that Frances Hacker would have had on when she escaped from that institution."

"That's not much to go on, Sis."

"I know it's not, and I'm not pushing it. But the third thing is more significant. Mrs. Hook—rather, Helga Milch—is a poisoner, and poisoners traditionally love the idea of poison. The appeal for them is not in murder *per se*, but instead in murder *by poison*. But what we've got operating around here is a killer with an entirely different mentality, someone who likes direct contact, who likes to see the blood flow."

Sebastian nodded and spoke slowly. "If Mrs. Hook is Frances Hacker, Mr. Ching must realize she's an impostor. He must have known it from the beginning, or. . . ."

"That's right," Violet said. "Or?"

"Or he's the accomplice we heard about."

Violet nodded.

"But if he's the accomplice, why did he get that note?"

Violet shrugged. "It could be to put us off the trail. Or it could be that things have got out of control, and as the only person who knows who Mrs. Hook really is, he's become a dangerous liability. As you probably know, the problem about getting involved with killers like Hacker is that you can never trust them. You can never be sure that they won't suddenly turn on you."

"I still say this is too confusing," Cerise said.

"Okay, let's look at it this way," Violet said. "Whether as Frances Hacker or as Helga Milch, our Mrs. Hook is a mass murderer. We've already had four murders. So . . . I'd say that it's about time we had a talk with Mrs. Hook. Has anyone seen her?"

Only no one had, since she had left the lounge. Nor had anyone seen Mr. Ching or Mrs. Argus.

As they were considering where Mrs. Hook might be and how they should go about locating her, Mrs. Argus came in from the terrace. After listening to the discussion, Mrs. Argus informed them with a laugh that she had seen the housekeeper. When asked where, she laughed again and went back outside, coyly gesturing that they should follow her. With considerable uneasiness and very little enthusiasm, they did.

They didn't have far to go, only about a hundred yards from the house. There, in the shelter of an evergreen bush, they found Mrs. Hook. She was lying face up in the mud, arms and legs spread out, hands clenched in fists.

Apparently a cleaver, or something very like it, had been used. She had been cut nearly in half. She appeared even more surprised than the people who were looking down at her.

"Wrong again, Violet," Sebastian said after a moment, flashing his sister a friendly grin.

Cerise began to sob hysterically, her body shaking with each new burst.

Sebastian moved to comfort her. "Take it easy," he said. "No use crying over split Milch."

Cerise stopped crying and stared at Sebastian, her green eyes round and startled. She began to giggle, then abruptly stopped, putting a hand over her mouth, looking surprised and puzzled and more than a little afraid. "What's the matter with me?" she said to herself. "It's happening. I'm going mad. I must be going mad." She hugged herself, rocking her body slowly forwards and backwards.

"I say! What's that?" Derrick pointed to the ground next to the body.

"Golly, you're right!" Sebastian said. "Look, Sis. It's the footprints of a gigantic duck!"

CHAPTER NINETEEN

THEY ALL STARED AT THE INDENTATIONS IN THE MUD AROUND the body. These did indeed resemble tracks made by the webbed feet of some tremendous water bird.

"The diving gear!" Derrick said.

"I saw Mr. Ching going in the direction of the boat-house!" Violet said.

Looks were exchanged, and without another word everyone ran to the boathouse. In the dim light they saw the two boats that could have taken them to safety had someone not put holes in the bottoms.

"The fins and the wetsuit were back there," Derrick said.

They all looked in the direction he was pointing, but it was obvious that the equipment was gone. After a quick search confirmed this, they went back outside. They scanned the lake, trying to catch sight of the swimmer, but the surface was smooth and grey, unbroken as far as they could see.

"So that's that," Derrick said.

"It was Mr. Ching all along," Cerise said.

"It has to be," Sebastian said. "Do you agree, Sis?"

Violet slowly nodded her head, frowning, looking as though she was giving the matter serious consideration. In fact, she was wondering if there was any way in which she could still get some benefit from this situation. Clearly, the Society-Girl Detective bit was right out; not only had she not come up with the solution, but the killer had got clean away, perhaps for good. Or perhaps drowned in the lake, which would be just as bad, especially if the remains were never found. No, it would be extremely difficult to have this reflect favourably on her detecting abilities, or to get any good publicity out of this.

On the other hand, she knew this would generate a hell of a lot of interest. There had to be some way she could capitalize on it. If she couldn't be the star, why shouldn't she be the one to provide the inside story? Yes, why not? This would be big news for weeks, maybe months. There would be a huge market for the story. And it was a natural: isolation, intrigue, strange characters, an escaped killer, violence, bloodshed, murder, even an ancient curse; it was just like one of those old-fashioned mysteries that everyone loved, only it was real. It couldn't miss.

Why, Violet thought, if she got right down to it, and if they weren't picked up for another couple of days, she could have the book fully outlined—if not completely written—by the time she set foot back on the mainland, and be all ready to entertain bids. With any luck, three million paperbacks would be on the racks while the story was still making front-page headlines. Looked at this way, her failure, and the escape of the killer, could even serve to make the story more challenging, mysterious, exciting. Christ, the film sale alone should be in the upper six figures. That would be enough to turn her company around. Hell, that would be enough to forget the company entirely! *The Tragedy of Komondor Island*. *Slaughter on Komondor Island*. *Komondor Island: Three Days of Murder and Terror as told by a Survivor*. Oh, yes. . . .

"What?" Violet said with a start when she realized Derrick was speaking to her.

"I asked if you have any ideas about all this. It's plain that it was Mr. Ching, but it doesn't really make sense to me."

Violet looked at Derrick, who was wrinkling his forehead in bewilderment, and thought that that was hardly a surprise. She certainly didn't have to worry about *his* scooping her. Sebastian, though, was another matter.

"Well, we don't have all the facts yet, do we?" she said.

"No, but does this mean that Mr. Ching is the escaped killer?"

"That's certainly one possibility," Violet said. "Though Francis Hacker is not one of your common Chinese names. That's one of the facts—whether this Hacker is Chinese, or even a man—that we don't know yet. But if I had to guess right now, I'd stick with Mrs. Hook being Hacker, and Mr. Ching being the accomplice."

"How do you figure that?"

"Well, maybe they came here because she knew the area and thought it would be a good place to lie low for a while. Disturbed individuals like that have a tendency to return to familiar territory. But once they got here, things started to get out of hand. Mrs. Hook/Frances Hacker lost control, and Mr. Ching got scared. Either he was going to be next, or he'd get caught along with her. He realized his only chance was to kill her and then try and swim for it."

"But you're just guessing again, Sis."

"That's true, but one thing is certain: whatever else he may be, Mr. Ching is not a cook. We've had—what?—five meals that testify to that."

Sebastian grimaced at the recollection. "You're right about that. If he's not a criminal, his cooking sure is. And something else is certain: the man knows his way around sharp weapons. You all saw the way he carved the roast the first night, and I saw the way he handled a cleaver. My goodness! Not to mince words, it wouldn't have taken him very long to turn us all into Big Macs."

Cerise giggled nervously, Derrick looked blank, and Mrs. Argus stared up at the grey sky.

"No, it wouldn't have," Violet said. "That's why I think he either killed or helped kill Mousey. I said at the time that I thought a skilled hand had been at work. And killing Mousey would have been necessary because she was the only one who knew Mrs. Hook and Mr. Ching were impostors. Then, if I'm right that Mrs. Hook was Hacker, all it took was that fresh taste of blood to start her off again. She did the next three on her own, Mr. Ching got scared, and he went back to his cleaver to take care of her. I know that's another guess, but it does fit what's happened. I also saw Mr. Ching sneak out of Drupe's room, and he's acted suspiciously at other times as well. It didn't make any sense before, but now maybe it does."

"And you know, Sis, I always had the idea that Mr. Ching knew more than he let on. He tried to look unconcerned, but I thought he was actually paying very close attention to everything. I think, though, that Mr. Ching may be this Hacker person, not Hacker's accomplice. Don't psychopaths often have a tendency to react violently to very slight provocations? Mr. Ching certainly did—positively exploded quite a few times for no apparent reason."

Violet nodded. That was a good point, and one that she hadn't considered. She made a mental note to be sure to include it in her account.

"I'm still confused," Derrick said. "Is Mr. Ching Hacker, or is he the accomplice? Is he a psycho, or is he someone who found himself in a situation that was more than he bargained for? All these different things you've said don't quite fit together."

"Maybe not," Violet said, "but there's no point in worrying about that right now."

"Thank God!" Cerise sighed, letting out a deep breath. "The nightmare is finally over."

"I say! It is, isn't it? At last!"

"That's right," Violet said. "We might as well all relax and try to enjoy ourselves until we're picked up."

Derrick, Cerise, and Sebastian nodded at each other, and smiled, and even laughed a little in relief. Their bodies suddenly felt loose and light, as the gigantic weight of tension and uncertainty and fear lifted, dissipating in the fresh cool breeze that had just started blowing across the water.

Violet smiled. Right, she thought, you all try to enjoy yourselves, and forget about everything that's happened; I've got an outline to work on.

Mrs. Argus sniffed at the wind, then grinned and nodded her head.

"What is it?" Derrick asked. "Is a storm coming?"

Mrs. Argus grinned again. "I smell mortality."

CHAPTER TWENTY

MRS. ARGUS'S CHEERY FORECAST DIMINISHED NO ONE'S SENSE of relief and release. Not only did Sebastian not make one of his usual comments, he even smiled somewhat tolerantly and sympathetically at the demented old bat. Even the task of carrying Mrs. Hook up to the house did not much dampen the rising spirits. For probably the first time since they arrived on Komondor Island, everyone felt pretty good.

After the body was deposited in the freezer, the others went off, but Violet lingered behind. She opened the freezer door and looked in. It was not a pleasant scene—large pieces of animals hanging from hooks and mutilated corpses lying on shelves and the floor—but Violet felt she had to study it in order to be able to describe it accurately. She thought that this might even be a good place to begin: "As I gazed into the walk-in freezer filled with the ghastly contents it was never intended to accommodate, I felt. . . ." Violet paused; what did she feel? She shivered. Chilled, mostly. ". . .I felt a frisson of terror move up my spine. The nightmare was over, but the violent, terrifying events of the last three days would not be forgotten for a long, long time." Hmm? Not bad.

Violet took Aunt Budgie's pocket camera out of her purse. Thus far she had diligently photographed all of the crime scenes, but it seemed appropriate that the last frame on the roll should record this makeshift morgue. No other single picture could so dramatically epitomize their ordeal. She had originally taken the pictures to provide the police with necessary evidence. Now, while they were still welcome to a set of prints, that was all they would get. Her photographs would be a valuable addition to the book—"With eight pages of dramatic photographs of the events on the death island"—not to mention the pretty penny they would bring in from international wire services.

Violet shifted around, trying to compose the picture, but the angle of the lens was not wide enough to take in everything. Determinedly gritting her teeth, she stepped into the freezer, took Mrs. Hook by the arms, and pulled her a foot and a half towards the centre of the floor. She was about to let the arms drop when she noticed something interesting. The housekeeper's hands had been clenched in fists at the time of death, and Violet now saw that there was a tiny piece of paper held between the thumb and the side of the forefinger. The fragment was so small that only a portion of one edge was visible, and thus it had been easy to overlook.

Taking a deep breath, Violet grasped the clammy hand and carefully pried up the stiffening thumb. The paper dropped to the floor. Violet put a card under it, picked it up, and examined it. The edges were ragged, but it was rectangular in shape, roughly one-half of an inch by one-quarter. From the smallness of the sample, it was difficult to be certain, but Violet thought the paper was the same as that used by Mousey for her letter accusing Mr. Drupe. The ink looked the same, too, as did the writing, though the fragment contained only five letters. While Violet was no longer actively detecting, she could not help being curious about the letters "illeg" that she looked at. Obviously, another page of that letter had turned up with Mousey accusing someone else of doing something illegal. But who? And what? And why did Mrs. Hook have the letter in her hand at the time of her death? Maybe she was a blackmailer after all, and the letter accused Mr. Ching of some illegal practice. But then neither Mrs. Hook nor Mr. Ching could be Hacker. Or maybe Mrs. Hook still could be if—

Violet shook her head. Derrick was right, this was awfully

confusing. Violet was glad she no longer had to have all the answers. In fact, in a way, the more mysterious, complex, and convoluted this got, the better.

She put the letter fragment into a small glassine envelope that she had in her purse, and put it with the other pieces of evidence that were similarly protected. She must remember, she thought, to have all this stuff photographed before she handed it over to the police.

Violet went back to the doorway, saw that the scene through the viewfinder was perfect, and took the shot with a satisfying click. She closed the freezer door, and went upstairs.

As soon as Violet stepped into her room she sensed that something was wrong. A look around verified this. Although great care had been taken, and although there were no overt signs of disturbance, Violet was sure that someone had been in her room, going through her things. So, she thought, someone else is doing a little snooping, too. It was fortunate that she never left anything important lying around. Still. . . . Another quick inspection, and Violet had the impression that something might be missing after all, though she couldn't figure out what.

She looked speculatively at the door to the bathroom connecting her room and her brother's.

"I wonder . . . ," Violet whispered to herself.

It was early evening when Cerise came into the lounge. Sebastian was alone there, seated on a couch. He had changed into a T-shirt, on the front of which was printed, "If you have nothing good to say about anybody, come and sit next to me."

Cerise smiled and did just that, bouncing a couple of times on the overstuffed cushion. The signs of strain that had been increasing on her face over the last three days had vanished, and she seemed happy and relaxed.

"My, my," Sebastian said. "We're certainly in a good mood, aren't we?"

Cerise again smiled broadly.

"What was it you were worried about before?"

"About being killed, of course!" she said quickly. "Weren't you?"

"Sure. But I also got the idea there was something else."

Cerise shook her head. "Don't be silly. What else could there be?" She suddenly seemed very interested in the pattern of the carpet under her feet.

"Nothing, I guess." Sebastian looked at her for a minute, then asked softly, "You thought it was you, didn't you?"

She stared at him, her eyes round with alarm, and started to protest. Then she stopped and silently nodded her head.

"Why?"

Cerise hesitated a moment, then shrugged and smiled weakly. "For a while now I've been worried that I might be cracking up. You know, really going crazy."

"Why in the world should you think that? Golly, compared to the people I know—even compared to the people around here—you could be selected Ms. Mental Hygiene without any competition."

Cerise tried another smile but didn't quite succeed. "Well, you see, I have these blank periods. I don't know if I black out or doze off or go into a trance or what. All I know is that some time has passed—usually not all that much—and I can't account for it."

Sebastian nodded. "I thought that might be it. Look, didn't I tell you this morning that that happens to me all the time? It's no big deal. Why, I once lost an entire year—1974, I think. I can remember being at a New Year's Eve party and feeling that I had to rest for a few minutes. When I woke up, the party was still going on—only it was a different party, a year later. Talk about blanks!"

Cerise looked sceptically at Sebastian, then laughed.

"No, really!" he said. "The only way I was able to reconstruct that year even partially was through a stack of credit-card bills and several lawsuits that were waiting for me." Cerise laughed again and Sebastian smiled. "Besides, what makes you think that you do something awful during these blanks? You probably go out for a walk, start thinking about something, get lost in thought, and the next thing you know you've gone several blocks and you have no idea how you got there. Everybody experiences that. Have you ever found yourself doing something terrible, something violent, something really out of character?"

"No, but—".

"Well, there you are."

Cerise seemed unconvinced. "There is some instability in the family."

"Welcome to the club."

"And there was an incident a few years ago. . . ."

"Connected with these so-called blanks?"

"Not as far as I know. But thinking about it now, I'm not so sure."

"Then stop thinking about it, silly. Look, as far as I can tell—and having had lots of experience, I'm a pretty good judge of these things—the only thing at all crazy about you is that you think you're going crazy. That in itself should reassure you. The ones you really have to watch out for are those who think they're on top of things and everyone else is out of step."

"You're sweet to say that, but still—"

"But, but, but!" Sebastian said. "You want more reassurance? Just look around you. Mrs. Argus has been listening to a different drummer for so long that she'll never get back to the parade. And speaking of blanks: our friend Derrick seems asleep on his feet half the time; that hum you hear when you stand next to him is the sound of disengaged gears. I've told you about my little adventures. My sister has had her share as well."

"Violet? Really? She always seems so in control of everything."

Sebastian shrugged. "Well, maybe she is now—I don't know—but it wasn't always that way, believe me. You talk about doing things you're not aware of, there were times when she was younger when her left hand literally did not know what her right hand was doing. This usually occurred during times of stress. Why, I can remember one time when she cut up all her clothes—ripped them to shreds in the midst of some adolescent trauma—and then had no recollection of doing it. So when she saw them, she naturally got very upset. She accused me of destroying her wardrobe, and I don't believe she ever accepted the fact that she herself was responsible. Very strange. And then there was the business of the butchered cat. . . . "

"Cat?"

Sebastian shook his head. "No, forget I said that. I may have had my suspicions, but we never knew for sure what had happened to the poor creature."

"You think that Violet. . . ."

"No, forget it. I don't think anything, and besides it was a long time ago. The point is, you can see that your fears are really pretty minor league, and seem to be based upon very little."

Cerise slowly nodded her head and relaxed. "I know you must be right. I guess I was just being neurotic. And besides, it couldn't be me anyway, could it?"

"Not any more, it couldn't. . . . By the way, I wouldn't mention any of this to Violet. She tends to be a little sensitive about such things. I mean, she won't even admit she's in therapy. Now, really! Who cares?"

Just then the subject of Sebastian's confidences looked in the doorway. "Did you notice that Mr. Ching laid out dinner on the sideboard before he left?"

"Yes, I saw," Sebastian said. "Very thoughtful of him. What do you suppose is in the big pot?"

"I think it's a stew of some kind."

"But it's all sort of green and slimy."

"Yucko," Cerise said with a shudder. "Considering the circumstances, I think I'll pass."

"Wise decision," Sebastian said. "But considering what we've been served so far, the circumstances hardly matter. Rather than eat another of Mr. Ching's creations, we'd be better off tucking into one of Mrs. Hook's strychnine soufflés, or her arsenic *en croûte*."

All except Mrs. Argus seemed to agree with this, and while the others opened a few cans for themselves, the old woman happily put away a large portion of what Mr. Ching had prepared. Sebastian remarked that that was proof of her severe derangement, but to his disappointment, Mrs. Argus apparently suffered no ill effects from her foolhardiness.

After their meal, the five remaining members of the house party were again in the lounge. Cerise and Sebastian sat together. She giggled almost continuously as he related an outrageous narrative involving people and events that might have been absolutely factual, heavily embroidered, or wholly wishful. She had no idea which, nor did she care. Violet scowled at each new burst of laughter, but continued to scribble furiously in the notebook resting on her knees. Derrick, deeply immersed in a book on eighteenth-century cryptography, occasionally grunted to himself and jotted down the odd note on a piece of scratch paper. Mrs. Argus sat quietly, hands folded, looking as though she were waiting for something. Outside, the wind was blowing harder.

Suddenly, there was a pounding on the front door that made everyone except Mrs. Argus jump in his seat.

"Thank God!" Cerise said. "Help has come at last! We can finally get away from this place!"

Mrs. Argus laughed indulgently. "There is no help. Death is at the door."

"Oh, shut up for once, you old bag!" Sebastian said. "Do you have any idea how tedious and boring you are?"

Led by Cerise, they left the lounge. Mrs. Argus, murmuring happily to herself, remained behind.

The light in the entrance hall was out. As they approached the front door, they felt that something sticky had been spilled on the floor, but in the darkness they couldn't see what.

"Well," Sebastian said, "Mrs. Hook's housekeeping was about as good as Mr. Ching's cooking. Sis, your friend Mousey sure could pick 'em."

There was another bout of heavy pounding on the door,

but for some reason, they all held back. Finally, Cérise took the last two steps and pulled open the door.

At first she was confused, not understanding what she was seeing. Then she understood. Then she screamed. Then she screamed again.

She was looking into the pale face of Mr. Ching. Only for the first few seconds it seemed to her that he didn't have any body. Then she saw that he was hanging upside down, his head directly in front of hers.

He was wearing the missing wetsuit and swim fins. He was suspended by a rope tied around his ankles. His throat had been cut, almost from ear to ear.

He was very, very dead.

CHAPTER TWENTY-ONE

"MY, MY," SEBASTIAN SAID. "HE'S CERTAINLY WELL HUNG. Which, in my experience, is unusual for Oriental—"

"Sebastian, will you please shut up!" Violet said. "There are times when your irrepressibility should be mercilessly squashed."

Irrepressibleness must have run in the family, though, because it seemed that the Society-Girl Detective was once more back on the case.

Or at least there was now a case to get back on...a thought that hit each of them almost like a physical blow.

"I hate to mention it, but what do you suppose it is we're standing in?" Sebastian said, shifting his feet with a sickeningly squishy sound.

"I say! My Guccis!" Derrick cried, leaping backwards.

Cerise was not worried about her canvas shoes, but she too backed away from the door, eyes riveted with horrified fascination upon the thing that swayed in the opening. She began to shake her head from side to side, as though in denial of some terrible accusation.

Sebastian moved next to her. "Hey, you're not thinking that you might have...I mean, you're not still worried about what we talked about before, are you?"

Cerise looked at him but said nothing.

"Well, you do know that we've all been together for quite a while. What were you doing before you came down?"

Cerise continued to stare at him, then said, "I took a nap."

"Well, then, there you are. You were asleep."

She moved back a step. "Was I?"

There was a peculiar look in her eyes, and an edge to her voice—as though inside her a harsh laugh was rising uncontrollably—that gave Sebastian a decidedly uncomfortable feeling. He went outside and joined Violet and Derrick, who were staring up at the window out of which the rope descended.

"Whose room is that?" Violet asked.

Sebastian looked up at the second floor. "There're so many rooms, I'm not sure, but I think it's the old bat's."

"Mrs. Argus's?" Violet looked around. "Where is she?"

"She's always disappearing," Derrick said.

"Never for long enough," Sebastian muttered.

"I guess we'd better have a look," Violet said.

They went back into the house, looking first in the lounge, but Mrs. Argus was no longer there. Then, with Violet leading the way and Cerise trailing, they went upstairs and found that Mrs. Argus's room was indeed the source of the rope. The end of it was tied securely around the foot of the radiator in front of the window.

They stood just inside the doorway for a minute, staring at the scene that, in its simplicity, was almost more sinister than the grisly spectacle down below. Then Derrick, with an interested expression, crossed the room, bent down, and examined the knot in the rope. He stood up and thoughtfully rubbed his sleek chin.

"You know, that's a sailor's knot," he said.

"Oh, really?" Violet said. "Didn't Budgie tell me that Mrs. Argus had been quite a sailor in her youth? Of course! And that Mousey's mother had died in an accident when they were out together."

"That's right, she did say that," Sebastian said. He started to add something, reconsidered, then decided to go ahead anyway. "I know this might strike some of you as being a little too simple," he smiled at Violet, "but might not this be another 'Purloined Letter'?"

"What?" Derrick said. "Is another letter missing?"

Sebastian, displaying remarkable restraint, merely sighed. "I meant, isn't it possible that the solution is so very obvious, so out in the open, that we've failed to see it?"

"Huh?"

"We've been looking for a maniac, right? Well, all the time, there's been one person flitting around who's unquestionably deranged."

"You mean one besides you?"

Sebastian smiled at his sister, who, he knew, had difficulty accepting with much grace a good idea not her own. "I'm not denying that I may be a bit off-centre, but still. . . ."

"You mean—" Derrick motioned to the room they were in, and Sebastian nodded.

Violet rolled her eyes. "Oh, come on. He's just saying that because he doesn't like the woman."

"Of course I don't like the old bag. She gives me the creeps. But does that mean she couldn't be the one? As I said, is it too obvious for you, Sis?"

Violet didn't answer, but sat down heavily on a small, chintz-covered armchair.

"I say, Violet. I think your brother may have something."

Oh, he undoubtedly had lots of things, Violet thought, none of which any sensible person would want to catch. However, she just looked at Derrick and asked, "Why?"

"Well, for starters—like your brother said—she is crazy. That's pretty clear."

"And?"

"And she's always disappearing and then popping up when we least expect it."

"And?"

"And she keeps saying things are going to happen, and they do. Why, not ten minutes ago, she said that Death was at the door, and it was."

"A dead person was at the door. That's not the same thing."

"It's close enough for me. And that's not the first time she's done that—said things were going to happen before they did. Now, how could she do that unless she was the one who was doing them?"

Violet made a face. "You just said she was crazy. One of the things that makes her crazy is that she says crazy things. If you want to attribute all kinds of meaning to her cryptic remarks, that's your affair, but isn't it more reasonable simply to ignore them as the ravings of a mad woman? 'Death is at the door.' What the hell does that mean? And because Mr. Ching was hanging there, it doesn't follow that she killed him. It seems more likely to me that she saw him, but didn't tell anyone." Violet shook her head. "No, if she's the one who's doing all this, what's her reason?"

"If she's bonkers, isn't that reason enough?"

"You're not suggesting that she's Frances Hacker, are you?"

"I don't know. She could be."

"No, she couldn't be," Violet said. "From things that Budgie said, she recognized her. So she knew her from before. So she's not Hacker."

"But she's still crazy."

"So what? You can be crazy without being a killer, and you can be a killer without being crazy. What's been happening here is either random, senseless slaughter, or it's been motivated, it's had a purpose."

It would have been difficult to fault the logic of this proposition, and even more difficult to blame Violet for not perceiving that it could be both at the same time.

"So far," Violet went on, "you haven't shown me anything to indicate that Mrs. Argus fits either of those possibilities."

"How about this, Sis?" Sebastian, who had been wandering around the room casually looking at things while Violet and

Derrick talked, now stood next to the built-in bookcase, holding a sheet of paper in his hand. "I was looking at some of these old books, and I found this stuck between two of them. It's another page of your friend Mousey's letter. Page one, in fact." Sebastian smiled pleasantly as he waited for the commotion to die down. "Relax. It's not about any of you. If you'll be quiet for a minute, I'll read it. It's not very long. It says: 'I have recently learned that my mother did not die in a boating accident. She *was* drowned, but it was not an accident. She was murdered. My godmother, Mrs. Cassandra Argus, killed my mother. She did this because she was in love with my father. She thought that if my mother was out of the way, my father would marry her. But he loved my mother and he wouldn't do this. And so to pay him back, Mrs. Argus killed him, too. Thus the oldest and closest friend of my parents killed both of them, and made me an orphan.'"

Derrick broke the shocked silence that followed Sebastian's reading. "I say! Do you think we might now have a motive, Violet?"

Violet shifted uncomfortably in her seat. "Possibly. But there was also a page in the letter about Mr. Drupe, and we know that he wasn't responsible for anything."

"But this is murder. That's really a secret to keep hidden at any price."

"Maybe."

"Come on, Violet," Sebastian said. "If the old bat had already killed twice, why wouldn't she kill a third time to protect herself? Don't you remember? You presented that at various times as a sufficient reason for murders presumably committed by both Mrs. Hook and Mr. Ching. Why isn't that good enough now?"

Violet again shifted position. "Okay. Maybe there was a reason to kill Mousey. But what about the others? Not only is there not a reason, there's nothing even to link her to those killings. And there's got to be, because I still say we're dealing with only one killer. Where's a link?"

"Mr. Ching was dropped out of this room," Derrick said.

"It could be a frame," Violet said, "to cast suspicion on Mrs. Argus."

"The sailor's knot?"

Violet dismissed this with a flick of her hand.

"And the letter?"

"Another frame."

"Okay, then. She was the one who found Mrs. Hook."

"So? Cerise found the Colonel."

"But Mrs. Argus never showed up when we found the Colonel," Cerise said, speaking for the first time since they had come upstairs.

"So? Neither did Derrick."

Derrick blushed, then looked down at the floor, and shuffled his shiny shoes.

"Come on, Sis. Just because the Society-Girl Detective didn't figure it out, doesn't mean it can't be right."

Violet moved uneasily in her chair as she narrowed her eyes and gave her brother a cold blue stare. "No, but you need more."

"All this taken together looks pretty good, Sis."

"I still say you need something more. Something less coincidental. At least one more good solid link." Violet again changed her position. "What the hell is that?"

She lifted herself up from the seat, put her hand under the cushion, and felt around. She found whatever it was she'd been sitting on and brought it out. She uttered a terse and not very polite exclamation of displeasure. In her hand, looking very much like a remnant of the Cheshire cat, were Mr. Drupe's missing dentures.

"What was it you wanted, Sis? Something solid? Something you could sink your teeth into?"

Cerise giggled.

"Actually, Sis, it looked like you were trying to sink your something into those teeth."

"Sebastian!" Violet stood up and gave her brother a look that made it clear that if he made another tooth remark, he might well find himself missing a mouthful of them.

"I say! Take it easy," Derrick said, trying to pour oil on troubled waters. "We've got to decide what to do."

"How about exterminating the old hag?" Sebastian suggested.

"Hee, hee, hee," Mrs. Argus laughed behind them.

Everyone literally jumped in the air, whirling around, and before they came down they were shouting accusations, demanding explanations. They wanted to know about the letter, the body, the teeth, her frequent disappearances, and all the other strange things she'd done and said.

Mrs. Argus's expression through all this was one of interest, but she seemed to be listening to something other than their questions. When they'd finished and were waiting for answers, she looked from face to face, giving each of them the same enigmatic, faintly unsettling, thin, bloodless smile. Then the smile broadened.

"No one will leave here alive," she said, quietly, as though passing on an obvious but still interesting piece of information

The four of them backed nervously away from Mrs. Argus.

Was it a threat? Or a prophecy?

CHAPTER TWENTY-TWO

LATER THAT NIGHT, ALL EXCEPT MRS. ARGUS WERE AGAIN in the lounge. While they would have liked to know where the old woman was and what she was up to, that uncertainty was still preferable to the uneasiness her presence would have caused, especially with her habit of regarding each of them as though his current animation was merely a passing phase. Best of all, of course, would have been to lock her up somewhere— Sebastian suggested some place with a very limited air supply— but Mrs. Argus had already gone off again, and no one much felt like looking for her.

Violet was writing in her notebook, but with less enthusiasm than before. Not only was she annoyed that *she* had not come up with the answer, she was also a lot less than thrilled with what that answer had turned out to be. In fact, the result was so unsatisfying that she thought it might well detract from the story's intrinsic interest (and, consequently, from potential sales). She could see it now: "...a marvelously intriguing situation; unfortunately, the ultimate resolution does not fulfil the expectations that were built up in the reader." No matter that she told it the way it had happened; that assessment wouldn't be far wrong. After all, Sebastian had settled on the answer effortlessly, like a butterfly on a flower, and even Derrick had been able to put together the elements of the solution. Maybe, she thought, she could work a kind of reversal in which the solution's very obviousness could be used to deflect attention from it.

Violet sighed. Unsatisfying though it was, it did seem to be correct. Still, even though the murderous rampage was an act of madness, Violet continued to believe that—at least initially—there had been a reason, a purpose, behind it all. Maybe the reason had been quickly lost or forgotten or abandoned, but it had been there in the beginning . . . and the beginning was Mousey. Violet remained convinced that Mousey's death was intended; whether to hide something, or to get something, or to keep the girl from doing something, there had been a reason for the murder. And, although Violet had downplayed it at the time, that page of the letter Sebastian had found made it clear that—mad or sane—Mrs. Argus had had a very good reason to kill Mousey.

More to the point, Violet thought, no one else—at least none of those left alive—seemed to have a motive. Certainly Sebastian didn't—he hadn't even known the poor girl. She looked across the room at Derrick and Cerise who were seated together on a couch, engaged in quiet conversation. She wouldn't put it past him, but even Derrick was bright enough to know you had to wait until you had actually married your rich fiancée before you killed her for her money; to do it before the wedding would just waste the effort expended on the courtship. And while Violet thought there was something strange about Cerise, she apparently had no more reason to kill Mousey than Sebastian did. That left only Mrs. Argus.

Or Frances Hacker, she thought, looking at Cerise. Or Francis, looking at Derrick. Or, looking up at the glassy-eyed animal heads, an intruder who had thus far managed to remain invisible.

Violet shook her head: no, no, no; it had to be the old woman. Now, if only there were some way to make it more interesting, a final twist, something. . . .

Violet frowned across at Derrick and Cerise, who seemed to have moved slightly closer together. He looked to be really turning on the charm, talking persuasively, while she appeared to be listening with considerable interest. Judging from Cerise's expression, Violet assumed that Derrick was no longer discussing old map-making techniques, about which he had droned on earlier.

"What do you suppose they're talking about?" Violet said to her brother.

Sebastian was sitting at the other end of the couch from her, turning the pages of an ancient magazine and wondering what it would have been like to live in a time when everything seemed so simple and straightforward. Boring, probably. He looked across the room and shrugged. "Whether it's his place or hers?"

"Hmm. I wonder. . . ."

Violet shut her notebook and stood up. Sebastian gave a big yawn and also rose. After saying goodnight to Derrick and Cerise, they went upstairs and into their rooms.

A little while later, the door to Violet's room slowly and silently swung open, and her head appeared. She checked the hallway, then stepped out, carefully closing the door behind her. Soundlessly, she went down the corridor to the front of the house, pausing outside Derrick's and Cerise's rooms, but hearing nothing. She stopped at Mrs. Argus's door, pressed her ear against it, then quickly opened it and went in.

Meanwhile, Sebastian was in his room, standing before the full-length mirror, admiring what he saw. He struck a pose and touched his blond hair. "Not bad," he said softly, moving closer to the mirror and making a minor adjustment. "Not bad at all, kiddo."

Later that night Mrs. Argus was walking across the gentle slope that ran from the stone terrace outside the lounge down to the water. Clouds hid the stars, and there were few lights on in the house, but despite the thick darkness, Mrs. Argus moved without difficulty. She seemed equally untroubled by the damp and the cold, even though she wore only her long black dress.

Near one of the large empty birdbaths—actually, it was more like a fountain, and big enough to accommodate a flock of swans—she suddenly stopped and held her gaunt body rigidly motionless. She sensed a presence close by. Slowly she turned, then stopped, then smiled.

"Oh, so it's you, is it?" she said. "You know, I thought it might be. I said so, didn't I . . . in a way, at least. . . . I really was pretty close, wasn't I?" Mrs. Argus grinned again. "Is it my turn now?"

CHAPTER TWENTY-THREE

WHEN VIOLET CAME DOWN THE NEXT MORNING, DERRICK, Cerise, and Sebastian were already in the dining room.

"Oh, there you are, Violet," Sebastian said cheerfully. "We were just wondering if maybe you'd bought it during the night."

"I appreciate your concern."

"Actually, it was a question of whether we should save this English muffin for you, or not."

Violet gave her brother a pitying smile and gestured that he was welcome to the muffin. She poured herself a cup of coffee and sat down at the place next to Sebastian. She took a couple of sips, then looked up. "Has anyone seen her this morning?"

Derrick and Cerise shook their heads. Sebastian suggested that perhaps she'd lost her grip while she was asleep and had fallen on her head.

"You know," Violet said, "we're going to have to figure out what we're going to do about her."

"What did you say to her last night?" Cerise asked.

"Who?"

"Mrs. Argus, of course."

"What are you talking about? I didn't say anything to her. I didn't even see her."

"Sure you did," Derrick said. "We saw you."

"What are you talking about?" Violet repeated.

"Cerise and I were sitting in the lounge, and we saw you and Mrs. Argus walking across the lawn outside."

"That's right, Violet," Cerise said. "It was pretty dark, but there was still enough light to see you. You had on that nice jumpsuit of yours."

"Yes," Derrick said. "The two of you walked together, and then you passed out of our line of sight. Cerise and I wondered what you were doing."

"That's right. We did."

Violet looked across the table at Derrick and Cerise. "All right. Just what's going on here?"

"What do you mean?" Derrick said.

"I mean just that. What's going on? What kind of game are you playing?"

"We're not playing anything, Violet," Cerise said. "We're just telling you what we saw."

"Only you didn't see it."

"Of course we did. Derrick and I both saw you. Besides, what reason could we have to make up something like this?"

"Yes, Sis. Why would they say they saw you if they didn't?"

"That's the question, isn't it? I'd also like to know how come they seem to be so chummy all of a sudden? And how come they happened to be in the lounge and just happened to 'see' me walk by? Awfully convenient, wasn't it?"

"Sis, what are you suggesting? That they really didn't see you but decided to make up this story together?"

"Of course that's what I'm saying, you fool!" Violet's voice rose shrilly, and her eyes flashed at her brother. "I know I wasn't wearing my jumpsuit last night. I know I wasn't outside. I know I didn't talk with Mrs. Argus. Therefore—if this is not too great a logical leap for you—they are lying when they say that they saw me."

"I say, Violet!"

"Yes, Violet," Cerise said. "Believe me, we're not lying. What possible reason could we have?"

Violet looked at Derrick and Cerise with considerable suspicion. "I don't know yet, but I know there's got to be one. And I'll tell what else I know. Last night, I didn't see Mrs. Argus, but I did go into her room. I wanted to see if there was something there that might help to tie all this up into a neater package. Well, I didn't find anything that provided any new explanations, but I did find this on the floor under the chair where I'd been sitting." From her purse she pulled out a small, pocket-sized binder which she put on the table. The cover was of sleek chocolate-brown leather, embossed with the letters DC.

"I say! That's mine!"

Violet looked expressionlessly at Derrick. "Yes, it is, isn't it? I wonder how it came to be in Mrs. Argus's room."

"I must have dropped it last night when we went up there."

"Only you didn't have it last night. I remember you were making notes on a loose piece of paper. And you also didn't go anywhere near that chair last night. So how did it get there?"

"How should I know? That old woman probably took it and hid it for reasons of her own."

"Probably." Violet stared steadily at Derrick until he blushed and looked down at what was left of his breakfast. "Except," she added slowly, as though thinking out loud, "it hadn't been hidden. It looked more like it had been accidentally dropped."

"Would you please give it to me?" Derrick held out his hand.

"And, do you know?—" Violet turned to Sebastian "—there's only one page that has anything on it."

"Please give it to me."

She opened the binder. "Here it is. See? The word 'GOLD' followed by the number 716147."

"Give it!"

"And then below that, a whole long string of letters." Violet pointed to a section that began, "TFPPBEHWNP TWLJGZBOGTIGMBKQCBKUR. . . ."

"Give it, you stupid bitch!" Derrick reached across the table and snatched the notebook from Violet's hands.

"Oh, sure. Take it." Violet shrugged unconcernedly. "I made a copy of it anyway."

Derrick pointed a manicured finger at her. "You've poked into everybody else's business, Violet, but I'm warning you, you'd better not poke into mine."

"Why not? What are you afraid I might find?"

"I'm not afraid of anything. Especially not a stupid bitch who does things and then doesn't remember she's done them. You're probably the one who stole this notebook, and then forgot you did it."

Violet's eyes seemed to bulge slightly, her lips were pulled back, and her fingers gripped the edge of the table. "At first I didn't know what was happening," she hissed between clenched teeth. "Now, it's looking more and more like some kind of conspiracy."

"Conspiracy!" Derrick's tanned face flushed even darker. "You must be mad. There's no conspiracy. I'll tell you what it is, Violet. It's frustration. Frustration is giving you delusions. What you need is a man. That's assuming you could find one who'd put up with you. But if you did, then maybe you'd stop behaving like a nosy, snoopy old maid."

"My God!" Cerise turned to Derrick. "You're not only a boring lout, you're a stupid boring lout!"

"I can defend myself, thanks!" Violet shouted at Cerise. "I don't need your help. And besides, it won't work. Whatever it is that's going on, I know you're in it with him."

"In it with him?" Cerise said. "I'm not in anything with him. I wouldn't spit on him if his hair was on fire. But believe me, Violet, we're not lying. We saw you—"

"Believe you?" Violet stood up, her eyes round and hot, glowing red spots on her pale cheeks. "I believe something funny is going on, is what I believe. And I believe you're right in the middle of it, sweetie. And I intend to find out exactly what it is. Then we'll all know just what to believe."

"Golly, Sis—"

Violet whirled to face her brother, and he forgot about trying to pacify her. She glared at him for a moment, her anger like a cold blue flame. Then she tilted her head and looked quizzically at him, and finally turned and stomped from the room.

Cerise looked at Sebastian. He merely raised his eyebrows and brought a silencing finger to his lips.

CHAPTER TWENTY-FOUR

ACTUALLY, THEY WEREN'T ALL THAT SURPRISED WHEN THEY found Mrs. Argus's body.

Violet had come back downstairs about half an hour after her outburst, once more composed, though displaying an odd air of expectancy. She told the others that Mrs. Argus was not in her room, and that her bed had not been slept in. With reluctant sighs but little discussion, they agreed that they'd better look for the old woman.

The search did not take long. It started where Derrick and Cerise said they'd last seen Mrs. Argus, and stopped about fifteen yards farther on, at a large concrete birdbath. There, lying on the dead leaves that covered the bottom, they found her. From the marks on her neck, and the horrible expression on her face, it was obvious that she'd been strangled.

They stood looking down at the corpse, nodding their heads. There were no shrieks, or cries, or hysteria. Perhaps they were beyond that, shocked to the point where numbed acceptance was the only possible response; certainly they were getting used to having their worst fears continually confirmed.

"What's that?" Derrick said, then stepped over the side of the birdbath and knelt by the body. From between the fingers of Mrs. Argus's tightly closed hand, he withdrew something.

"What'd you find?" Sebastian asked.

Derrick went back to the other three, holding out something between his thumb and forefinger. When he got close enough, they could see it was a single hair, about nine inches long. It was blond.

"Golly, Sis, it sure doesn't look good for you."

"No, it doesn't, does it?" Violet said evenly. "Two witnesses to place me with the victim not fifty feet from the crime? A blond hair clutched in the victim's death grip? You're right. It looks pretty bad." She stared at her brother, then smiled. "In fact, Sebastian, it looks just the way you intended it to look. You did a pretty good job. Just not quite good enough."

"What are you saying, Sis? That I—"

"Yes. That you're the one, Sebastian. You're the killer."

"I say, Violet! Really!" Derrick said. "Sebastian? It doesn't make any sense."

"Precisely," Violet said. "That's why we haven't been able to figure it out. We've been trying to make sense of it, when all along there was no sense, only confusion. And who here has devoted his whole life to confusion, to chaos, to absurdity, to demonstrating the pointlessness of everything?"

"Oh, come on, Sis. I've never devoted myself to anything."

"Right. Perfect nihilism—a common attitude of those who kill without conscience." Violet turned to Derrick and Cerise. "From the beginning I've been thinking it was someone with a reason to kill Mousey. Of everyone here, only Sebastian didn't know her, therefore he was the only one I didn't suspect. Now, it's obvious I was wrong . . . just as I was supposed to be. It was a classic case of the least likely suspect. Christ! I should have realized what was going on right at the beginning, when Sebastian kept reminding everyone that he couldn't have done it because he was the outsider who didn't know anyone." Violet shook her head disgustedly. "If a character in a book said that, it would be like waving a red flag at the reader. Only I didn't see the flag. If I had, maybe more of us would be alive. But I mistakenly agreed with him—which by now I should know better than to do—and never considered him as a possibility. Until now."

"But Violet," Cerise said. "Why would he do this?"

"Yes, why, Sis? This should be interesting. I must say, you're really outdoing yourself this time."

"Well, I said before that Sebastian never needed a reason to do anything. That he had a whim was usually sufficient justification. This, too, may have started as a perverse whim, but the reasons behind it are now clear. Obviously, one of his purposes was to get me, to show me up. You see, ever since I became successful, Sebastian—who's never had to do anything except amuse himself—has been envious of what I've accomplished. Every chance he gets, he tries to make fun of me, mock me, cut me down. He wants to see me fail, and when we got here, he saw it as a perfect opportunity to make the Society-Girl Detective fall flat on her face."

"Oh, Violet," Cerise said, sadly shaking her head. "You're saying he killed seven people—seven innocent people, seven total strangers—just to make you look bad? Don't you think that's a bit extreme? For someone to do that, he'd have to be absolutely insane."

"That's right. Just because Sebastian jokes about how unstable he is, doesn't necessarily mean that he's not. He learned early on that any abnormality you cheerfully acknowledge is rarely taken very seriously; in fact, it tends to make people discount it completely."

Sebastian was still smiling pleasantly, but Derrick and Cerise began to look more serious.

"Another favourite trick of my brother's," Violet went on, "is to attribute his own symptoms and aberrations to someone else. That's what he's doing when he talks about me behind my back—just another of his attempts to get at me. He doesn't make things up; no, it's much more effective to tell the truth. So he tells about all the strange things I supposedly did—only they are really things that he himself did." Violet looked at Cerise. "Oh, so he's tried that on you, has he? What'd he tell you? Have you heard the old chestnut that I used to do things without knowing I did them? That's one of his favourites. Did he tell you about my ripped clothes? Oh, he did? But did he tell you that everyone thought he'd done it?"

"Not everyone, Sis," Sebastian smiled. "Only you."

Violet looked at Derrick and Cerise, and shrugged. "I never said he wasn't convincing. It's not surprising. Considering all the ways in which he's indulged himself over the years, I doubt that he even has a clue any more what's real and what he's imagined. But I don't mean to suggest that he's not responsible for his actions. On the contrary. I think he knew exactly what he was doing. And there's an even more important explanation than his desire to see me fail. In fact, I suspect making me look bad was just a bonus."

Violet paused and Sebastian said, "Well, don't keep us waiting, Sis. What did motivate the Master Crook besides a desire to humiliate you? Which, believe me, could be accomplished with a whole lot less than seven murders."

Violet looked at Derrick and Cerise. "I've been hearing rumours for some time that Sebastian is running out of money, but I never took them seriously. Now, I'm not so sure. Certainly, his star is rapidly dimming, waning almost as fast as his finances. By creating a sensational murder case, he could propel himself back into the spotlight. By framing me for the murders, he could remove me permanently from the scene, and then take over my company and restore his fortunes."

"Oh, come on, Sis. Talk about leaping into the fire. Even assuming I needed money—which I don't—in taking over Cornichon Cosmetics I'd be going from merely reduced circumstances into outright bankruptcy. If anything, I might very well kill to *avoid* getting that white elephant, not the reverse."

Sebastian laughed, but Derrick and Cerise did not join him. They looked uncertainly from Violet to Sebastian and back again.

Sebastian sighed wearily and shook his head. "Knowing you as I do, Sis, I assume that your ridiculous accusation is based upon something more than your paranoid delusions and the very unlikeliness of my candidacy."

"You see what I mean?" Violet said to Derrick and Cerise. "He's very good at this. And he's right—there are a few other things. . . . First, he had opportunity."

"So did everyone else, Sis. No one has a decent alibi for any of the murders."

"That's right," Violet agreed. "But Sebastian has one that's especially bad. When Budgie was killed—remember? Sebastian was supposed to be searching the top floor, from which Budgie was thrown out of the window. When I asked him how it was that he didn't hear anything, he said that he never got up there—some excuse about a call of nature. It was clear to me he was lying."

Sebastian smiled and shrugged. "You got me there, Violet. I was lying."

"I say!"

"My God, Sebastian! You don't mean——"

"No, of course I don't mean that. I didn't get up to the attic because I wanted to take a look at the equipment Violet said Budgie and the Colonel had."

Violet sniffed sceptically.

"Well, of course I didn't say so, Sis. You know, nothing much usually bothers me, but—golly!—that embarrassed me even while I was doing it. Especially when I found out that Budgie had been killed at that very moment. I mean, how tacky."

"You see," Violet said. "He readily admits to one aberration in order to deflect your attention from the others. But it's not going to work this time. . . . There are also the curious circumstances surrounding Mousey's letter. Remember, Sebastian found the empty envelope, and also the page concerning Mrs. Argus. All very convenient. So convenient, in fact, that I think Sebastian knew where to look for them. Because he had hidden them. And he had them to hide because he killed Mousey, and discovered the letter, and realized that it was a potential gold mine."

"But Violet," Derrick said, "you found the letter about Mr. Drupe."

"Yes, in his dresser. Where—subsequent events have

shown—it must have been planted. Planted by the person who killed Mousey. Planted by a person who figured I would look there. Planted by a person who wanted me to go off course. Planted by a person who wanted to embarrass me, who loved it when he could chortle out, 'Wrong again, Violet!'"

"My, my," Sebastian said. "My cleverness astounds me."

"There were times when I think it astounded all of us, Sebastian. In fact, I think you may have been a little bit too clever." Violet turned back to Derrick and Cerise. "Didn't either of you wonder about Sebastian's reactions whenever we found another corpse? About why he didn't react normally? Never seemed scared or surprised or shocked? Never seemed to take it very seriously, but instead always had some kind of joke ready?"

"Golly, you're right, Sis. The fact that I deal with tension by trying to make a joke, and the fact that I happen to enjoy a certain verbal facility—a flair for the *bon mot*—are highly incriminating."

"I hate to tell you, Sebastian, but your *mots* are not so damn *bons*. Your flair, as you call it, is for the feeble and childish, which is precisely how I would characterize—among other things—the removal and eventual reappearance of Mr. Drupe's teeth. Out of which, I should also mention, you got a great deal of mileage. No, Sebastian, I don't think your remarks have been spontaneous. They were thought out beforehand because you knew beforehand what we were going to find. In fact, judging from some of the things you've said, I wouldn't be surprised to learn that the particular modes of death were selected solely to provide you with the opportunity to make your outrageous remarks."

Sebastian shook his head and smiled. "I was right, Sis. You really are outdoing yourself this time. I've heard of people being killed for a song, but for a laugh? Really, Violet!" He held out his arms, wrists together. "Clamp on the old irons. It's a fair cop."

"You see: even now he's clowning." Violet looked pityingly at her brother. "You really are diseased, Sebastian."

"Gimme a break, Sis! It's a little bit difficult to take all of your desperate scramblings seriously. Especially since there are two witnesses who saw you do everything but throttle the old crow."

Violet smiled broadly at her brother. "I was wondering when you'd bring that up. That was your one mistake, Sebastian. If you hadn't done that, I still wouldn't have caught on." She turned to Derrick and Cerise. "Before, I said that you were lying. I was upset, and I apologize. After I said it, I realized there was another possibility."

"Huh?" Derrick said.

Violet went over next to her brother and positioned herself in a way that duplicated his stance. The similarity—the near-identicalness—was unmistakeable and undeniable.

"At night, from a distance," Violet said, "it would be difficult to tell us apart, wouldn't it? Especially if Sebastian had on something distinctive that you'd immediately associate with me, like my jumpsuit."

"I say, Violet! You could be right."

"Of course I'm right. I knew that I wasn't the one you said you saw. Therefore, either you were lying, or it was someone impersonating me for the purpose of casting suspicion on me. After all, there can be only one killer, so if you knew who did one murder, you'd know who did them all. Sebastian was just waiting for the opportunity to link me with the crimes. And how much better for you to make the link, than for him to do it—you who have no connection with me and nothing to gain. Yesterday, somebody went through my room. I had the feeling then that something had been taken, but I didn't know what. Now I realize it was my jumpsuit. Sebastian must have laughed himself silly thinking about the headlines: 'Society-Girl Detective Goes Berserk, Kills Seven.' Nice try, Sebastian."

Sebastian rolled his eyes. "Really, Violet! If it had been your silver lamé party dress, perhaps . . . but I wouldn't be caught dead in that jumpsuit thing. Besides, that's got to be your hair that Derrick found."

"Or yours."

"Mine's too short."

"What about this?" Violet reached in her purse and pulled out a blond wig that was almost exactly the colour, length, and shape of her own hair. "I found this in your room twenty minutes ago."

"I say!"

"My God! Sebastian!"

Sebastian blushed, then went pale. He shrugged, and tried a laugh that didn't come out quite right. "So? I never denied that I like to dress up every once in a while. Didn't any of you ever want to pretend you were Doris Day? I know it's kinky, but it's not a crime."

But it was clear from the way Derrick and Cerise were regarding him that they thought he was guilty of a lot more than a little harmless make-believe.

"Hey, wait a second!" he said. "Don't you see what's going on here? Violet's turned everything around. She's doing exactly what she claims I did. Every reason she's given for my guilt can apply equally well to her. She desperately needs a success. Her reputation—and consequently her business—is sinking fast. The only way she can reverse things is by having a spectacular triumph. Since no appropriate situation presented itself, she had to create one, and the more complicated the problem, the greater the glory when she solved it. But she had to solve it. It wasn't enough to have a series of bizarre and sensational and apparently insoluble crimes. She also had to have a perpetrator. But since *she* was the perpetrator, she had to come up with somebody she could frame—which you just saw her do with a most interesting double bluff. She intended that you see her with Mrs. Argus last night, so she could turn it around and say it was me posing as her. Really quite impressive, Violet. And what a solution it gave you! As if the situation wasn't extraordinary enough, the detective's very own brother turns out to be the culprit. Sensational! They'd beat down the doors to get the Society-Girl Detective's own story. What were you going to call it, Sis? *My Brother's Catcher*? Have you already got yourself a good literary agent?"

"No, Sebastian, I do not have an agent." Violet tried for a

condescending tone, but merely managed to sound strained.

"No, of course not. It would look a bit peculiar if you got one in advance." He looked at Derrick and Cerise. "Violet says I'm jealous of her success. Well, for years now, she's been eaten up with bitterness over the fact that circumstances gave me all of our parents' estate while she was left with nothing. Even though this wasn't my fault, Violet has never forgiven me. Now, it looks as though she thought she'd finally found a way to get even. By pinning the murders on me, she not only gives herself a wonderful triumph with a stunning twist, she also gets her revenge on me for being four minutes older. And as my only relative, she'll get control of my assets when I get put into the loony bin. Yes, Violet, there is still more than enough left to bail out Cornichon Cosmetics several times over."

Violet stood with arms folded, tapping her foot and looking bored. Derrick and Cerise, however, looked anything but. Their eyes moved between Violet and Sebastian, and their expressions displayed growing confusion, puzzlement, and uncertainty.

"And speaking of motives," Sebastian continued, "I never made any secret about my feelings for the late, unlamented old bat." He nodded towards the birdbath. "But what about Violet? She had only contempt for her so-called friend, Mousey, who apparently was no longer going to let Violet take advantage of her. She despised Mr. Drupe. She hated the Colonel on sight and was furious when he tried to grope her. She probably thought that Budgie was such a pitiful creature that she should be put out of her misery. Mrs. Hook talked back to Violet and did not treat her with proper deference and respect. Mr. Ching? I'm not sure about him. Maybe Violet saw him as an interesting bit of plot development. And Mrs. Argus was necessary to frame me. If I were you," he said to Derrick and Cerise, "I'd be very careful. You've both made Violet angry at different times. You may have noticed that she angers easily. She also tends to bear long grudges. Maybe her new therapist told her to express her anger—let it all out—and this is the result."

"I told you," Violet said, barely moving her lips, "that I've never been in therapy."

"And I told you, Sis, that Binky Edwards saw you coming out of that office."

"Then he's either lying or mistaken. As far as I know, it was you that he saw."

"Well, Sis, you're so loopy that as far as you know, it could've been you that he saw, only you don't even know you're in therapy." Sebastian stopped and looked quizzically at Violet. "Maybe I've done you an injustice. Or else given you more credit than you deserve. Maybe there is no plot here. Maybe you never meant to frame me. Maybe you've been seriously following the trail, all the while never realizing that the trail leads back to you. The Society-Girl Detective finally solves the crime, only to discover that she herself is the murderer—that through the whole thing, the murdering half was laying false clues for the detective half to follow. How's that for a twist, Sis?"

"Highly implausible," Violet said, "unless you'd like to apply the principle to yourself."

Sebastian started to say something in rebuttal, then stopped and nodded to his sister in acknowledgement. He turned to Derrick and Cerise and smiled. "Well, there you are. Quite a situation, isn't it? Right out of Pirandello. Which of us is it? Which twin do you believe? Who is lying, and who is telling the truth? Maybe we both *think* we're telling the truth, but one of us is mad. How can you tell which? We're both pretty convincing . . . both ways. It's a poser, all right. Unless one of us turns up dead, it will be difficult to resolve the matter. My advice would be to—" Sebastian suddenly stopped, looking very surprised. He gazed up at the slate-grey sky, then snapped his fingers. "Of course!" Slowly he looked from Violet to Derrick to Cerise. "I know who did it," he said, smiling smugly. "It is the least obvious and also the most obvious. It is the only person with a motive for all the crimes, ample opportunity, and the necessary familiarity with the different methods employed." He smiled at each of them again, then said, "Toodle-oo," and started towards the house.

The three of them watched in silence until he disappeared inside.

Two hours later, it was Derrick who discovered Sebastian's body. He'd been killed in a most unpleasant way.

CHAPTER TWENTY-FIVE

VIOLET, DERRICK, AND CERISE STOOD IN ONE OF THE
pantries next to the kitchen, looking at Sebastian's body. Or
rather, at the lower half of his body, which was what hung over
the top of the barrel of vinegar into which he'd been put head
first and drowned.

"Well," Violet eventually said, "it looks like the murderer shares Sebastian's sense of humour."

Cerise looked at Violet, then started to giggle. Derrick
said, "Huh?"

"Don't you see?" Cerise said, still laughing. "A Cornichon
is in a pickle."

"Huh?"

Violet looked at Derrick, shaking her head, then turned to
Cerise and regarded her with more than a little curiosity. "It
also looks," she said, "as though Sebastian was right when he
said he knew who it was. Certainly, someone's silenced him."

Derrick moved a couple of steps away from Violet, and
looked at her with a serious expression. "Your brother also said
that we'd be able to tell which of you was lying if one of you
turned up dead."

"So that means I'm the one?" Violet shook her head. "All
it means is that it wasn't Sebastian. He's innocent . . . of everything, including masquerading as me last night."

"Then you're saying that it was you we saw."

Violet looked coldly at him. "It didn't work the first time. It hasn't improved with repetition."

"But Violet," Cerise said, "we did see you."

With an effort, Violet swallowed the roar of hatred and fury that was rising in her throat, and kept her voice and her gaze level. "All right. We're back to where we were this morning. The lines have been drawn. You have your story. I just have to find out why. And when I do, I guess you'll have to shut me up as well. Or try to."

"Please, Violet," Cerise pleaded. "You're wrong. We don't want to hurt you."

"Of course you don't. If something happened to me, there'd be only the two of you left. That could be awkward, couldn't it?"

"Violet, please——"

Derrick cut Cerise off. "Don't discuss it. If this is the way she wants to be, let her. Just be sure that you're never alone with her, or that you never let her get close to you."

"But it's all right if she gets close to you?" Violet said. "Is that it? You know, when we were speculating about it being Mrs. Hook, you seemed to react very strongly against the idea of a conspiracy. That struck me as odd at the time, but now I see your reason. You wanted to divert attention from the idea of a conspiracy, because that was exactly what was involved."

"You're mad," Derrick said. "I reacted that way because the idea was ridiculous then, and it's even more ridiculous now."

"Is it?"

"Violet, there's no conspiracy," Cerise said.

"You won't convince her of that," Derrick said. "She's been chasing shadows from the beginning, because she can't face the truth."

Violet's eyes narrowed. "And what have you been chasing, Mr. Slick? Mr. Gambler? Mr. Deadbeat? Mr. Lady-Killer?" Violet paused, then smiled. "Mr. Fortune Hunter?"

Derrick flushed. "You stupid, meddling bitch! If you don't——"

"If I don't what? Mind my own business? I already have a pretty good idea of what your business is. 'GOLD—716147.' Have you figured that out yet? I have." Violet smiled as Derrick tried unsuccessfully to appear indifferent. "But what I haven't figured yet is where Cerise fits in."

"Violet, I don't. There's nothing for me to fit into."

"I told you it does no good talking to her," Derrick said to Cerise, moving over next to her. "Violet's already made up her mind, and is not interested in having reality interfere."

Cerise looked at Violet, then at Derrick, then nervously stepped back from him. "Keep away from me!" she shouted. "I don't know what Violet's doing. I don't know what you're up to. I don't know what's going on. But I do know that you'd both better stay away from me."

Violet smiled. "Nice try, sweetie, but it won't wash."

Cerise looked desperately from Violet to Derrick. "My God!" she sobbed. "Is this a dream? When will it end? Or are we all mad? Don't you see what's happening? Mrs. Argus was right: none of us will leave here alive." Crying, she ran from the pantry.

Violet and Derrick warily eyed one another.

"You'd better go after her," Violet said. "Your partner seems to be fraying a bit around the edges."

Derrick stood for a minute, then quickly strode out of the pantry and turned in the opposite direction from Cerise.

Violet remained in the small room, looking at her brother's legs hanging out of the barrel but with her thoughts elsewhere. It was no longer a question of success, or her reputation, or publicity, or even paperback rights. No, none of that seemed important any longer. Now, it was a question of her life.

Violet slowly nodded her head once, as though accepting a challenge, and left the pantry.

So much had happened so quickly that Violet knew there must be a good deal that she had overlooked . . . not to mention the many things she had noticed but couldn't make sense of.

Maybe, she thought, if she went over everything from the beginning, she could find some detail that she'd missed, and that would give her the key that she needed. Thus, later that afternoon, Violet was in her room going over the notes she had made when she'd been planning to turn author.

She had not gotten very far—only to the notes about the first morning—before she found something. And it was no trifle either, she thought, making a face, and then laughed. She'd hoped for a key, and she'd gotten a lock . . . or rather a locked room. In the excitement of the moment, the fact that Mr. Drupe had been found in the classic locked room had somehow failed to register.

Only locked rooms were never really locked; they were merely apparently locked. Violet knew that if you could discover the means of entry—or exit—you could probably determine who'd employed it.

She thought back to that morning—just over three days before but already seeming incredibly distant. They had all run to the study, but the door had been locked. Then . . .? Then Cerise—Cerise!—had said she'd check the terrace windows, and before anyone could stop her, she'd run off. And, if Violet remembered correctly, it had taken her an unaccountably long time to return, and she had seemed slightly winded and flustered. Violet wondered if this was what Sebastian had been thinking of when he talked about one person having the opportunity. She still couldn't see the *why*, but if she could find out the *how*, she'd have the *who*. And then the reason would no longer matter.

Violet hurried down to the study. Everything looked exactly the same as on that morning. She quickly crossed to the french windows, but a careful examination of them convinced her that, unfortunately, what had seemed a good idea upstairs had nothing to support it down here. Both windows were securely bolted at the top and bottom, and the other windows in the room were fixed and could not be opened at all. No, unless some terribly complicated mechanism had been employed, which Violet very much doubted, Cerise could not have entered the room, killed Drupe, and left, locking the windows behind her, in the time available. So much for that theory.

Likewise, the door from the corridor did not seem to lend itself to any manipulation or sleight of hand. It had truly been as it had seemed—locked and bolted.

Violet, a puzzled expression on her face, went back to the desk and sat heavily in the chair in which Mr. Drupe had been found. As she pondered this latest complication, she let her eyes roam over the papers the lawyer had taken out of the safe.

Absorbed as she was in the problem of the locked room, Violet at first failed to notice a familiar name on one of the sheets. Indeed, she was two pages beyond it before she realized what she had seen. She flipped back, and there it was among some of the old household accounts, in a list of the servants who had worked for Mousey's father. No, Violet thought, it couldn't be coincidence; it had to be the same.

The *why* that had thus far stymied her was no longer a mystery. There was a reason—a reason for murder, a reason for conspiracy, a reason that explained a great many things, including a reaction at the dinner table the first night that Violet had wondered about. Two reactions, she corrected herself, as she suddenly recalled the details of a particularly nasty story that Mousey had once told her. And that letter fragment she'd found in Mrs. Hook's hand! With a laugh, Violet realized it was not about Mr. Ching, nor had it concerned anything illegal. Oh, yes, she thought, it all fits together.

Purposefully, Violet stood up and began walking around the room. During that stunning explosion of insight and inspiration, she'd also remembered something she'd once heard about Mousey's grandfather and this house.

Once Violet started tapping on the oak walls, she located the right spot almost at once. It took her much longer to find the hidden switch that caused the section of panelling to slide open, giving access to the secret passage behind. Violet smiled and shook her head: no, a "locked room" was never really locked.

Taking a pocket flashlight out of her purse, she entered the passageway, shutting the secret door behind her. She didn't have to go very far to discover that the passage she was in intersected with several others, and that the house was, in fact, honeycombed with a hidden network of them. Well, Violet thought, the house that old Augustus Sill built had certainly made it easy for him to indulge his twin passions—eavesdropping and jumping out and scaring people; no wonder guests had been less than thrilled to receive invitations to the island. And no wonder, she added, as she climbed a built-in wooden ladder to the second floor, that Mrs. Argus had been able to disappear and reappear so unexpectedly. No doubt she had discovered the passages when she'd stayed at the house years before.

Now Violet needed to know who else had discovered the secret. And, in a passage on the second floor, she found what she was looking for. There, beside one of the passage's access points, was the old map that had been taken from the wall of the study. On the floor next to the map was the Colonel's cane, its silver lion's head all brown and crusty.

So this is the end of the line, Violet thought as she turned off her flashlight. Wondering into whose room she would emerge, she opened the sliding panel.

At first she couldn't understand why it was so dark. She put her hand out in front of her and almost cried out when she touched something soft and furry, then realized that she was in a large wardrobe. She listened a moment before opening the closet door. From the fine fabrics she had brushed up against in the closet, Violet already knew she would step into Derrick's room, and she did.

The temptation was great, but Violet didn't linger in the room. She doubted that she'd find much of anything, and anyway she already had more than enough.

She crossed the room and opened the door. She stepped out, then froze as she saw a door open at the other end of the hall. It was the door to *her* room. It was Derrick who came through it. He too stopped in place as he saw Violet. They stared the length of the hallway at each other but did not speak or move. Then they each shut the doors and went in opposite directions, so they would not pass one another.

It was late afternoon. Cerise was walking alone on the shore, gazing out at the water. For the first time since their arrival, the clouds had lifted. The air was cold, but brilliantly clear. It was so clear that, even at a distance of several miles, Cerise could see a light on another island. Indeed, it was so clear that, as she looked in that direction, she thought she could almost make out a figure moving in front of the light.

Suddenly it came to her, as clear as the late-afternoon weather. It all fit. She knew the answer.

She considered trying to signal. If that light was visible, a light from her would be as well. Then she laughed sadly, maybe even ironically, as she realized that it would be pointless even to try.

CHAPTER TWENTY-SIX

It was the morning of the fifth day on Komondor Island. The three survivors sat well apart at the dining-room table, uneasily eyeing one another.

After a long and tense silence, Violet looked at Cerise and casually asked, "How's Rebecca?"

"Who?" Cerise said, but Violet had seen her stiffen momentarily, and she knew she was right.

"Rebecca Redford. Isn't that your mother's name?"

Cerise stared at Violet, then said, "Yes."

"The same Rebecca Redford who used to work here as a maid?"

Cerise looked down and mumbled something.

"What'd you say?"

Cerise looked up again. "I said, 'Yes, it's the same Becky.'" Her voice was hard and flat.

Violet looked at her for a long while, nodding her head, then asked softly, "Where is it . . . ? The mark?"

"All right! If it will make you happy." Cerise pushed up the sleeve of the blue sweatshirt she was wearing. Just below her shoulder was a small, fin-shaped strawberry birthmark.

"I say!"

Violet looked disgustedly at Derrick. "Oh, cut out the act! You're not very good, and it's a little late to try and pull that one."

"Okay, Violet," Cerise said. "You found out. Yes,

Rebecca Redford is my mother. Yes, she worked here. Yes, I'm a bastard. Yes, that son of a bitch, Ripley Sill, was my father. Yes, I am Rosa's half-sister."

"I say!"

"Shut up!" Violet said, not turning to Derrick, but keeping her eyes on Cerise. "I told you I'd find the reason, and that when I did it would all be over."

Cerise smiled sadly. "Oh, it's all over, all right. But what is the reason? That I'm the one?"

"Yes."

Cerise shook her head. "For quite a while I was afraid I might be."

"But now you're saying you're not?"

"No, I'm not. It doesn't make much sense for it to be me, does it . . . ? Oh, I admit I came here planning to have it out with Rosa, and absolutely determined to get half the estate. If she didn't share it, I was going to sue. And I also admit that I grew up hating Rosa, because I thought that she had such an easy life while my mother had it so rough. Now, of course, no one cares that much about this sort of thing, but when I was born it was a much bigger deal. When I got to know Rosa, though, I found that in most ways her life had been much worse than mine. I even felt a little sorry for her."

"How touching."

Cerise shrugged. "I don't care if you believe me, Violet. It really doesn't matter any more. I won't deny it looks as if I had a reason to kill Rosa. Maybe if I had confronted her—if she got upset and we fought—maybe under those circumstances it could have happened. But I never saw her here alive."

"That's what you say."

"Well, it's true. Don't you remember? I told you that I heard Budgie and the Colonel in their room. So I couldn't have had the opportunity."

Violet nodded. "That's what I assumed for quite a while. Until I realized that at the time you made your assertion, the Colonel was dead and Budgie was gaga. So neither of them was in a position either to verify what you said you heard, or to say in turn that they heard *you* in *your* room. No, you provided your own alibi, and that's not good enough."

"All right, Violet," Cerise sighed. "So I might have killed Rosa, presumably either by accident, or in anger, or to get the estate. But assuming that I did, what would be the point of continuing? The estate's worthless. Actually, after all my plans, all my anticipating, I found it quite funny when we learned that there was nothing left."

Violet smiled. "But there would be a point if the estate was not worthless. If, in fact, there was—at today's prices— several million dollars' worth of gold buried somewhere on the island. It might be worthwhile killing quite a few people for that, mightn't it?"

"What are you talking about?"

"Oh, give it up. I'm talking about the other half of the arrangement. I knew you two were in something together, but I couldn't make it fit together until yesterday. Now, it makes perfect sense. I don't know whether it was planned beforehand, or decided upon after you got here. It hardly matters. It's a natural partnership, though—the heir to a seemingly worthless estate, and the person who thinks he knows where a treasure is buried on property that belongs to the estate."

"What are you talking about?" Cerise repeated.

"So you want to play dumb? Suit yourself," Violet said, and turned towards Derrick. "You haven't located it yet, have you?"

Derrick looked at Violet without much warmth, then said, "No."

"Where did you get that code? Did you have it before, or did you find it here?"

Derrick hesitated, then shrugged. "I'd seen a catalogue of Augustus Sill's collection of historical papers. The catalogue showed that there was a cryptogram among the papers that had belonged to a Loyalist who I remembered was supposed to have taken part in the theft of the Continental Congress' treasury. As you know, that gold was never found, nor does anyone know what happened to the Loyalists after they came to this island. I thought the cryptogram might have the answer."

"But you haven't managed to decode it yet, have you? Is that what you were doing in my room? Looking for the translation? Is that why you took my notebook?" Derrick stared at Violet, but did not speak, and Violet took a piece of paper from her purse. "I would never leave something like this lying around. You know, it was really very simple. Two hundred years ago they weren't very sophisticated in these matters. I'm surprised that book on cryptography you were looking at didn't help you, since this is about as basic as they come. After all, the key is given right with the code. 'GOLD—716147.' Each letter has a numerical value. G is the seventh letter of the alphabet, and its number is seven. O is the fifteenth, but its number is 16, and L is the twelfth while its number is 14. Each letter in the word increases by an additional increment. The same thing was done in the cryptogram proper, only there all letters were used instead of numbers, and it was all run together. Thus the first three letters of the cryptogram are 'TFP'. T is the same because it starts the word, F is one letter beyond the correct one, and P is two letters beyond. So the word is 'ten'. The only problem is figuring out where each new word begins in order to get the progression right. Your message starts off, 'Ten paces northeast of the main cairn.' Then it goes on to relate distances to the great oak and the round rock."

"Oh," Derrick said.

"Not much good, is it? Unless you know where those things are. Unless you have an old map that shows where at least some of them had once been located. Unless you know enough about old surveying techniques to be able to relate a map to the real thing. I assume that is why you were studying those books on map-making practices."

"Violet," Cerise said, "are you saying that Derrick and I have been working together in order to get this treasure? But it doesn't make sense. Why kill all those people?"

"Still playing dumb, sweetie? Okay, by the numbers. One,

Rosa: so you can inherit. Two, Drupe: because he might have known about you; or perhaps because you had to get the map and he just happened to be in the way. Three and four, the Colonel and Budgie: so your alibi remained intact, so there'd be no question of sharing the estate with the aunt and uncle, and so the Colonel didn't get to the treasure first. Five, Mrs. Hook: because she somehow got hold of Mousey's letter naming you as her illegitimate half-sister. That would be enough for her to figure out that you were involved in what was going on. Especially if Mousey also included that story about your expulsion from medical school."

"That was a lie!" Cerise screamed.

"Was it? What had Mousey told me? That you were kicked out because you got a little too much pleasure out of dissection? Wasn't that it? What did they call it? Just a touch of sadistic psychosis? Wouldn't that kind of personality disorder fit with the way people keep getting carved up around here? You certainly put your training in dissection to good use on Mousey, but you got a bit sloppy with the others."

"I told you—and I told Rosa—that story was a complete lie. You want to know what happened? One of the professors made a play for me. I turned him down and reported him. So the creep, to get off the hook, made up that story about my being a sadist. Naturally he was believed, and I was out. That's why I'm sensitive about references to med school. Another piggish man messing up my life."

Violet nodded. "You know, I believe that by this point you have convinced yourself of the truth of that story. Of course, in view of everything that's happened, you might have some difficulty convincing anyone else of it. . . . Now, where was I? Number five, Mrs. Hook. Number six, Mr. Ching: I don't know, maybe Mrs. Hook had told him what she'd learned, or maybe he was going for help and you couldn't permit that before you were ready. Seven, Mrs. Argus: because, no matter what you thought about the man, she still killed your father, and you had to repay that. Eight, my brother: he figured it out— I don't know how—and you, who always found him so amusing, killed him in a way he would've appreciated. Did that help to ease your conscience? Though I guess you're not often much troubled by guilt, are you, sweetie?"

"Are you through, Violet?"

"Oh, yes. I think so."

"Then why don't I tell you who's doing this?" Cerise stood up, went to the sideboard, and poured some coffee in her cup. "It came to me yesterday afternoon when I was standing by the water."

She paused and took a sip of her coffee. At that instant Derrick jumped to his feet and cried, "Wait! Don't drink that!"

Cerise looked at him, then swallowed. "It's—" Suddenly her eyes opened wide. Her hands clutched at her throat, and liquid gagging sounds came from her mouth. Her face contorted in a spasm of pain. A tremendous convulsion seized her body. She fell to the floor, writhing, then went still. And rigid. And dead.

Violet and Derrick looked at one another and slowly moved even farther apart.

CHAPTER TWENTY-SEVEN

LATER THAT MORNING, VIOLET STOOD ON THE SLOPING lawn below the house, looking out at the grey water. Her body was tense, her senses alert, her eyes and mouth hard with determination. As Derrick approached her from the house, she drew a gun—taken from the display of weapons in the lounge—out of her purse and trained it on him. As he got close, she saw that he, too, held a revolver, which he pointed at her.

"I think that's far enough," she said when he was ten feet from her. "What's your plan now? Kill me, hunt for the treasure, then somehow get away before anyone comes for us? Just disappear, leaving ten bodies and a giant mystery behind, and hope that in the confusion no one ever connects you with this island? Maybe use Drupe's plane ticket to get down to South America?"

Derrick looked at Violet without reaction, his gaze and the gun both steady. "I came down to tell you that I intend to leave here alive. If I have to kill a rabid bitch to do so, I will. So you'd better keep your distance."

"You really had me fooled," Violet went on, as though he had not spoken. "I must have assumed that anyone who seemed so dumb and always acted so suspiciously and guiltily couldn't possibly be the one. I still don't know if you are inept but lucky, or if this was all a pose to distract us. You know, that's an interesting approach—to look so uneasy and to make it so clear that you're hiding something that no one ever takes you seriously, because it's all too obvious. If you can bluff like that, I'm surprised you haven't done better at poker. Or do you lose your money at other games?" Derrick neither moved nor spoke, so Violet shrugged and continued. "I'm not yet certain which ones you did and which Cerise did. At first, I thought that she had done most. Now, seeing that I may have underestimated you, I'm not so sure. That was certainly a nice manoeuvre you made the first night, after we found poor Mousey. You'd forgotten all about the boathouse. If we'd been able to get away from here, your plans would've fallen apart, but you covered nicely. You volunteered to check it out, and left before anyone could stop you. That was when you destroyed the boats, wasn't it?"

Derrick did not reply, and his expression remained blank and unchanged.

"I guess you were the one who did Drupe," Violet said. "After all, your dislike of him was pretty clear, and he knew enough about you and your relationship with Mousey to make things very awkward. You obviously also killed the Colonel. Although why I accepted your ridiculous story about falling in the mud right before we found the Colonel in that hole I'll never know. I guess that, once again, you were so obvious I couldn't even consider you as a possibility. Budgie? I should have realized that you were the only one strong enough to tear that room apart. . . . " Violet paused for a reaction, but still there was none. "I think that maybe things started falling apart at that point. You tried to frame Mrs. Hook using the handkerchief, but she wouldn't co-operate, so you had to eliminate her. And Mr. Ching as well, probably for the same reason. But things had to stop sometime, and you still needed a scapegoat. Who better than mad old Mrs. Argus? You threw suspicion on her by identifying the knot in the rope as one used by sailors. I didn't think of it at the time, but now I see that if you could identify it as a sailor's knot, that meant you could also have tied it. Then you must've decided it would work better to have it be me, so you killed Mrs. Argus in order to set up the frame. Then my brother became a threat, so exit Sebastian.

"As I said," Violet went on, "Cerise may have had a hand in some of those, but the latest one was all yours. Any lingering doubts I may have had entirely disappeared after that. What was the idea? You knew I'd figure it all out, so you had to silence me? What'd you do—put poison in the coffee the last time you took some? Intended for me? Only Cerise drank it before I did, and you reacted too slowly to stop her?"

"I didn't put any poison anywhere," Derrick said.

"No? Then, if you didn't poison the coffee, how do you explain your attempt to warn her?"

Derrick looked at Violet for a long time before speaking. "You don't know, do you? You really don't know. Your brother was right after all."

"What are you talking about?"

"I knew the coffee was poisoned because I read that it was."

"What?"

"I read it in your notebook, Violet."

"What do you mean? What are you playing at now?"

Derrick sadly shook his head. "I'm not playing at anything. I was looking for that code yesterday in your room. And I took your notebook to see if it was in there. As you said, it wasn't. Instead, I found a summary of all the murders."

"Yes. I made those notes. So?"

"So this was yesterday, Violet. And the last entry was for a murder that did not take place until today."

From inside his coat Derrick took out Violet's notebook. He tossed it across to her and it dropped at her feet. Keeping a close watch on Derrick, Violet cautiously knelt, picked it up, and stood again. She turned to the last page with writing on it. There, following her account of Sebastian's death, was one further sentence: "On the morning of the fifth day, Cerise died from swallowing an unknown, untraceable poison."

Violet threw the notebook down. "What are you trying to do? Isn't it obvious that that's not my writing? It's not even close. You just put that in this morning. What do you expect to accomplish with a feeble stunt like that?"

"It's not my writing, Violet. And it was there yesterday."

"Do you expect me—or anyone else—to believe that? Come on!"

"You'd better believe it, Violet, because it's true. Just as it was true that Cerise and I saw you with Mrs. Argus. Face it, Violet. Your brother was right. It's been you all along, only you haven't known it. You've been chasing yourself, Violet."

"Don't be absurd."

"It's not absurd, it's the only explanation. You've got some kind of split personality. Half of you is a detective and the other half is a murderer. How else were you always able to find *the* bit of incriminating evidence that you needed each time? You knew it was there because you planted it. Or your murdering personality planted it in order for your detective half to find it."

"No," Violet said, shaking her head from side to side. "No. It can't be."

"Violet, it is. What else is there? That note cinches it. It was written by that other personality inside you. It knew what was going to happen."

"No, I didn't write that! I would know about it if I had, and I didn't."

"You wouldn't necessarily know, Violet. And who did write it, then?"

"What about Hacker?"

"There is no Hacker, Violet. There is only us."

"I see what you're trying to do!" Violet cried, her voice rising to a scream. "You're trying to drive me mad. That's how you're going to get away. You're going to pin it on poor mad Violet. Well, it won't work! You'll see! You'll be sorry! Now, you just stay away! Keep back! I'm warning you!"

Suddenly a shot rang out. Derrick's lower jaw dropped and his eyes rolled upwards as a wet red hole appeared in the centre of his forehead, and he crumpled to the ground.

Did I do that? Violet wondered; I guess they must be right about me. Christ!

She looked at the gun in her hand.

It had not been fired.

CHAPTER TWENTY-EIGHT

VIOLET DIDN'T SCREAM OR SOB OR TREMBLE. SHE HARDLY even reacted.

She looked down at the corpse and clicked her tongue a couple of times. "So that's that," she said, then smiled. "Guess it wasn't old Derrick," she added with a giggle.

She went up to the house. One of the french windows to the lounge was open, and a still-smoking rifle lay on the floor.

"Okay, whoever you are," Violet called out. "Let's get this over with."

Silence.

Then a roll of thunder, like rumbling laughter, broke near the house.

"Come on!" Violet shouted, looking up at the ceiling, feet spread apart, hands on her hips. "Come on!"

Suddenly, Violet felt herself picked up, seized as though in a giant hand, shaken. A unbelievable force, superhuman, godlike in its strength, hurled her across the room.

So powerful was the force that when she struck the wall she was killed instantly, on contact. The impact was so great that it compressed her spine, and when she dropped to the floor, she was several inches shorter than she had been in life.

As Sebastian might have said, for the first, last, and only time, his normally gregarious, outgoing sister could now genuinely be called a shrinking violet.

Again the big house was silent.

Then the thunder rolled again, another peal of cosmic laughter shaking the house, filling it, echoing down empty corridors.

The thunder passed and the house became still.

With a crackle of static, the ancient radio in the lounge came back to life. "We bring you a news bulletin," it announced to the empty room. "Francis Hacker, the fugitive psychopathic killer, has been apprehended trying to cross into Mexico. We repeat: Francis Hacker has been caught. The danger is over."

EPILOGUE: CONVERSATION IN LIMBO

I

VIOLET CORNICHON walked down the long corridor. At least she thought it was a corridor. Certainly it felt like one, although the pale, luminous, faintly iridescent grey that surrounded her provided no indication of where the walls stopped and the floor and ceiling began.

She came to an arrow hanging on the "wall" pointing in the direction she was going. Superimposed on it were the words, WAITING ROOM. What the hell is happening? she thought.

She continued walking and soon saw a figure in the distance. As she drew closer, she saw it was an elderly man dressed in a priest's cassock. He had a fringe of bright white hair, merry twinkling eyes, and a friendly welcoming smile. He seemed to be expecting her.

"Come along, Violet," he said with a pleasant Oxonian accent. "They're all waiting."

"Where the hell am I?"

"Not there, I can assure you. Now, come along, please."

Violet held her ground, feet spread, hands on her slender hips, rising defiance showing in her eyes. "Just who are you?"

"Oh, forgive me," the priest said, smiling and shaking his

head. "Most inconsiderate of me. My name's Knox. Ronald Knox.* Now, please come along."

Making a face and shrugging, she followed Father Knox through a doorway (though again she could perceive no lintel or jambs) into what seemed to be a much larger open area. Violet had an impression of space, but without any point of reference to provide a focus or a sense of scale; it was like being inside a giant glass ball surrounded by glowing but impenetra-

---

*Unlike the other characters in this book, Monsignor Ronald A. Knox (1888-1957) was a real person. He was Catholic chaplain at Oxford for many years, and a lifelong devotee of the mystery story, who wrote several detective novels himself. Knox was also the subject of a biography by Evelyn Waugh, but he may be best known as the author of the Ten Commandments of Detection, published in 1929.

"A Detective Story Decalogue"

I. The criminal must be someone mentioned in the early part of the story, but must not be anyone whose thoughts the reader has been allowed to follow.

II. All supernatural or preternatural agencies are ruled out as a matter of course.

III. Not more than one secret room or passage is allowable.

IV. No hitherto undiscovered poisons may be used, nor any appliance which will need a long scientific explanation at the end.

V. No Chinaman must figure in the story.

VI. No accident must ever help the detective, nor must he ever have an unaccountable intuition which proves to be right.

VII. The detective must not himself commit the crime.

VIII. The detective must not light on any clues which are not instantly produced for the inspection of the reader.

IX. The stupid friend of the detective, the Watson, must not conceal any thoughts which pass through his mind; his intelligence must be slightly, but very slightly, below that of the average reader.

X. Twin brothers, and doubles generally, must not appear unless we have been duly prepared for them.

ble fog. It was warm and comfortable, though, and Violet assumed that this was the Waiting Room.

"Come along, Violet."

She followed the priest and soon saw a long conference table, coming from which she heard the sounds of a heated discussion. As she came nearer, she saw that the nine people around the table were her former companions from Komondor Island, all apparently restored to their original state, unbloody, unhacked, unbludgeoned, unshot, all whole and hale and hearty.

Violet moved closer, and conversation at the table trailed off, then stopped entirely as, one by one, the speakers noticed her.

"You see! I told you it wasn't Violet," Sebastian said, then turned towards his sister. "Violet, some of them have been saying that you were the one who done it—I mean who did it. Why, Mr. Drupe, here, and Derrick have even taken to calling you Violent. That's not entirely inappropriate, but I insisted that they were wrong. It wasn't you. And now you're here, so I guess I was right. It wasn't you, was it?"

Violet stared coolly at her brother, shook her head, sighed, then sat down at the empty place. "No, it wasn't me."

Sounds of surprise, confusion, and puzzlement greeted this simple statement. Sebastian flashed a big smile at Mr. Drupe, who merely sniffed and clicked his teeth twice.

"Wait a second," Violet said. "Do you mean that none of you knows who did it?"

"Well, I think I know," Sebastian said. "And Cerise thinks she knows."

"But didn't anyone see who it was?"

"Hee, hee, hee," Mrs. Argus said. Her eyes were glazed, and her hair stood straight out around her head in a wild electrified halo; even more than usual, she resembled Charlton Heston after his conversation with the burning bush.

"Mrs. Loony Tunes here did, but all she'll say is that she was glad she met her Maker."

"Hee, hee, hee."

"Oh, shut up!" Sebastian said.

"You mean, none of us is a murderer?"

"Now, Sis, I didn't say that. There are at least two that I know of for sure. Mrs. Argus and Mrs. Hook."

"Then. . . . But they couldn't. . . . How . . . ?"

"I didn't say they were *our* killers, Violet. It was a long time ago."

"What?" Violet said weakly, slumping in her chair, her pale, pretty face looking utterly confused.

"Maybe I'd better summarize so you'll know what's what." Sebastian looked around the table to see if there were any objections, but everyone indicated he should go ahead. "First, your friend Mousey was only half-right in her accusation against Mrs. Argus, and even then for the wrong reasons. The death of Mousey's mother was a genuine accident, for which Mrs. Argus—wrongly—felt so responsible that it unbalanced her. The father, though, was another story. Apparently old Ripley was a prime candidate for the Swine Hall of Fame. He was so busy chasing the ladies that he barely noticed his wife's death. On top of everything else, this was highly upsetting for Mrs. Argus. But when he started chasing *her*, it was too much. She figured Mousey had to be better off as an orphan, and one fine morning she dropped a gargoyle on Ripley's head. I gather that the sounds of cheering and celebration were heard across four counties.

"I don't blame you at all, dear," Budgie said, patting Mrs. Argus on the arm while looking steadily at her husband.

The Colonel shifted in his seat, hmphed and cleared his throat, but said nothing. Mrs. Argus said, "Hee, hee, hee."

"Mrs. Hook," Sebastian continued, "is in fact that Milch woman—though she'll always be Hook to me." He smiled at her, but received only a stony gaze in return. "She did wipe out the nine members of that family she worked for, but she still insists it was an honest mistake. While I do not want to suggest that I in any way doubt this assertion, I still intend to eat nothing but canned food that I open myself when La Hook is around."

"Fine," she said, glowering. "Less work for a body."

"So neither of them had anything to do with anything?" Violet said.

"That's right."

"Then it must be——"

"Hold on, Sis. Don't go jumping to conclusions again, until you have all the information. Mr. Drupe is, of course, a sleazy, corrupt, contemptible, crooked, pettifogging shyster. He is not, however, an embezzler. Or, at least from Mousey, he's not. There was nothing left in the estate, because it had almost all gone by the time Ripley died. He must've spent money even faster than me. It was only exceptionally good management on Mr. Drupe's part that made what remained of the estate last as long as it did. He was fleeing down to Rio, all right, but that was in connection with an entirely different matter. In fact, he delayed his departure so he could explain to Mousey Squeak just how things stood."

"But what about all of his nonsensical obstructionism?" Violet asked.

Sebastian shrugged. "The habits of a lifetime. Also, he really couldn't afford to get involved in a criminal investigation; the authorities were on his tail, and he had to get out fast." He looked at the lawyer, who nodded and indicated that Sebastian should go on. "Also, Violet, he finds you to be a self-centred, selfish, nasty, vindictive, greedy, grasping, self-promoting young woman who has a grossly exaggerated idea of her own importance, intelligence, and ability." Sebastian smiled pleasantly. "In other words, Sis, he thinks you're a stupid bitch——"

"Hear, hear!" said the Colonel.

"—and he enjoyed doing anything he could to get in your way, even when it involved acting stupidly himself. Apparently, he feels much the same way about you that you do about him."

Violet, eyes flashing, looked into the smiling faces of her brother and the lawyer for a long time before she nodded once and relaxed. "And the Colonel didn't kill him?"

"Hmph!"

"Of course not, Sis. Haven't you figured out that the

Colonel is nearly a total fraud? He was never in the Far East, never in the war, never wounded. Probably never even in the army. He is definitely an insufferable bore, a boor, and a pig. Like most people who are completely unaware of anything outside of themselves, he is wildly insensitive to other people, and rides his hobbyhorses roughshod over them with monomaniacal dedication. Still, for all of his talk about violence, his only involvement with it is whatever he can get poor Budgie to inflict upon him. You could say that he's a typical product of British public schools. Besides, Violet, why would he kill Mr. Drupe?"

"I don't know. Something to do with the treasure?"

"Oh, he is indeed obsessed with that. However, since he can never figure out which direction is north, all the maps in the world aren't much help."

"Then maybe he was afraid that Drupe knew about what he did to Mousey."

"Entirely unsubstantiated hearsay, Miss Cornichon," the lawyer said with a thin-lipped smile.

"That's right, Sis. The Colonel is a foul, disgusting old man with abundant malignant kinks, but child molestation is not necessarily one of them. I'm not saying that it's not true; just that we don't know, and that it doesn't enter in here."

Violet rubbed her blue eyes and shook her head. "I suppose you're going to tell me next that Aunt Budgie doesn't hate the Colonel."

"Of course she hates him! Don't be silly. How could she help it? She just didn't kill him. No matter what she says she'd like, she'd never leave her husband—never. She detests him, but she also knows that without him her life would be empty, meaningless, and quite without focus. Surely you recognized that theirs is a symbiotic relationship of mutually satisfying misery, antagonism, and conflict. His role is to make waves; hers is to smooth them over. Maybe she hates the role, but it's the only one she has. That's why she fell apart after he was killed. She realized that she'd lost her purpose." Sebastian turned to Budgie. "How'd I do?"

"Just fine, dear."

"Then," Violet sighed, "Derrick must have killed the Colonel."

"I say!"

"Why, Sis? The treasure again? Come on. Oh, he might well have killed to protect the treasure if he'd found it, but since he hadn't. . . ."

"But he returned to the house all muddy, just after the Colonel was killed."

"What did he say? That he fell?" Sebastian shrugged. "He fell. It's that simple."

"But—"

Mr. Drupe cleared his throat with a rasping sound. "Perhaps, Miss Cornichon, it is your involvement in the cosmetics field that is responsible for the difficulty you have distinguishing between what is and what seems to be. Surely you, of all people—since your business is solely concerned with appearance—should know that appearance is not necessarily indicative of anything . . . except itself. Yet, you persist both in reading more into the appearance of things than is actually warranted, and in ignoring the fact that other possibilities may well lie beneath the surface."

Violet gave the lawyer a chilly smile. "I suppose I should listen to you, Mr. Drupe, since you, too, have made a career out of covering up your clients' blemishes."

Mr. Drupe's dentures snapped closed with a brisk click.

"As I was explaining," Sebastian hastily put in, "Derrick might have killed to protect the treasure. His situation is desperate. He's a gambler, deeply in debt. Even worse, he's not been a very fortunate fortune hunter; the word was getting around on him, and his little Pinky was just about his last chance to score. Derrick's character is certainly not very appealing or classy. And he's definitely not all that swift. Oh, I must admit that he's not as dumb as you and I made him out to be, but he's not precisely top-of-the-line in that department either. But still, the only thing he's guilty of is being interested in his Pinky's money. As were you, Violet; as was Cerise. Though at least she had something of a legitimate—or illegitimate, if you wish—claim to part of the estate. She'd even developed some interest in and affection for her half-sister. You and Derrick, however, had no real interest in the Pink Mouse, except insofar as you could manipulate her. Now, don't get upset: I'm hardly one to pass judgement; I'm just trying to get things clear."

Sebastian paused for a moment. "Now what else is there? Oh, yes. Violet, you and I are both pretty far around the bend, though not necessarily the same bend. We are both seriously disturbed individuals. I, at least, have never denied it; I recognize it, accept it, perhaps even revel in the cachet it gives me. Besides, I'm basically harmless. While I can be annoying and selfish and inconsiderate, mostly I'm just frivolously self-destructive. You, though, have a real capacity for violence—as Mr. Drupe and Derrick rightly perceived—over which your control is at best tenuous. You dislike being thwarted, you have a tendency to lash out at anyone who gets in your way, and I do believe that you are capable of just about anything if you think it will further your interests. It's quite conceivable that you could have killed the lot of us—or most of us—in order to get some much-needed publicity."

"Only I didn't."

"I know you didn't. And besides, bad as it is, your mental health is not much—if at all—worse than anyone else's. Indeed, I suspect that Cerise—who was the only one who worried about cracking up—is probably the least crazy, most decent person here."

"You only say that because she laughs at your jokes," Violet said.

"Well, she does have marvellously good taste and a wonderful sense of humour."

Violet rolled her eyes. "Give me a break. Are you through yet, Sebastian? It seems as though you've been running on forever."

"Yes, I guess that's it. . . . No, it's not. I forgot Mr. Ching." He turned to the cook. "Sorry about that."

Mr. Ching folded his muscular arms and growled something in Mandarin.

"You were right, Sis, to be suspicious of his cooking.

Certainly, that was the most suspicious-looking kedgeree that I've ever seen. But, except for the quality, there was nothing sinister about it. Mr. Ching is actually a very accomplished cook. It's just that he has the idea that Occidentals only like bad food. So that's what he prepares."

The Colonel loudly cleared his throat.

Sebastian nodded. "Right. I should also point out that the Colonel was pretty close when he accused Mr. Ching of being an enemy agent."

"What?"

"Calm down, Violet, you're starting to squawk. He's not an *enemy* agent, more like a friendly one. Besides being a good cook, he's also a trained psychologist. He was put in place by Mr. Drupe in order to observe Mousey, and also to keep an eye on the predators that were circling around her. When Mr. Drupe was killed, he felt that he had some obligation to figure out what was going on. That's why he kept making notes. And his mad kung-fu act was to make sure that people kept their distance and didn't penetrate his cover."

"But what about the footsteps next to Mrs. Hook's body?"

"He's a powerful swimmer, as his arms and shoulders suggest. He decided he had to try to reach the mainland for help. He'd put on the wetsuit and fins, and was about to leave, when he heard Mrs. Hook scream. He went to investigate, but it was too late."

"Misleading appearances again," Violet sighed, shaking her head. "Are you going to tell me that it was Hacker after all?"

"No, it wasn't, Violet," Father Knox said. "He—it turned out to be Francis with an 'i'—was far away. He's now back in his cell, heavily sedated."

"So that's it," Derrick said. "It wasn't Hacker. We're all here. It wasn't any of us. What's the story?"

Suddenly, Violet sat up straight, eyes gleaming, and snapped her fingers. She had an idea...or the glimmer of an idea. All was not yet lost; damn! she thought, I might still be able to redeem something from this mess.

"No, we're not all here," Violet said. "One of us is missing. Though it's easy to see why this was not commented upon. Since her presence was almost never noticed, it's hardly surprising that her absence should go unremarked."

"I say! You mean——"

"Of course! I mean your fiancée, my friend, Budgie's niece, et cetera, et cetera. I mean the person who was responsible for our all being together in the first place. I mean the person who—rightly or wrongly—felt she had grievances against us, who thought we were using her, taking advantage of her in different ways. I mean the person who—and here I must, however reluctantly, acknowledge Mr. Drupe's earlier contribution—has provided abundant evidence of her paranoia, her neuroses, her delusions, and her generally unbalanced condition. I mean the person whom I've been calling 'poor little Mousey', but who not only started to roar, but turned into a goddamned avenging Fury."

"I appreciate your acknowledgment, Miss Cornichon, however belated," Mr. Drupe said. "But while this latest analysis is certainly dramatic and unexpected, you seem to be ignoring the fact that we all saw Miss Sill's terribly mutilated body. You're not suggesting she reconstituted herself while lying in the meat locker?"

"Obviously I'm not suggesting that, Mr. Drupe. Look, I'm not saying I have all the answers, only that I see the direction in which we have to look. To begin with, there was the very awfulness of the corpse itself. Not exactly conducive to lingering contemplation, was it? What did you all do? You took in the birthmark, the decapitated head, the rest of it. You were all expecting Rosa, so you saw Rosa, and then you averted your eyes. Hell! I examined the body, but I didn't gaze into Mousey's dead little bloodshot eyes. Did any of you?"

"I say! She's right about that. I caught a glimpse of what lay on that coal pile, and that was enough. I looked at the wall, or the ceiling, or my fingernails, but I wouldn't look down."

"Neither would I, dear."

"Sis, are you saying that that wasn't Mousey?"

Violet smiled and nodded. "Precisely. Think about it: if it

wasn't Mousey, then it all makes sense. We all know that Mousey's father—dear Ripley—spread his genes lavishly around the countryside. The Colonel said that there must be dozens of little bastards around, all bearing the distinctive Sill birthmark. Well, if Ripley passed that along, why not other characteristics as well? Look at Cerise. If you took off her make-up, and changed her hair style and colour, she'd look a lot like Mousey. The similarity wouldn't stand up to much scrutiny, but if you saw her only briefly, at a distance and in poor light, you could take her to be Rosa. Especially if you were expecting to see Rosa."

There were murmurs of surprise as everyone studied Cerise, and realized that Violet was correct about the resemblance.

"Hey!" Cerise said. "You're not saying that I'm involved, are you?"

Violet shook her head. "You're here, therefore you're not."

"Or that I'm Rosa, or something?"

"Hmm. That's an interesting idea. . . . But no. I'm saying that with such a large sample to choose from, it wouldn't have been that difficult for Mousey to have found someone who looked sufficiently like her to serve as a stand-in. Especially since death—particularly violent death—can dramatically alter appearances. Especially when she could ensure that the remains would be so grisly that no one would look closely at them. And especially when she knew that people tended to look through her, that no one ever paid enough attention to her to know what she really looked like anyway. And if all that was not enough, a little judicious application of make-up would take care of the difference."

"Oh, dear," Budgie said, putting a little hand on her bosom. "Another pair of doubles. This is getting too confusing for me."

"So you're saying that was not little Pinky that we found, but——"

Violet nodded to Derrick. "But another illegitimate half-sister."

"But why? Why would Pinky do this, kill an innocent stranger?"

"It's clear Mousey was deeply disturbed and bore festering grudges against most of us. It's equally clear she went right over the edge. She decided to get even once and for all. She decided to kill us, came up with a plan, and put it into action. Not only did she want to kill us, but she wanted the pleasure of seeing us struggle, groping blindly after the answers. And what better way could there be for a murderer to deflect all suspicion from herself than to appear to be the first victim? We would look in every direction, but never at Mousey...the pieces of whom, after all, were sitting in the freezer. And once she'd decided to kill ten or so people, I doubt that she troubled herself much about the innocence of the eleventh."

"My little Pinky?" Derrick said, pale beneath his dark tan. "But how could she manage it all?"

"That's the other half of it," Violet said. "She's the only person who could manage it. The house was a labyrinth of secret passages, as I discovered too late. Apparently old Augustus liked to spy on his guests or jump out and scare them...a nice host. But Mousey did him quite a few better. There were stairs and tunnels and passages going all over. Mrs. Argus knew all about them—and used them—because she'd been in the house before. The only other person who could've known about them was Mousey herself, either from seeing her grandfather's plans, or from coming out to the island and investigating. With the freedom of movement that the secret passages provided, she could do virtually anything. That's why we thought someone was looking at us. That's why the murderer was able to strike at will and remain invisible and undetected. Think about it," Violet said, smiling, feeling pretty good about things. "It all fits. It can only be Rosa herself."

The stunned silence that greeted Violet's pronouncement lasted only a few seconds before Sebastian merrily cried, "Wrong again, Violet!"

"Oh, I'm wrong, am I?" Her eyes flashed. "If I'm wrong, why isn't she here? Huh? Where is she?"

"Actually, Violet," Father Knox said stepping forward, "it

was determined that Rosa didn't have to stop here. She went right on to her final destination."

"Oh," Violet said softly, and then pointed up, raising her eyebrows.

Father Knox shook his head.

"Then where the hell is she?"

"Right you are, this time."

"What? You don't mean——" Violet pointed downwards.

Father Knox nodded.

"But Mousey didn't do anything. Oh, she was a drip and a twerp, but that's all. Everything was done *to* her. If she was crazy, it was only because we—and everyone else and everything else—conspired to make her so. She was the victim."

"Be that as it may. . . ." Father Knox shrugged.

"But it's not fair."

The priest stared incredulously at Violet, then put his hand over his mouth and turned away so he wouldn't laugh in her face.

Sebastian, not nearly so polite, did laugh.

"Real funny, huh? You think you're so damn smart? You think you can do better?"

"Maybe not better," Sebastian said. "But certainly more correctly."

"Oh, yeah? Then enlighten us. Please."

"Well, Sis, it came to me when I realized we really were being observed. It wasn't nerves or imagination; we were being watched. Still are, if you'll notice. And you were right that someone wanted to see us squirm, liked seeing us stumbling around in the dark. Enjoyed watching our discomfiture, enjoyed seeing us dance to a lunatic tune. This is someone who's a voyeur, who's obviously a sadist, who possesses abundant knowledge of the ways in which pain and death can be inflicted. Who likes to see it done. I said it was someone who is simultaneously the most and least obvious suspect, and it is. It is someone who is always with us, looking at us so to speak, but who is invisible, whom we can never see."

"Get on with it, would you?" Violet said. "Who is this spectre?"

Sebastian looked around the table, then stood up. He began to pace, eyes straining to pierce the pearl-grey empyrean overhead. With a satisfied grunt, he located the spot he was seeking, and pointed. His back arched, and he pointed.

His arm stretched out, a long elegant index finger extended, and he pointed.

He pointed through the glowing grey canopy, through the luminous firmament, and beyond.

He pointed right off the page you are now looking at.

He points, in fact, directly at you, Reader.

He points right into your face.

He points, and he glares at you, and he shakes his finger, and he screams, "*J'accuse!*"

II

"OH, DEAR."

"I say!"

"Damned cheek!" the Colonel said, brandishing his cane while straining unsuccessfully to see through the greyness overhead. "If I get my hands on you—whoever you are—you'll be damned sorry, I promise you."

Mr. Drupe sniffed. "Most irregular."

Violet sighed and shook her head resignedly. "Perhaps irregular, Mr. Drupe, but none the less effective. We were led on a merry chase, all right, and I was always in the front. Damn! How could I have been so foolish?"

"Practice, Sis?"

It was a sign of Violet's almost total dispiritedness that this remark passed without rebuttal. "But you know what really gets to me, Sebastian? It's that you didn't work at it. I looked for clues, I followed trails, I pieced together facts, I tried to make sense of the whole thing. But you? You didn't do anything. It was just inspiration. Intuition. A goddamn lucky guess."

"Well, Violet, as your career until now has amply demonstrated, it's far, far better to be lucky than to be good."

Violet sighed again. "Sebastian, I never thought I'd hear

myself say this, but I'm afraid I have to agree with you. About everything."

Sebastian smiled sympathetically at his sister, hardly gloating at all.

Father Knox stepped forward and put a comforting hand on Violet's shoulder. "There's something you should know, Violet."

"What?"

"About your agreeing with Sebastian."

"Yes?"

"I'm afraid you're wrong again."

Violet looked up at the priest, blue eyes alarmingly round and large. She opened her mouth, but the only sound that came out was a kind of whimper from deep in her throat.

"She is?" Sebastian said. "I am?"

"Hee, hee, hee."

"Oh, shut up!" Violet snapped, recovering quickly. She heard herself sounding very much like her brother, and she wondered what—considering where they were—would happen if she throttled the damned old bat.

"What do you say, Cerise?" Father Knox asked. "Is Sebastian right or wrong?"

Cerise looked at Sebastian and smiled apologetically. "You're wrong."

"Really? Golly, and I was so sure I had it. Oh well, easy come, easy go."

"Actually, Sebastian," Father Knox said, "you did quite well. You were right as far as you went; you just didn't go far enough. But you were certainly correct to comment on a highly suspicious situation. The reader must bear his or her share of the responsibility for what happened to you all on Komondor Island. After all, the reader encouraged those events, indeed expected them, and looked forward to them. Had the reader not wanted them to happen, they would not have happened. In fact, if the reader had not been there, they would never have occurred at all. And then, once things started to happen, once the bodies started falling, the reader enjoyed seeing it, and wanted it to continue. Certainly the reader made no attempt to stop it. And it was within his or her power to do so, merely by slamming the book shut in disgust. The fact that this was not done signifies at least tacit approval. So the reader most definitely has a share—perhaps a significant share—in the guilt. But it is that of accessory, both before and after the fact. It is not that of perpetrator. For no matter how much the reader wanted the murders to occur, and no matter how familiar the reader may have been with the methods employed, the reader still lacked the opportunity. No, only one person had all three: motive, means, and opportunity."

"Why does everyone feel obliged to draw this out as long as possible?" Violet said. "Get on with it, already. Who the hell was it?"

Father Knox looked at Cerise.

"There's only one person left, isn't there?" she said, smiling. "The author, of course."

"What?" Violet squawked.

Mr. Drupe looked up at the grey canopy and said, "I would advise you to remain silent."

"Oh, dear."

"It's a damned outrage!"

Sebastian laughed. "Well, Mrs. Argus did say she'd met her Maker."

Father Knox smiled. "Exactly."

"Oh, come on!" Violet said. "What's going on here? This is hardly fair."

"Fair? Fair!" Father Knox said, his cheeks shaking and flushing, his fringe of white hair bristling. "Fair! My dear Violet, that's the second time you've used that word. And you of all people should know better. Weren't you the one who, in Chapter Ten, contemptuously said to your brother, 'Since when is anything in this world fair?' Well, didn't you?"

"Maybe. I don't recall. But still——"

"Still! Really, Violet! As far as I'm concerned, anyone who places his or her trust in some unknown writer's sense of fair play either deserves whatever happens, or needs to be placed under supervision. This poor retarded dolt will also probably believe in the institutional advertising of oil companies and the half-baked pie-in-the-sky promises of sleazy, power-mad politicians. Fair play? It's about time all these innocents were introduced to the real world, where self-interested madmen are leading them by the nose right to the hamburger factory." Father Knox paused, took several deep breaths, then smiled sheepishly. "Sorry about that. That subject always sets me off."

Violet, who had scrunched down in her chair, grumbled, "I still think it's pretty crummy."

"Come on, Sis, loosen up. Don't be so stuffy."

"Yes, don't," Cerise said.

"Oh, keep quiet. It's all right for you two. Sebastian almost got it, and you did figure it out."

"It's no big deal," Cerise said. "It was just luck. It started at the end of Chapter Four, when I had the feeling—no, the conviction—that we were being watched. I knew it wasn't just atmosphere, but something real. As things progressed, that belief strengthened, and I began to get the idea that it was not someone like us, but an individual much more powerful. Just after Budgie was killed—when the room looked like it had been torn apart by a giant hand—I even said that it was like we were being manipulated in somebody's fiendish game. I kept thinking about all this, and about some of the other things that were said. Then, that evening after we found Sebastian in the barrel, I was walking down by the water. It was a clear night for a change, and I could see a light from a neighbouring island. Then I saw a figure, and I knew it was *her*. She lives alone on an island close to Komondor, you know."

"Not for much longer," Father Knox said. "But go on."

"There's nothing more. As I said, I knew it was *her*. At first I thought about trying to contact her, but I realized her mind was made up, and that it would do no good. I knew it was just a matter of time. I didn't see much reason to wait, so the next morning I forced the issue. I started to tell what I'd guessed, but I knew she wouldn't let me finish. She didn't."

"It is very obvious," Sebastian said, "once you see it. The

killer did seem to be invisible, ubiquitous, and omnipotent. For a very good reason: she was."

"Unfair," Violet muttered, sulking.

"Well, Sis, I hate to say it, but I think you're wrong about that, too."

"Oh, yeah?"

"Yes. Besides the things Cerise mentioned, quite a few of us had feelings or premonitions that pointed in the right direction."

"That's right, dear," Budgie said. "I said that something awful was going to happen."

"And you were right," Sebastian said. "Violet, even you had a strange feeling at the end of Chapter Two."

"Big deal."

"No, Sis, it's not a big deal. But if you take all these little things together, it starts to add up. Why, you remember that Mrs. Argus said that Death was present, and that Death was a woman, and that *She* was walking the halls. Well, *She* was."

"Christ! Who pays attention to the ravings of a demented old woman?"

"If you'll recall, Violet," Father Knox said, "no one believed the prophecies of the original Cassandra either. Like her namesake, Cassie here only spoke the truth and was always correct."

"That's right!" Derrick said. "Only we never listened. We just naturally assumed she was nothing but an annoying character who was there solely to make an uncomfortable situation even creepier."

"It would have been hard to think otherwise," Father Knox said, nodding. "And, without getting too philosophical about this, what conclusions can you draw about a world in which curses and prophecies come true?"

Mystified silence greeted this question, until Cerise said, "That prophecies come true suggests that events are not casual or random, but that there is a controlling power in effect."

The priest smiled. "Exactly. A controlling power. If not actually a divine power, then someone who occupies that role in relation to all of you. After all, who else but your creator could—as Cerise said—manipulate you however she wanted for her little game?"

"And not just us!" Sebastian said excitedly. "She manipulated everything. She put physical objects—all the clues we kept finding—wherever they'd do the most good, where they'd be the most suspicious or dramatic. Even the weather—or especially the weather—was controlled for maximum dramatic effect. Why, she even had the thunder provide cosmic commentary. We should have noticed. Any world in which pathetic fallacy operates is hardly one where you'd look for realism, self-determination, or common sense."

Father Knox nodded and smiled.

"Theological mumbo-jumbo!" Violet said. "This was just a goddamn little mystery, and you're handing out anagogic analyses. Gimme a break!"

"Don't take it personally, Violet," Father Knox said. "This is just the nature of the beast. In an ordered universe, there can be no accident or freedom; only manipulation and control. Why else would so many of you act so consistently contrary to your own best interests? Even so, Violet, you were not subjected to anything different than what hundreds of thousands of your confrères have experienced in similar stories."

"So? For all your talk about order, this looks very much like anarchy to me."

The priest shrugged. "Perhaps it just depends on your point of view. You were so sure that one set of principles was in operation that you failed to see that it was another set entirely. Why, Violet, you even recognized this possibility yourself in Chapter Fifteen. Remember? You realized that 'with the right frame of reference, things that otherwise seemed isolated and incomprehensible were suddenly seen to fit together and make perfect sense.' Unfortunately, you immediately went on to discount the possibility that you were in a world that—how did you put it?—was 'buffeted to and fro according to the whims of laughing, indifferent deities.' Which was, of course, precisely the world you were in."

"Oh, how very ironic," Violet said sarcastically. "*Très amusant*."

"Well, Sis, speaking of irony and amusement," Sebastian said, "you do realize now, don't you, that you actually had the solution at one time?"

"What do you mean?"

"Do you remember, right after you saw my body in the vinegar barrel? You said the murderer shared my sense of humour."

"But I didn't think that—"

"No, but you could have. You're so stuffy and pinched-mouthed that it's obvious that a sense of humour doesn't run in *our* family. Therefore I had to get it from somewhere. Therefore I share it with the person who gave it to me. Therefore. . . ."

"He's right, Violet," Father Knox said. "Your author may not always have been completely forthright but, like Mrs. Argus, she never, ever lied."

"No?" Violet said. "What about right after we found the Colonel? Cerise said that there must be a homicidal maniac on the loose. Then our dear author, *in her own voice*, said, 'She wasn't, as it turned out, far wrong.' What about that?"

"Damned right!" the Colonel said. "What about that?"

Cerise looked at Sebastian, who indicated that she should field the question.

She shrugged. "How else would you describe someone who brutally and senselessly slaughters eleven more-or-less innocent people for no reason other than a perverse sense of humour, and to satisfy the desire to feel superior to those around her?"

"Superiority is precisely the right word," Father Knox said. "And like other homicidal maniacs—Jack the Ripper, for instance—your author occasionally enjoyed demonstrating hers by taunting you, making tantalizing yet cryptic remarks, saying in effect, 'Here I am, but you can't see me.' Violet, do you remember that in Chapter Eighteen you said that all the things that didn't seem to make sense either would fit together if you found the right perspective from which to look at them, or were a smoke screen? Then your author smugly stated that you couldn't have known that the alternatives you proposed were in no way mutually exclusive. Which, I assume you now see, they are not."

"Oh, I suppose they're not," Violet grudgingly agreed. "But only if you look at it from the point of view of this laughing indifferent deity of yours. And I still say there was no reason to consider that possibility."

"No?" Father Knox asked. "In that same Chapter Eighteen just a few pages further on, you—not unreasonably—noted that the delusion of invincibility and omnipotence was a common characteristic of the personality type you must be dealing with. Then your author commented parenthetically that it wasn't precisely a delusion. If it wasn't a delusion, that means the person you were after *was* invincible and omnipotent. I don't see how it could be stated much more clearly than that."

"Who the hell pays attention to remarks like that?"

"If you had, maybe you wouldn't be so upset. As I said, your author was virtually shouting, 'Here I am, here I am!' And then once again, in Chapter Twenty-one, Violet, you say that everything has been either random, senseless slaughter, or it's been motivated and purposeful. After which your author tauntingly and condescendingly remarks—and you can almost hear her giggling as she does so—that you really couldn't be blamed for not perceiving that it could be both at the same time."

"Oh, she's really quite a card, isn't she?" Violet said.

"Damned woman's a menace!" the Colonel growled. "Needs a good thrashing."

"He's right," Derrick said. "How come a woman like that is still running around loose?"

"Actually," Father Knox said, "I believe the police are— or soon will be—on her trail."

Suddenly Sebastian let out a whoop of laughter.

"What now?" Violet asked sourly.

"Sis, do you remember how this whole thing started?"

"No."

"Sure you do. What was I doing?"

Violet glared at her brother for a minute, then reluctantly said, "You were reading from the back of that old-fashioned mystery."

"That's right. Then what did I do?"

Violet looked at him, then looked down, and mumbled something.

"What'd you say, Sis?"

She looked up at him and made a face. "I said, 'You threw it away.'"

Cerise looked from Violet to Sebastian, then started to giggle.

"That's right," Sebastian said. "We were told right from the beginning how we should look at all this."

"Yes, beginnings and endings can often be extremely significant," Father Knox said. "And in fact, you were told even before that exactly how things stood."

Sebastian looked puzzled for a minute, then snapped his fingers. "Of course! Golly! At one point, I even said we were dropping like flies."

"That's right, you did!" Cerise said, laughing again.

"What are you two talking about?" Violet grumbled.

"Never mind, Sis. You wouldn't appreciate it." He turned to the priest. "Have we missed anything?"

"Actually, there are a couple of small but not totally insignificant points to be mentioned. Did none of you wonder about the name of the island?"

"Komondor? It's an Indian word, isn't it?" Derrick said.

"Of course it's not, you dope! Had anyone troubled to look it up in the dictionary, you would have found that it is a breed of Hungarian sheepdog. If there had also been a picture, you would have seen that the komondor is unquestionably one of the world's shaggiest dogs."

"Oh, dear," Budgie said, and tittered.

"I say! The cairns!" Derrick said, sitting up straight.

"Yes?" the priest said.

"The house was built on the site of the ritual cairns.

Besides being a ceremonial pile of stones, a cairn is a kind of terrier—a very long-haired, shaggy kind of terrier."

"Right you are, and very good! Just a little late."

Sebastian laughed. "Is this tale going to wag again?"

Father Knox smiled merrily and winked. "Well, there is one more item. Weren't any of you curious about the name, Rosa Sill? What it meant?"

"Not really," Violet said.

"Actually, Violet, if you had been, you might have saved yourself a lot of wasted effort. Names of characters can also be quite significant. 'Sill' is clearly a word from a European language, and equally clearly not one of the Romance languages. That means it's from a northern European language. With that determination, it would require no great effort to discover that it is a Swedish word, and that it means 'herring'."

"Rosa! Red!" Sebastian shouted, clapping his hands.

"Christ!" Violet said. "First metaphysics and now linguistics! Impossible!"

"I'm not so sure about that," Cerise said. "Remember, you were told that every member of the Sill family bears a fin-shaped strawberry birthmark."

Mr. Drupe cleared his throat. "And it was clearly stated that old Augustus Sill began his career selling pickled fish out of a barrel."

Sebastian laughed again.

"Still more, Sebastian?"

He smiled broadly at Violet. "Well, Sis, I was just thinking that, no matter what, you really can't say that old Runa didn't play Fairleigh."

In that instant, Sebastian's future was decided. Even before the groans died down, he was plucked from their midst and deposited into a place of eternal fire and darkness, inhabited solely by utterly solemn people who had no wit, no sense of humour or irony, and who regarded everything as deadly earnest and serious.

EDITOR'S POSTSCRIPT

CONSTABLE EDWARD ATKINS and Sergeant Horace Sutton were the two police officers who investigated the disappearance of Runa Fairleigh. As we know, the only things out of the ordinary that they found in the house were the manuscript of *An Old-Fashioned Mystery* and a note left in the typewriter.

Constable Atkins found the note. He read the two short lines several times, but could make no sense of them. He removed the sheet from the roller and showed it to Sergeant Sutton.

"What do you make of this?" he said. "Suicide note?"

Sutton read it over, and shook his head. "No idea. It doesn't sound like one, does it?"

"What do you think it means?"

"How should I know? I think it's poetry. Shakespeare, or one of those guys."

"Oh? It doesn't make any sense."

"Look, Atkins, the only place things ever make sense is in books. Right? What we've got is a crazy old lady who vanished, leaving behind a crazy note. So why don't you just put that note with those other papers over there, and let's get out of here. We do have some real crime to investigate."

Atkins did as his sergeant suggested. He placed the note with the stack of papers, putting it beneath what seemed to be a title page in order to keep it clean. He looked at the note once more, and again shook his head. What the hell does that mean, he wondered, and what does it have to do with anything? It was a real mystery, all right. He shook his head, and read the words yet one more time.

> *As flies to wanton boys, are we to the gods;*
> *They kill us for their sport.*

CHARLOTTE MACLEOD

Masterful Mysteries
By The Mistress Of Murder
DOROTHY L. SAYERS

featuring the inimitable LORD PETER WIMSEY

BUSMAN'S HONEYMOON	62489-3/$2.95
CLOUDS OF WITNESS	64394-4/$2.95
DOCUMENTS IN THE CASE	58263-5/$2.50
FIVE RED HERRINGS	62109-6/$2.95
GAUDY NIGHT	65037-1/$3.95
HANGMAN'S HOLIDAY	58669-x/$2.50
HAVE HIS CARCASE	58305-4/$2.95
IN THE TEETH OF THE EVIDENCE	62943-7/$2.95
LORD PETER a collection of Peter Wimsey Short Stories	59683-0/$7.95
LORD PETER VIEWS THE BODY	63503-8/$2.95
MURDER MUST ADVERTISE	60913-4/$2.95
STRONG POISON	59329-7/$2.75
UNNATURAL DEATH	58420-4/$2.50
THE UNPLEASANTNESS AT THE BELLONA CLUB	67132-8/$2.95
WHOSE BODY?	62240-8/$2.50

Also the first authorized biography of Dorothy Sayers

DOROTHY L. SAYERS
James Brabazon   58990-7/$3.95

Delightfully Baffling Mysteries From

CHARLES MERRILL SMITH

REVEREND RANDOLLPH AND THE HOLY TERROR
60707-7/$2.50

Reverend Randollph's marriage to a ravishing redhead marks the beginning of a series of murders which put the ex-quarterback and sometime sleuth on the trail of a "holy terror" who is murdering Chicago's priests, Rabbis and Bishops.

REVEREND RANDOLLPH AND THE FALL FROM GRACE
58832-9/$2.50

After eating food sent to TV preacher Reverend Prince Hartman, two aides die from poison. And when Reverend Randollph is called in, he realizes he must catch the poisoner before the charismatic Hartman becomes the third victim.

REVEREND RANDOLLPH AND THE AVENGING ANGEL
58933-8/$2.50

The wedding of a former flame turns to tragedy when the bride is found dead in her hotel suite. An investigation uncovers illicit love affairs and near incestuous relationships before the Reverend gathers the suspects and solves a difficult case.

REVEREND RANDOLLPH AND THE WAGES OF SIN
57174-9/$2.50

The wife of one of the church trustees disappears with ten million dollars of church funds and is then murdered. Reverend Randollph begins to investigate, and when he discovers Mrs. Reedman's pastimes, he realizes what kind of person might want her to pay for her sins.

AVON Paperbacks

Randollph 2-83

COLLECTIONS OF TALES FROM THE MASTERS OF MYSTERY, HORROR AND SUSPENSE

Edited by Carol-Lynn Rössel Waugh, Martin Harry Greenberg and Isaac Asimov

Each volume boasts a list of celebrated authors such as Isaac Asimov, Ray Bradbury, Ron Goulart, Ellery Queen, Dorothy Sayers, Rex Stout and Julian Symons, with an introduction by Isaac Asimov.

MURDER ON THE MENU   86918-7/$3.50
This gourmet selection offers a fabulous feast of sixteen deliciously wicked tales, sure to please the palate of everyone with a taste for mystery, menace and murder.

SHOW BUSINESS IS MURDER   81554-0/$2.75
Get the best seat in the house for the most entertaining detective fiction from Hollywood to Broadway. The curtain's going up on murders that ought to be in pictures, and crimes that take center stage for excitement.

THIRTEEN HORRORS OF HALLOWEEN   84814-7/$2.95
Here are a devil's dozen ghoulish delights, filled with bewitching tales of murder and the macabre.

THE BIG APPLE MYSTERIES   80150-7/$2.75
An anthology of thirteen detective stories set in the vibrant, electric—and sometimes dangerous—city of New York.

THE TWELVE CRIMES OF CHRISTMAS   78931-0/$2.50
When twelve masters get into the holiday spirit, it's time to trim the tree, deck the halls...and bury the bodies. Here are a dozen baffling tales of murder and mischief committed during the so-called merry season.

AVON Paperbacks